THE HUNT

CHRIS WARD

THE HUNT

ISBN – 10: 1537475428
ISBN – 13: 978 – 1537475424

CHAPTER 1

The twenty-five-year-old slight, wiry young man placed both dirty-finger-nailed hands on the off-white chipped window ledge and looked out through the grimy glass. Handsome, with a middle-eastern colour, he had short, jet-black hair that accentuated his fine bone structure. Women always gave him a second glance.

On this cold, wet, miserable mid-January afternoon, the thickly painted, grey, old-fashioned radiator underneath the window ledge didn't even manage to get lukewarm, though the heating should be on.

He watched as cars sped noisily up and down the local roads, exhausts trailing thick black and grey smoke. The branches on the trees swayed viciously as the strong winds whipped around them. He didn't notice straight away but then recognised that the cars all looked predominantly up-to-date with many German built BMWs and Mercedes, and this in a working-class area. His thoughts turned to the old jalopies at home in his village, virtually held together by string. This must be a rich society where even low-income working-class people could drive expensive modern cars.

Yousef El-Sayed wore his trademark hardly-ever-washed, scruffy, blue, torn-in-the-knees jeans, a plain dark green tee shirt with sweat marks under the armpits, and a thick, dirty silver puffy anorak to keep warm. He inhaled deeply on the Marlboro cigarette that seemed glued to his lips and blew out smoke rings one after the other. His mind wandered back to the lengthy and demanding trek across Turkey, Bulgaria, Romania, Hungary, Austria, and — ultimately — arriving in Germany.

Then he laughed. The Merkel woman was completely mad, just like all the other Kafirs. He'd even recognised two other brother fighters on the journey. It had been an exhausting passage, lasting weeks with just enough food and water, but it had all been worthwhile in the end.

Yousef recollected the rain-lashed day when he had been smuggled into the UK in the back of a lorry containing children's playground swings. Now, he stayed in a tiny, dingy, one-bedroom flat on the fifth floor of a tower block in Canada Way, White City, in West London, near Queens Park Rangers Football Club.

From the paint-peeling ledge, he picked up his steaming-hot Maxwell House instant coffee and held it in both hands to warm them. He slurped at the scalding, sweet, strong drink, which brought him partly back to life. His gaze roamed the room. Everything seemed old and dirty and worn out.

Wednesday today. Food parcels came on Wednesdays and Saturdays at five pm, and the anticipation brought a smile. Yousef had asked for some Arak — the clear, colourless, unsweetened anise-flavoured alcoholic drink he so loved, and he prayed that it would be in the parcel. One thing that had improved enormously in the three days he had been in London was the food he ate.

Brought up in a small, white-painted terraced

—

2

house in Al Arfi Street, near the Deir Ezzor
Cemetery in the dusty, sun-bleached village of Deir
ez-Zur in South East Syria, food had often proved
hard to come by. The famous Euphrates River split
the village in half. The civil war and the rise of Isil
had both made sustenance more and more
problematic to find and expensive to buy. The
Syrian pound had lost half of its value against the
American dollar and it would, without question,
get worse before it got any better.

The young man would never forget the warm,
star-lit night when Abd Al-Ala Hashemi had
suggested that he travel to London and become a
fully-fledged terrorist fighter in the Jihadi war
against Jews and Christians alike. It hadn't taken
much to persuade him. He had commenced at the
age of ten as an Al-Qaeda errand boy, had
progressed to Al-Qaeda arms training, graduated
to becoming a fully-fledged foot soldier at the age
of fourteen, and then had executed his first
Christian at the age of fifteen by shooting a fifty-
five-year-old Grandfather and fruit shopkeeper in
the back of the head, and then kicking him into a
twenty-foot-deep pit full of dead and dying and
moaning bodies.

At the age of nineteen, he became a trusted Isil
captain and fought in countless battles against Iraqi
and Syrian government forces. His latest training,
in bomb construction and how to live as a deep
cover agent in a foreign country, he had picked up
quickly and grown proficient in (as with
everything else he had trained for). He hadn't
believed his luck when told the location of his

target, and if the worst happened and he died, then he would be remembered forever, and the seventy-two virgins made for a glorious prize.

Yousef himself remained a virgin, having dedicated his life to the cause of Jihad. He sipped at his now-only-very-hot coffee again. Suddenly, a loud-mouthed uproar erupted outside the flats. A glance through the grimed window showed a gang of wild teenagers attacking a young boy and stealing his bright-red BMX bicycle. The young man enjoyed looking through the window, as they didn't allow him out yet. The day before, he had seen a young couple having sex behind a garage. The girl had lifted her navy-blue skirt and slipped her pink knickers down, and had then leant against the black garage door while the boy entered her from behind. Over in seconds, he had felt momentarily excited and also shocked, and the scene had confirmed all that he had heard about the base animal instincts of the British youth.

He drank the rest of his coffee, and then took the chipped mug to the kitchen, where he turned on the tap. The usual clanking noises reverberated through the pipes. Yousef washed up and left the cup to drain. The kitchen, disgustingly dirty, had old and rancid fat an inch thick stuck to the oven and cooker hob. When he'd turned the electric oven on to see if it worked, within seconds, thick black smoke billowed out, and he turned it straight off. Stood in the centre of the tiny kitchen, he resolved to clean it from top to bottom. They planned for him to stay in the flat for weeks, if not months, and he had no inclination to live like a pig.

—

Lips pursed, he wandered into the lounge and sat in the old, but still comfy, green lounge chair. Within a minute, he'd fallen asleep, and slept solidly for an hour and twenty minutes. A soft knock at the door awoke him. Yousef glanced at his gold Rotary watch; a present from a dead Christian. Five pm. As per instructions, he waited for the minimum of two minutes, and then opened the front door. Two bulky cardboard boxes sat in the hall. He carried the largest in first, placing it on top of the small Formica table in the kitchen, and then collected the second, taking it into the kitchen and setting it down on the black-and-white plastic tile floor.

How could such insignificant points become the focal point of a day and feel so exhilarating? Yousef took his time in studying the first box — plain brown cardboard, no labels, and no indication where it had come from or who had sent it. Then he took a Stanley knife out of one of the dresser draws and ran it across the tape at the top of the box. It sliced through effortlessly, even though the knife wasn't particularly sharp. Gently and slowly, he pulled back the two flaps of cardboard, savouring the moment and imagining all sorts of luxuries waiting inside the box.

A sheet of greaseproof paper lay at the top, which he lifted it out and took a step, then folded it and placed it on the workspace. His training had taught him never to waste anything because you never knew how useful something could be in the future. The anticipation felt exquisite. His heart pounded, and his breathing deepened, as he looked inside

5

and reached for the first item. A jar of Maxwell House instant coffee, which pleased him.

Next, came cans of lamb stew, long-life pitta bread to eat with the lamb, fig jam (he licked his lips), a thick, white sliced loaf of Sainsbury bread, a large tub of hummus, olives, and—they hadn't let him down—a bottle of Arak. He pulled it out the box and ran his hands lovingly around it, caressing the neck as though it were the most precious object in the world, which at this precise time, it was.

Butter, milk, orange juice, cereal, and then ... a carefully wrapped pastry. Oooh, Baklava, a rich, sweet filo pastry with nuts and held together with delicious honey. He would feast this night, and he smiled while he brought out other mundane items like soap and toothpaste. Emptied, he lifted the box, tore the tape off the unopened end, flattened it, and leant it against the wall. Then he hoisted the second box onto the table. Though smaller, it felt heavier.

With care, he cut the tape at the top, not sure as to what he'd find inside. Again, he eased back the cardboard flaps and looked in. His idea of what it could be proved correct. Yousef lifted out the four plastic-wrapped parcels of brick-red Czechoslovakian high-explosive Semtex 10. Yousef felt content. He had trained extensively using Semtex and loved its malleability and waterproof properties. It would have come from Libya, and always remained the explosive of choice due to it being almost impossible to detect.

Meticulously, he deposited the four parcels into a drawer and went back to the box. From it, he

—

6

retrieved a selection of yellow wired electrical detonators, electrical and non-electrical blasting caps, pliers, a set of screwdrivers, two digital watches, an array of specialist miniature tools, a tiny soldering iron, solder wire, two 12-volt batteries, two coil relays, two solar igniters, and two mobile phones. They all went into the next drawer down from the Semtex.

At seven-thirty, Yousef stood in the middle of the kitchen, ready. He had scrubbed the table clean and laid out his dinner. On edge, he licked his lips, and his breathing came shallow and fast. Hummus and olives for the starter, followed by a can of lamb stew — which heated on the stove — and to finish, a piece of Baklava for dessert. The pitta bread ejected from the toaster. When he grabbed it, the bread felt so hot that he juggled it before setting it down on a white, chipped side plate. Then he opened the hummus, tore the bread in half, and dipped it in, scooping up a generous dollop, which he placed slowly in his mouth, savouring the chickpea and lemon taste.

Unable to resist, he ate two of the pittas with the hummus and a few olives, saving one more piece of bread for the lamb. Mouth watering, he took the pan from the stove and placed it on the table, dipped in the pitta, and enjoyed the succulent taste of meat and vegetables.

After he'd scraped the pan clean, he put it in the sink and went back to the table, where he opened the Baklava, which he just sat and looked at. Would it taste like it did at home? He took a bite. A Syrian had made this. Delicious. Yousef finished

7

the Baklava and retired to his comfy chair in the lounge. Earlier, he'd washed a glass tumbler shiny clean and placed it with the bottle of Arak, sitting on a small wooden stand next to the chair. He poured the Arak, smelt it, and took a sip. With eyes closed, he drifted back to his village in Syria, where he walked amongst the olive trees and strolled on the banks of the Euphrates River in the glorious sunshine.

While watching a seemingly endless glut of trivial, boring television programs on BBC1 and ITV, he drank half the bottle. With one last sip, the glass emptied. Yousef felt good; a full stomach and several glasses of Arak solved so many problems. Satisfied, he ambled into the bedroom and lay on the rickety, old metal-framed bed, and within two minutes, snored contentedly.

—

CHAPTER 2

'Get your own coffee. What did your last servant die of?'

Richard Carpenter laughed loudly while he spoke, and David Morgan — one of his colleagues — sauntered off toward the coffee machine area. Richard sat in one of the numerous, uninteresting meeting rooms at MI5 Headquarters in Thames House, on the banks of the famous river with the same name. At six foot three, he looked attractive with short, dark hair, despite a few grey strands that had appeared above the ears. He believed it gave him a distinguished look, while others proved somewhat less complimentary.

Richard always wore the obligatory dark-blue suit, crisp white shirt, and black brogue shoes. Ties being optional, nobody wore them. He had been with MI5 since they recruited him during his tenure at Oxford University, where he'd studied science and maths. Now thirty-three, he lived in Camden Town, married to tall, slim, brunette Serena, with five-year-old twin boys, Andrew and Harry. Life had become more and more difficult over the years, with no work-home balance. All work. The latest terrorist atrocity, in which a hundred and thirty had died, at the Bataclan Theatre and Restaurants in Paris, had reawakened fears of mass gun attacks in the UK and particularly London. Multiple gunmen attacking a sporting venue, an airport, a theatre, or a shopping centre now posed a real threat.

Sir Philip Jones, the Welsh Metropolitan Police Commissioner, had requested another two hundred armed officers to patrol high-risk areas. The Prime Minister had pledged on television that the UK stood prepared for any such terrorist attacks, and that the public need not worry. Of course, he *would* say that, but he only wished to pay for an extra hundred officers and said to put them in cars so that they could get to trouble spots quickly. Rumours did the rounds that SAS teams routinely patrolled Heathrow, Gatwick, and selected tourist venues as an added precaution.

Richard, a senior MI5 Case Officer, worked in the UK and International counter-terrorism section. Responsible for running numerous surveillance teams and counter-terrorist agents throughout the UK and abroad, he formed part of the Joint Terrorism Analysis Centre (JTAC) team, who reported to the MI5 Director General, Sir Terence Brady. Richard sat and waited for Jack Taylor, the Deputy Director General, who had requested a meeting between him and David Morgan, his colleague of similar rank.

David Morgan, of a close age to Richard, had let himself go a bit too much. Cream cakes and continual snacking had piled on the pounds, and less exercise over the years hadn't helped. He had a bald patch right at the top of his head and looked older than his thirty-six years. He came back into the meeting room and sat down next to Richard. His white shirt bore a food stain on the front, and he looked tired while he sipped at his machine made Latte coffee.

David asked Richard, 'So, what have you heard?'

'Not much. They're no nearer to finding the terrorist bastard that escaped from Paris. Seems he's disappeared. My bet is he's already back in Syria or Iraq.'

David raised his brows in surprise. 'I heard he's definitely in the Kuregem area of Brussels, and it's only a matter of time before they flush him out.' He shook his head and raised his well-plucked eyebrows once more. 'Never believe anything anybody tells you and you can't go far wrong.' Then he laughed quietly.

Richard replied in an almost conspiratorial manner, 'What's the meeting for? You heard anything?'

'No idea, but it's all rather hush-hush. Something interesting is taking place, that's for sure.'

Just as David finished speaking, Jack Taylor pushed open the door.

As Deputy Director General, Jack had a direct line to the Director General and, if needed, to the Prime Minister. At fifty-five, he'd been in MI5 for thirty-five years. Though short, he seemed built like a challenger tank. Even at his age, he made for a formidable opponent both physically and mentally.

'Good morning, gentlemen,' Jack said in his almost-Sargent-Major-parade-ground voice, which blasted over one's ears rather than washed.

Richard and David returned the greeting and waited with baited breath to hear what the meeting was about.

Jack sat and opened a file, flicked through a few of the pages, and then found what he had been looking for. 'So, we have twenty thousand odd Syrian refugees turning up, and for me, it's all taking place a little bit too quickly. The good news is that someone at the Prime Minister's office is actually paying attention to what we say for a change. The refugees will be families from the Baharka and Erbil refugee camps in northern Iraq. So, parents and children, but of course, we don't know who they are, or where they may or may not have come from. Their pasts cannot be checked reliably, so we have a problem. And, I'm sure you know exactly what I'm talking about?' He eyeballed Richard and David, waiting for them to speak.

Richard said, 'Obviously, any of them, men or women, could be Al-Qaeda or, now, more likely Isil terrorists.'

Jack looked down at his nails and then back up. 'Exactly, and to further complicate matters, millions of so-called refugees have inundated the whole of Europe. Germany, alone, has taken over a million.' He raised his voice to get his point across, 'With no checks, no fucking checks, and thousands of young single men … how many of them are terrorists? Of course, we have no idea, but if I were in charge of embedding terrorists into Europe, then several hundred would be sleepers.'

He shook his head in exasperation, and then continued, 'We are currently monitoring—no, I'll amend that—we are currently endeavouring to monitor approximately a thousand people of interest in the UK alone. That problem will get worse, and we don't have the manpower. As is customary, we will cross off names that we feel are less interesting than others. In the camps, British staff will interview and photograph the Syrian families chosen from Northern Iraq, and will fill out forms. Those forms and images will arrive in London, and we and GCHQ will assess them. Any remote feeling that someone seems suspicious will result in them getting knocked off the list of immigrants we'll take.

'When they arrive at Heathrow, they will have to fill out identical new forms, which we'll compare to the ones they did in the camps. You won't be surprised to hear that this simple process will throw up a number of anomalies, and those people will be detained and interviewed thoroughly by border control staff. And, of course, we will have a permanent presence at Heathrow to assist.

'As I see it, the real issue is identity. They give us a name, but is it real? And how do we find out if they are who they say they are?' Jack took a breath. 'With difficulty, I think, *but* we are getting some help, which will prove invaluable. Two new recruits will join us from Syria.' Jack turned a few pages over and took out an A4 sheet. 'Hesam Atallah and Badi al Zaman Siddique.'

Both Richard and David cringed at Jack's appalling pronunciation.

'Are these new recruits? Or have they worked for us in Syria?' Richard asked.

'Atallah has been with us for six months. The Siddique character is new. If they do a good job,

---

the powers that be have promised them that they can stay and bring over their families.'

David said, 'Even they could be plants.' He shook his head. 'It's messy. Very messy.'

Jack nodded. 'I agree, David, but we have to do something, and this is the best we could come up with. You will take Atallah, and Richard, Siddique. These Syrians are not just here to help identify the refugees, but also to help in all matters relating to the security of the UK against terrorist threats and particularly from Isil. They will arrive at Luton tomorrow. It's much quieter than Heathrow or Gatwick. And our staff will pick them up and drive them to a safe house.' Jack checked his notes again. 'Custom House.'

'Where the hell is that?' David asked.

Richard got in before Jack, 'It's near Newham Hospital. Plaistow Way, I believe?'

'That's correct.' Jack smiled. 'All the information on the new chaps will be in files, which you can pick up from my office later today, say two-ish, okay?'

The two men nodded; working with Syrians would offer a new challenge for them both.

CHAPTER 3

Meticulously, on Friday, Yousef had cleaned the flat. It took the best part of the day, but when he had finished, he felt extremely happy and celebrated with two glasses of Arak. Now, on Saturday morning, he had written a shopping list for the man who brought his groceries at five. He had asked for fresh lamb to roast, which would be an unbelievable luxury, and just the thought of the aroma made him lick his lips. In truth, he expected more cans of lamb stew, but if you didn't ask. ... Also, he had also requested a laptop with internet connection, a tourist book of London, a tube train map, and every available book with diagrams of the House of Commons, particularly the internal rooms and chambers. In addition, he'd included a note, asking when he would be allowed to go out. Waiting proved a skill that had to be learnt. It's not easy waiting for an indeterminate period, doing the same things over and over again, and not growing frustrated, impatient, or angry. Yousef, a master, focussed on the goal. The waiting would not last forever and, of course, he had prayer.

Like all good Muslims, when he could, Yousef observed prayer five times a day. As soon as he awoke, he would drop to his knees and start the day with the remembrance of God, with a prayer called Fajr, which should be performed before sunrise. Dhuhr, the second prayer of the day, is performed just after noon to remember God and seek his guidance. The third prayer, Asr, he observed in the late afternoon to remember God and the greater meaning of life. Then, just as the sun went down, Yousef would remember God again as the day drew to a close, through Maghrib. Isha made the final prayer, just before retiring for the night, and he, again, took time to remember God's presence, guidance, mercy, and forgiveness.

Yousef took comfort in prayer, but in his line of work, sometimes prayer had to be taken where and when possible. This Saturday felt not dissimilar to a weekday, but as five pm drew closer, the anticipation of more luxuries to eat and drink grew. At four, the young man sat in his comfy chair and waited.

And waited.

When it got to five-thirty, he became angry. In an effort to control his frustration, he closed his eyes and prayed for patience. It worked, and he relaxed. At five-forty, a hard knock sounded on the door. Alert, Yousef listened. The person was late, and the knock sounded different. Obviously somebody new. He waited the two minutes and, as he stood, another hard knock came on the door. Yousef tiptoed to the kitchen, opened a drawer, and took out the Stanley knife. Then he pushed the blade open and edged toward the front door. Once he'd disengaged the security chain, he tensed while he gripped the door handle and turned it, readied to strike with the knife. Then a quiet voice, a Syrian voice, said, 'I am a friend. Do not do anything rash.'

Yousef paused for half a second, and then eased

open the door. A tall, broad-shouldered, younger man with a thick mop of hair stood there wearing a short dark coat with the collar pulled tight around his neck.

'I am Kaashif Bashara. Let's go inside.'

Yousef stepped to one side. 'I don't want to know your name, you fool.' Although fuming, he shut the door quietly, and then kicked the man's legs into the air. The man landed on the old, worn hall carpet with a thud and a moan.

Yousef had the Stanley knife at his throat in a split second. 'You fucking amateurs.' Yousef studied the young man: smart, casual clothes and expensive-looking brown leather shoes, but he smelt like he hadn't had a bath in a month. 'What is my codename?'

The man shook and struggled to speak.

Yousef pressed the knife into his flesh. 'Calm down, or I'll cut you open, and you'll bleed to death.'

The man controlled himself. 'Beacon, your codename is Beacon.'

Yousef glared into the eyes of the young man, who'd given him the correct code, and then he speculated as to why they had employed such a fool for the job.

'What shall we call you, then? I know … Adhan because you are a messenger, is that not correct?' Adhan was the Islamic call to prayer.

'Yes, Master, very correct. And I like Adhan very much.'

'I don't give a fuck if you like it or not.' He withdrew the knife from Adhan's throat and stood.

'Get up and go and sit in the lounge. I'll be a minute.'

'Yes, Master.'

Yousef walked to the kitchen, poured himself a moderate-sized shot of Arak, and downed it in one. Now, he felt ready. He picked up the one wooden kitchen chair and strolled into the living room, where he sat opposite Adhan, who occupied the comfy chair.

'Report,' Yousef said.

The man reached into his coat and took out a large brown package and handed it to him. 'Money, one thousand pounds. You are to be careful. It is a large sum and should last you a considerable time. From now on, you are to buy all your groceries. You should commence travelling on the tube and plan your strike. Anything else you need, you tell me, and I'll get it for you as quickly as possible. This is an emergency number.' Adhan gave Yousef a piece of paper. 'You call. Let it ring only once. Exactly two minutes later, you ring again. If it is safe, I will answer, and you must say "Beacon", nothing else. If not safe, I will call you when I can.'

'I need a weapon, preferably a Glock G30S, and three-hundred rounds of ammunition, you understand?'

'Of course, I understand simple instructions. I—'

'Don't talk. Go and do your job and bring the items when you're ready, you understand?'

'Yes, I understand.' Unsure as to whether Yousef had concluded or not, he continued to sit there.

'What are you waiting for?'

'We have finished, Master?'

'Yes, now hurry up and get out.'

Adhan jumped up and made for the door. Before he opened it, he turned back. 'Master, I am delighted to be helping you in our great cause. If I can help in any way, just let me know. I am your servant.' Then he bowed his head and smiled.

Yousef jumped up and shouted, 'Get out, you, you imbecile.'

The door slammed, and Adhan had gone.

Yousef smiled. He liked the boy and decided that he would take him under his wing and train him.

The crisp new notes sat in small piles on the table. Yousef had counted out twenty stacks of fifty pounds, made up of two twenties and a ten. He liked things neat and accounted for, and he folded and secured each stack with a paper clip and placed them in an old Mars Celebrations tub that he'd found on top of one of the cupboards. Fifty pounds, he'd put in his pocket, as he planned a trip to the local convenience store.

Desperately, he had tried not to get too excited about going out, but it proved difficult. Just to walk in fresh air. To smell life around you. He couldn't wait. By seven-thirty it had grown dark. The young man had looked out of the window a hundred times, to check that no one watched the flat, and hadn't seen anyone. A light drizzle fell, and it remained cold like it had all day. Yousef pulled his anorak collar tight around his neck. The time had come. He pulled the security chain off, turned the lock, and opened the front door, then he moved outside and slowly and quietly closed the door.

Three other doors led from the hallway, for flats seventeen, eighteen, and nineteen, and he'd heard noises throughout the days and nights of children running and playing, adults shouting—sometimes at each other, sometimes at the children—and even a couple grunting and screaming during coupling. Always, he'd been taught to melt into the background, and so didn't want to know his neighbours and had no intention of making any friends. As Yousef wanted to stretch his legs, he ignored the lift and descended the cold, dirty concrete steps. Someone must have cleaned the stairway, as a strong smell of disinfectant settled in his nostrils.

Halfway down, noises warned him that somebody was coming up. He moved to the right side and kept going. A huge bald-headed black man appeared and brushed past, seemingly not even noting his existence. It pleased Yousef that this was the type of area where people didn't ask questions, and the police made for a common enemy. He got to the bottom of the stairs and emerged into the night. The pavement lights mostly worked, throwing shadows across the concrete walkways and giving them an eerie appearance and feel.

A corner shop operated about three hundred yards away, around the corner. Yousef took a deep breath and strolled along, taking in the sights and sounds of what had become his neighbourhood. Teenagers zoomed past on bikes, men and women made their way home from work, and he could see that it was a working-class, multi-cultural area, perfect for him to assimilate into. When he turned the corner, what could only be described as a feral gang of young, white and black girls confronted him. He walked on, and they spread to both sides of the pavement to let him pass. They glared at him, and just as he was about to pass, the last girl moved right in front of him, blocking his way.

'Got a spare fag, mate?'

He lied, 'Sorry, I don't smoke.' Then he went to go past her, but she moved again, blocking his path.

'Got any booze, then? We can come to your place.' The gang had surrounded him and stood laughing.

'I don't drink either.'

The gang went quiet, and the leader at the front frowned, and then shouted, 'Don't suppose you fuck either then?'

They burst into howls of laughter.

'Bet you wouldn't say no to a blowjob, though?'

Cue more laughter.

Yousef grew concerned. He wanted to get on his way without drawing attention to himself.

One of the girls taunted, 'Which one of us would you like to suck it for you? We've all done it before.'

Silence descended once more, as the girls preened, hoping to get chosen.

''Course, you'll have to pay. Twenty quid for a good blowjob. Bargain.'

Twenty quid would buy plenty of fags and a

bottle of vodka. The obvious leader of the gang said, 'What do you say, then?'

'I only have enough money for a loaf of bread and some milk. Two pounds is all I have. I'm so sorry.'

The girl moved out the way. 'Fuck off, you prat. I wouldn't suck your tiny cock for a hundred quid. You're probably a faggot anyway.'

They hurled abuse at him while he strode toward the shop. Yousef felt unnerved, as one or two of the girls struck him as pretty, and he imagined pushing his erect cock in and out of their mouths. He would love to have given that bitch a powerful slap but had done well to keep his temper under control. It had given him a good test. Hopefully, they would have moved on by the time he made his return journey.

Finally, he arrived at the shop, a typical open-all-hours, small convenience store. Iron bars covered the windows. Yousef pushed open the door, and the stale smell of curry and sweat met him. With his nose scrunched, he looked around. All the essentials he would need seemed to be on the shelves, so he picked up a green plastic basket and began to shop. As he selected his items, he kept an eye on the people that came into the establishment. Most of them bought cigarettes, vodka, or beer.

He knew about working-class people. Unemployed, and with no hope of a better life, the only things that made it bearable for some were the fags and booze. When he'd finished, he took his basket to the till and asked for a bottle of Arak. The elderly Indian man couldn't understand what he wanted, so in the end, he changed it to a bottle of vodka, and then added whisky as well. Also, he bought two packets of Marlboro's. The Indian man passed the items through a scanner and put them in two plastic bags. The bill came to forty-nine pounds and fifty-two pence. Yousef stood there, shocked: fifty pounds gone, just like that. Tight-lipped, he paid and reflected that the booze and fags would last some time and so it wasn't so bad.

Bags in hand, he opened the shop door, and the fresh air swept away the curry smell. With a deep breath, he walked out for the return journey, praying that the girls had moved on to another victim elsewhere. When he got to the corner, he slowed right down. Not hearing any noise, he peeked to see if any of the girls lingered. Upon finding the street girl free, he quickened his pace, wanting to get back to the safety of the flat as soon as possible.

After taking several deep breaths of fresh air, he then entered the communal entrance, and decided to take the lift. He pressed the button, one of the three cars arrived within seconds, and the doors slid open. Yousef got in and pressed 'five'. The smells in the lift disgusted him; urine and stale sweat. When the doors opened, he felt relieved and stepped out. After just one stride, number eighteen's door opened, and Yousef felt momentarily fazed. The leader of the gang emerged. In a pink mini-skirt and matching top, with short dark hair, a pretty face, and what appeared to be a lovely firm body, she looked about sixteen.

Over her shoulder, she shouted, 'Bye, Mum.'

A woman's voice filtered through the fast-closing door, 'Bye, Mandy.'

Evidently, she lived here.

Mandy turned, took a step, and stopped. They stared at each other, and then she shocked Yousef further when she smiled and spoke to him. 'Sorry about earlier. Didn't know you were a neighbour.' The girl glanced at his two shopping bags. 'That two quid went a long way?'

Yousef felt unsure what to say but eventually opened his mouth, 'No problem, and yes, it's surprising what good value you get at the corner shop.' He smiled and continued to his front door. Mandy got in the lift, still smiling and watching him until the doors slid closed.

In the flat, Yousef unpacked his shopping. It had proven an interesting and exciting evening, and he felt exhausted. Seated in his comfy chair, he turned on the TV and sipped at a glass of whisky. A film played, something to do with vampires and werewolves, and he found it fascinating, but then it went to adverts. Though not paying that much attention, he found it strange that people would want to throw away money by betting online; surely, a clear sign of the stupidity and abhorrent behaviour of Western cultures. The advert changed, and Yousef sat up straighter when he heard the name Syria mentioned. Unicef appealed for British citizens to give three pounds a month by texting 6672. The actor described how Syrian children needed warm clothing for the winter. Yousef, of course, had seen the aid agencies working, but this was something new, and it disturbed him. His enemy collecting money to buy clothes for Syrian Children? Why would they do that?

CHAPTER 4

With a thousand operatives sitting at individual workstations, housed in a cavernous room the size of a football pitch, the main operations centre at MI5, Thames house, looked an extraordinary sight. People of every age, from every nation in the world, tall, short, thin, fat, redheads, blondes, and baldies, all sat in front of four thousand computer screens. Richard always marvelled at this immense scene when he entered the room. The area, split into different functions, had different numbers of personnel in each section. By far the largest department was Counter-Terrorism, followed by Counter-Espionage, Cyber Threats, Protective Security, and Counter-Proliferation of Weapons of Mass Destruction.

Richard headed toward Counter-Terrorism and his personal boss, codenamed Bunny. Bunny, AKA Francis Matthews, a forty-four-year-old University Russian languages graduate from Oxford, behaved in a traditional, old-school manner. A stickler for punctuality, form filling, dressing correctly, and doing things the British way (which meant professionally and legally most of the time), she had never married and worked twenty-four-seven in the defence of her country. The same as nearly every other day, she wore a dark-blue trouser suit with a light-blue silk scarf. Bunny had a spacious office separate to the main area, which had an impressively large desk and also a conference table for meetings.

Richard said hello to numerous staff seated at their desks and soon stood outside Bunny's door. After he knocked, she shouted for him to enter.

'Hello, Richard. How are you?'

'Fine, thank you, Ma'am, and you?' He sat in the chair in front of her desk.

Bunny smiled at him. 'As well as can be expected at this busy time.' She paused and opened a notebook. 'So, you will soon have a Syrian partner, name of Badi al Zaman Siddique?'

Richard felt confused. 'I've just come from a briefing with Jack Taylor. I have a new Syrian working *for* me. He most certainly is not going to be my partner.'

'Fine, Richard, if you want to be pedantic, you know very well what I mean, and I bet he didn't tell you that Siddique was working for the Americans up until September, and they dropped him.'

Richard became more interested. 'He must have forgotten to mention that, and why was he dropped, Ma'am?'

'Something to do with his friends, one or two undesirables, apparently, and he wouldn't shop them.'

'All sounds a bit flaky, doesn't it?'

Bunny shook her head. 'We'll never know the complete truth. Anyway, you're to get on with it as best you can. Now, to something more serious. What's happening with Aashif Jamal?'

Richard hadn't looked forward to this. 'We lost him yesterday. We're on the case.'

For what seemed like an eternity, Bunny didn't say anything and just stared at him. Then, eventually, she spoke, 'On the case? That does not inspire me with confidence.' She leant forward. 'What the fuck is going on?'

Richard grew agitated at the tone Bunny used. 'We had one man on him yesterday, Kevin Connolly — a good man. Jamal went to prayers at Green Lanes Mosque, and we lost him.'

'You mean Connolly lost him?'

'It would be unfair to blame Connolly. The numbers have hit us —'

Bunny interrupted him in sharp tones, 'I know all about the numbers. I don't want excuses, Richard, I want answers, and I want them quickly. Do we understand one another?'

'We do, Ma'am, but one white Caucasian man on a direct surveillance against a Muslim will not work. We need more of their kind to help us.'

'We all know that and have to find answers to overcome the problems. Jamal poses a serious threat, so what about comms? Anything from his phones?'

'Nothing from his home phone, and he's got so many mobiles … changes them every day.'

'His friends?'

'We have three houses under direct surveillance, but no unusual activity.'

'Great, so when everybody suddenly disappears, then we know we have a problem, and of course, it will be exceedingly challenging to solve. Get this Siddique chap squared up, and then let him loose into the community. Maybe Central London

Mosque for starters?'

'I'll give it some thought, Ma'am, and let you know.'

'I've asked for more Syrians and Iraqis who've lived in the UK to come back and work with us. We have people out there now, working on it.'

'Ma'am, we have to be so careful. If they got just one man into our network, it would cause havoc.'

'I know. We just have to be cautious. So, I want Jamal found, and quickly. No excuses, Richard. Okay, last matter on the agenda; it seems GCHQ picked up some serious chatter, something about a new man coming to London, some reference to a big job. They have nothing concrete, but I thought I'd mention it. Put the word out that we want to know of any new arrivals. That's it then. How's the family?'

'I have no idea. I never see them.'

He watched her scowl and expected a verbal lashing. She said, 'We all have to make sacrifices. By the way, did you see the news? An Isis bombing in Jakarta—two killed, but five terrorists got their just desserts.' Bunny positively glowed as she continued, 'Always gives me a warm feeling when I hear such enjoyable news. Good day to you, Richard.' Then she snatched up a piece of paper and started reading.

'Thank you, Ma'am.' Richard rose, feeling like his old housemaster at boarding school had just dismissed him.

Richard left Bunny's office and called a meeting with two of the senior Counter-Terrorism Operations Team. Word would be sent down to all field agents that the whereabouts of Aashif Jamal was a top priority, and they were also to make enquiries about any new arrivals in London.

Richard needed something to eat, so he made his way to the staff canteen for a snack and coffee. He purchased a cheese salad sandwich and a Latte, and sat in the corner near the back, away from anyone else. He glanced up to watch the news on one of the three large-screen televisions. With nothing of any interest, he tucked into his sandwich.

Richard, musing over the new developments, suddenly heard a shout and glanced up. People at other tables jumped up and looked and pointed at the screens. More shouting ensued: 'Turn it up, turn it up.' He felt confused for half a second, and then he leapt up and moved closer to the nearest screen.

Then images of fire engines and ambulances hurtling through London streets came on screen, and then the newscaster, Jeremy Ford, appeared. Then came the words that Richard had dreaded for weeks.

'A bomb has gone off at Kensington High Street tube station. We have no more news at the present time but believe there have been a large number of fatalities. We now cross over to the scene ...'

Richard sprinted to the nearest office, threw himself into one of the hot-desk chairs, and logged into his account. Hurriedly, he punched in the passwords and gained entry. It would only take him a second. He looked for the code, found it, and deleted it.

All hell would break loose, and he was almost certainly already too late.

CHAPTER 5

The steel battering ram hit the lock, and the door crashed in. Ten strong and dressed in full combat gear, the swat team stormed into the house. Three women in the lounge, dressed in traditional black Hijabs, screamed at the sight of the police officers, who wielded machine guns and shouted at the top of their voices.

'Get on the floor, get on the floor.'

The women pretended not to understand, and so the officers threw them to the ground and pressed their faces into the carpet. Babies in prams and cribs joined in the screaming when they heard their mothers in distress. Methodically, the police officers made their way through all the rooms on the ground floor and, finally, declared it clear.

The lead officer, Terence Browne, a fifty-two-year-old veteran, then inched up the dirty blue-carpeted stairs, deadly machine gun pointed straight ahead ready for any threat that emerged. It all happened in the blink of an eye. An Arab-looking man dressed in flowing white robes jumped into view, brandishing a massive curved sword, and then charged down the stairs, screaming, 'Allahu Akbar, Allahu Akbar.'

Terry's instructions said that it was imperative to capture anybody in the house alive. He fired instantly, and twenty rounds thudded into and around the assailant's legs. The man flew into the air and landed in a heap at the feet of the firearms officer. Terry grabbed the man by his robe and threw him down the stairs. Other officers then dragged him into the lounge and dumped him next to the women. When the females saw all the blood and mangled legs, their screams and wails recommenced more loudly than before.

Slowly, Terry continued up the stairs. Two officers came behind him, also pointing machine guns ahead. The most dangerous point came just as they got to the top. He decided not to take any chances, as they had one man alive and that might be enough, so he opened fire, spraying bullets in every direction. Then he pushed forward, and just as he crested the top of the stairs, a man leapt at him with a long knife. Terry fired a short burst, and the man's head disintegrated into a mass of blood and pulp.

The firearms officer stopped to take a deep breath, shattered, but the adrenalin flowed. Then he moved forward again. All the doors on this floor stood closed. 'Fuck,' he said. Terry signalled to the man behind him for smoke and stun grenades. They inched further along the landing, listening for any noise. None came. Four officers took station next to the doors, and Terry gave the signal. They kicked in the thin wood simultaneously and threw stun grenades. A bang resounded in the narrow landing space, and one of the officers took a hit in the chest and crashed to the floor.

Another white-robed man hurled himself at the police officers, firing a pistol wildly. Hundreds of bullets smashed into his body at devastatingly short range and just about cut him in half. The swat team cleared the upstairs rooms and, eventually, went back downstairs. Soon, they left the house, and new officers took over to secure all the women prisoners. Social workers then arrived and took the babies, at which point the women tried to attack the social workers, but the officers manhandled and herded them into black people carriers with smoked windows.

A medic team worked on the man with the badly damaged legs; he wouldn't be able to walk for a long time but was alive and precious because of it. They took him under armed guard to a secure unit at St Thomas' Hospital.

MI5 officers, wearing dark suits and white shirts, entered the house next. Close behind them came the home office special crime scene technicians. Matt Barlow headed up the team, and he and his three agents would tear the house apart looking for clues to identities and the possible whereabouts of Aashif Jamal. All four would do room-by-room. They began in the lounge and tore all the soft, brown easy chairs, the three-seater sofa, and numerous multi-coloured cushions to pieces. They ripped up the threadbare green carpet and pulled up the floor boards, breaking many in the process. Then they opened every drawer in the welsh dresser and emptied them onto the floor. An assortment of batteries, plasters, cellotape, biros, magazines, and table mats flew in every direction. The team became frenzied, as time was of the essence, and Aashif Jamal could be planning more bombings.

One of the officers paced around the room, tapping the walls and listening for a hollow sound that would indicate a false room or secret safe. All the family photos, they saved for referencing individuals, living or dead. Then they took down the pictures on the walls and checked them, and then threw them into a heap. Next, they removed light bulbs. And, finally, they'd done. Nothing found. They moved into the dining room. The compact space contained hardly anything, other than a small oak table and six straight-backed chairs. Matt stood at the door. He could smell something.

'There could be something in here.' His hunches had paid off before.

They went through the same process: carpet, floor boards, and chair linings — until they had nothing else to smash and nowhere else to look. Matt stood watching while his three agents moved toward the kitchen.

'Wait.'

The three men stopped and returned.

'The coving. It's plastic. Pull it all down.'

The men set to it, and then one of them shouted, 'bingo.' The others stopped. The man had ripped a piece of the corner coving down and found something, which he passed down to Matt, who took it to the kitchen. He placed it on a worktop and pulled broken bits from the end and looked inside. Then he tipped it upside down. A plastic bag containing several items fell out. Matt opened the bag and removed five blank British passports, a roll of fifty-pound notes, two keys (one that looked like a house key and the other, maybe, a left luggage or storage site key), a mobile phone, and last, a Quran. All in all, a disappointing find. He took his mobile out and pressed speed dial.

'Richard, it's Matt. One male alive, three dead, and we have three women. He's at St Thomas'. Once he's stable, we'll take him to the house. We have the women en route already.'

After a breath, he continued, 'One bruised casualty; his bullet-proof vest saved him. Some passports and a couple of keys.'

Matt listened for a moment, and then said, 'Thanks, Richard. Yes, see you there tomorrow.'

Richard had been delighted to have a live one to interrogate for a change. Both men knew the women would prove a waste of time and would have no idea of what was going on. Still, they had to interview them, just in case. At last, Matt had given him good news for Bunny, a big plus.

CHAPTER 6

The morning dawned sunny but freezing, the ground remained wet from night-time rain, and Yousef felt thankful that it had stopped. Dressed in his usual shabby blue jeans and a plain white tee shirt, with his silver anorak buttoned up for warmth, he had walked down to the Queens Park Rangers Football Stadium. He'd wanted to see inside and marvel at the lush green pitch, but couldn't, so made do with strolling around the perimeter as much as he could.

An avid premiership football fan, like most of his friends in Syria, he supported Manchester United. He wanted to get a match ticket at some point but would have to return, as he didn't have enough cash on him. Yousef concluded his short excursion and strolled back along South Africa Road and turned right into Wood Lane. His destination, White City tube station, lay just down the road. In two minutes, he arrived and spent a second looking down to the vast BBC television studios. They would have made a superb target that would have received massive worldwide publicity.

Regretful, he turned and climbed the steps into the station, where he bought an all-day travel ticket for eight pounds, and then made his way down a lengthy series of steps and onto the platform. He took everything in about his local station, as he needed to know every step, every door, and every possible hiding place. You never knew what might happen in the future.

He sat on one of the three new-looking wooden benches on platform two and waited. The station being in the open and not underground surprised him. Later, he discovered that it was one of only a few such stations in London. People strolled down onto the platform, and Yousef didn't feel out of place; South Americans, Europeans, Arabs, Africans, and Asians milled about. It seemed that the whole world lived in West London.

Five minutes later, the train pulled in, and he boarded the third carriage and sat in the first seat on the right-hand side. Other passengers embarked and took seats on both sides of the car. The train pulled away and, three seconds later, entered a tunnel. The carriage dropped into inky blackness, and the tunnel walls looked impossibly close. The noise seemed louder than he had imagined it would, rattling, thudding, and screeching as the train careened around corners, seemingly travelling at a hundred-miles-per-hour.

Yousef studied the other passengers. He glanced at a woman sitting directly opposite him; she appeared English, had dark hair and a pale complexion, and seemed nicely dressed in a short red skirt and blouse with a short black jacket. When she lifted a limb to sit cross-legged, he got a glimpse of white knickers, which excited him. The woman challenged him with a stare, and he glanced to the side.

With interest, Yousef noted that the woman seemed unafraid about confronting him. The train settled into a recurring rhythm, only broken by the frequent station stops. It took seven stops to reach Oxford Circus, and the time flew by. Amidst a mass of heaving people all rushing for the escalators, he stepped off the tube. The crowd carried him along, and once on the escalator, he stood firmly on the right-hand side. Some people, obviously in a great hurry, ran up the free left side. Yousef would have to spend hours on the tube trains to familiarize himself with when busy and quiet times occurred.

At the top, he stepped off the escalator and joined the stampede that headed for the ticket barriers. There, he shoved in his ticket and walked through the open doors. After he'd gone ten paces, he remembered his ticket and turned around, only to see people streaming through the barriers. With a curse, he decided to buy another one, as he didn't want to draw attention to himself by fighting against such a crowd. Instead, he continued walking, following the signs to the exit. He emerged from the station into Oxford Street, and the air felt so damn cold that he would need to invest in new clothes to keep warm. After a glance left and right, he strolled right. So many shoppers thronged the street, and seemingly, most of them foreign. He passed a newspaper stand and got the shock of his life. A billboard exclaimed:

93 Killed in Kensington Station Terrorist Bomb
Attack

Utterly shocked, Yousef stopped. People knocked into him. He gathered his thoughts and moved to the stand, where he bought a Daily Mail from the old man, and then stood and studied the headline.

Isil Murderers Kill 93 Defenceless Shoppers

How amazing. There must be another lone sleeper, or even a cell, already working in London. Yousef read down the report: Ninety-three killed and another seventy injured—fifteen seriously. He smiled and felt like jumping in the air and shouting, 'Allahu Akbar, Allahu Akbar.' However, he managed to calm his urge. Then it struck him that the timing seemed strange. The police and secret services would go on even higher alert now as a result of the bombing.

Yousef needed answers, and the sooner, the better. Over the next few hours, he wandered up Oxford Street, marvelling at the designer shops and admiring the beautiful women, who strolled with their arms full of shopping bags. All so far removed from the tower blocks of White City, and even more so from his village in Syria. At Oxford Circus, he bought another tube ticket and boarded a train for the return journey. Soon back at White City, he left the station and took out his mobile.

'Come to the office at eight pm,' he said and clicked off.

Yousef got back to the flat at six o'clock and made himself a small dinner. It tired him, this living under constant threat of detection, and it made his senses alert at all times. That in itself proved exhausting, and training seemed the only way to combat it. And that meant being able to, somehow, relax.

Adhan arrived at exactly eight and tapped on the door, as Yousef had commanded. Yousef sat in his hard-backed kitchen chair, and Adhan on the comfy chair. This would repeat many times.

'Report.'

Adhan just looked at him.

'I said, report.'

Adhan waved his hands from side to side. 'There is nothing to report.'

Yousef looked at him and had to control his anger. 'What about the fucking bomb that went off in Kensington tube station?'

'I heard about it but know nothing.'

'Were they ours?'

'Master, I don't know, I only do as I'm told, nothing more.'

It would be a waste of time interrogating Adhan, as he was just a dispensable low-life messenger. 'You see, Adhan, if this was us, then I should know about it, don't you think?'

'That would seem to make sense, Master.'

'Then ...' Yousef stopped and thought for a moment. It must have been home-grown, that's why he hadn't had any warning. A couple of locals, perhaps, from the mosque, deciding to make a name for themselves.

Yousef shifted in his seat. 'Send a message up the line that I want to make contact with the rogue bombers. They can find out who it is with ease, do you understand?'

'Yes, Master.'

'Good, be off with you, and when you have answers, come back to me.'

'Yes, Master.'

Quietly, Adhan let himself out of the flat.

***

Fifty minutes later, Adhan turned the key in the lock of his up-market two-bedroomed flat in Richmond Avenue, Islington. He had friends and talked to his neighbours. His deep-cover story said that, as the son of a wealthy Arab, he attended University in London. He took his coat off and strolled to the lounge, where he sat in one of the expensive leather chairs and took a deep breath. Then he retrieved his phone and logged into the latest high-tech security app, from which he sent an encrypted message. The moment it got opened and read, it self-destructed. Done for the night, a large whisky was called for, and he poured himself a good measure. Adhan thought about Yousef. The man seemed clever. Mmm, cunning would be more the right word for him. The sort that could smell danger a long way off. A man not to cross, for certain. In need of an early night, he drained the glass and went to take a shower.

CHAPTER 7

As soon as the emergency message arrived from Richard, the teams raided the three houses on the Aashif Jamal watch list. The result entailed the one injured man and three women from the earlier house, and the other two buildings proved empty. Although the operatives ripped them to pieces from top to bottom, they found nothing of any interest. Aashif Jamal owned one of the empty houses. The injured man and the three women had been taken to a gated house in Acre Road, Dulwich, near the park, and a secret location. The spacious detached house had been refurbished into an interrogation centre. The downstairs lounge became the interrogation room, and the dining room a mini theatre-type viewing room. At the push of a button, everything that passed could be recorded onto audio and film. The big, five-bedroom, old-style Victorian house had large sash windows, high ceilings, and fireplaces in every room. It had been used as a safe house for witnesses and, on occasion, for agents. British agents, using interpreters, interviewed the women. Just as Richard had thought, it proved a complete waste of time, as they had no idea what their husbands did, where they went, or with whom they met.

Leather strappings secured the man onto a secure wood-and-steel chair in the lounge, and they left him to stew. He wore a plain white shirt, black pullover, and baggy, grey tracksuit bottoms. Plaster casts encased his legs, and he suffered from extreme pain because of the wounds, for which he took a strong hospital-prescribed, morphine-based opioid painkiller.

They left him for two hours and, finally, someone checked on him. The man had peed himself. In hospital and delirious, he had given his name as Abdul Muta'al Hassain, which fitted the name on the Electoral Roll, British Telecom, British Gas, and Council Tax accounts. Most importantly, his genuine British passport, which had been found at the house, also confirmed his name.

Richard opened the old wooden door and climbed the three steps into the viewing room. Four men already sat chatting. Matt Barlow, the two bodyguards that had transported the prisoner to the house from St Thomas' Hospital, and the fourth, a specialist MI5 interrogator called Duncan Parr. Richard had met Duncan before and introduced himself to the bodyguards. At eleven in the morning, he wanted to get started, as it could turn out to be a long day.

'Okay, Duncan, go to it. I'll join in later. Maybe we'll do the old good-cop, bad-cop routine. Remember, he is probably home grown, so will not have the tradecraft or resilience of a professional terrorist.'

'We'll start with the basics for an hour or two, and then I'll come out.' Duncan picked up his notes and left the room. Five seconds later, the door to the interview room opened, and Duncan entered. The prisoner looked up, and had trepidation written all over his face. Duncan strolled around the obviously nervous prisoner, supposedly reading the notes. Every so often, he would look up and eyeball the man, and then return to the notes once again. After three minutes, he sat at a small wooden table, about five feet in front of the man.

'So, your name is?'

The man put on a determined face. 'I want to know where I am. I want to see my lawyer. I am entitled to representation. And I demand my rights.'

Duncan took his time, as he wanted to unsettle the man. 'You are terrorist murdering scum; therefore, you have no rights. You might have noticed that you're not in a police station, and that is because you are off the radar. We can do with you whatever we want.' Then Duncan raised his voice, 'And, if needs be, we will stay here for days, and yes, your legs will get even more painful because you're not getting any more painkillers, and that's before we consider other measures. So that you co-operate, you understand that lives are at stake?'

'You fucking bastards. I'm saying nothing.'

'Your name?' Duncan looked at his notes for a minute.

Then he spoke slowly, 'We have interviewed your wife, and she proved incredibly helpful. She tells us that your name is Abdul Muta'al Hassain, and that name is on the Electoral Roll. Your passport gives the same name. So, now, what is your fucking name?'

The man shook his head. 'Of course, yes, that's my name, but I won't say another word until I've seen my lawyer.'

Duncan referred to his notes once again. 'What is your name?'

The prisoner raised his eyebrows. Then his shoulders sagged. 'Abdul Muta'al Hassain.'

'Good. I ask the questions, you answer. So, we've interviewed your wife, Aisha, and just this morning picked up your beautiful fifteen-year-old daughter, Adeena. We'll bring her here later today.'

'You bastards. This has nothing to do with my daughter. You fucking piece of shit. Leave her out of this.' The man spat a huge glob of phlegm at Duncan, which missed his face by millimetres.

Duncan picked up the file and smashed it onto the table top. 'Answer the questions, and we'll leave Adeena alone, I guarantee it.'

'You're all fucking liars, you filthy Jew lovers and perverts. I don't believe a word you say.'

Silence held for a minute.

'I forgot what your name is?'

The man screamed, snot hung from his nose, and tears welled in his eyes.

'My fucking name is Abdul Muta'al Hassain.'

Duncan smiled. 'Good, now we can move on. You have lived at this address for ...?' He looked directly at Hassain, 'How many years?'

'You know all this. Fifteen, sixteen years.'

'And you live in the property with your wife, two daughters, and baby son.' He paused, again referring to the notes. 'Your other daughter, Hana, currently resides abroad, is that correct?'

'Yes.'

'Where, exactly?'

'Syria.'

'Thank you.'

Duncan already had the names of Hassain's parents, his brothers, and some of his cousins but wanted to confirm the information. 'What are the names and addresses of your three brothers?'

'Hamza, Amir, and Caleb. Get the addresses from my wife.'

'Your cousins?'

'There are so many … ask my wife. I am tired. I need painkillers.'

'Once we've finished with the names, we will give you the painkillers, okay?'

'Aaban, Eshal, Rehan, Aamir, … ask my wife for the others. There're so many. Now, the painkillers.'

'Eshal is a girl, I believe?'

'Yes.'

'Who else has visited or lived at your house … let's say, in the last twelve months?'

'No one. For God's sake, the painkillers.'

Duncan looked at the notes. 'You had a visitor only last week. Yes, Thursday, at eleven pm. A bit late to be receiving visitors, don't you think? Who was that?'

'I don't know. I can't remember.'

'Let me jog your memory, then.' Duncan took a photo out of the file, got up from his chair, and held it in front of Hassain.

Surprise lit Hassain's face. Now, he knew they had watched his home and taken photos of any visitors.

'So, who is that? He's not a relative, is he? I'd say he was about thirty. Looks Syrian or Iraqi. Who is he?'

'I need my painkillers, please, my legs.' The man let out an anguished cry.

'We haven't finished the names yet. The man left at eight minutes past twelve, he stayed for over an hour, and you don't remember? He didn't come to fuck your wife, did he? Is that what you like? Do you take photos or video?'

'You deviant filth.'

'What was the man's name?'

***

In the viewing room, Richard cursed. He remembered the incident well. One of the surveillance team had gone off sick, and the man had been allowed to leave without being followed. Subsequently, the number plate on his old red Ford Escort had turned out to be false.

***

Back in the interrogation room, the prisoner said, 'He's from the Mosque. I needed powerful prayer.'

'Which Mosque, exactly?'

'I'm not sure. I go to many different ones.'

'No, you don't. You always go to Central London Mosque. You have to understand; there is no point in lying or trying to hide things.' Duncan proceeded to exaggerate the truth somewhat, 'I have photos of every single person who's gone in or out of your house for the past three months. I have listened to every call from your house and mobile phones for the same period. The man who visited you drives a red Ford Escort. I already know where he lives and what his name is because we followed him. Right now, I need you to confirm it so that we can establish trust here, Abdul.'

Duncan paused again, and then said, 'Trust is so very important, don't you think, Abdul?' Duncan looked at his watch, making sure that Hassain saw him. 'By the way, Adeena should be here any minute.'

'You are worse than a stinking dog. You are all bastards.' Hassain spat again.

'So, the man's name and address?'

'I need the toilet.'

'When you give me his name and address, you can go.'

'I'll shit myself here, and you'll have to clean me up.'

'If you do that, you will sit in shit for as long as you remain in that chair. His name and address?'

Hassain closed his eyes. He looked tired and in terrible pain.

'His name …' Hassain closed his eyes. 'His name is Ibrahim Muhammad. I don't know his address. He lives in London. Now, I need the toilet, and I want some painkillers.'

'Same name as your son? That's nice. One thing at a time, eh, and that will be the toilet.' Duncan left the room, and the two guards entered and carried him to the downstairs bathroom.

***

Richard felt happy with progress. 'Good job, Duncan. Well done. He won't last much longer. He's a novice.'

'Yes, I agree, but the big question is, does he have any idea where Aashif Jamal actually is?'

'He's killed and maimed hundreds. Gloves can come off if needs be. Bunny authorised it as a last resort.'

'Well, we can always end up there. Let's hope we don't have to, but should the need arise, he has badly wounded legs. They would make a good place to start.' The interview-room door opened, interrupting their conversation, and the guards dragged in Hassain and strapped him into the chair.

Duncan smiled. 'Are you coming in?'

'Not yet. Let's see what happens for half an hour, and I'll decide then.'

Duncan went back to work.

***

'I need painkillers. I'm in terrible pain.'

'Hassain, you make me want to vomit. You moan pathetically about your bit of pain, yet you just killed ninety-three men, women, and children. Dozens more lay in hospitals all over London with limbs torn from their bodies. Do you, seriously, think I give a fucking shit about your little bit of pain?'

Hassain spoke quietly, 'I didn't kill anybody.'

'You're just as guilty. Where were the bombs made? And where is Aashif Jamal?'

Through his pain, Hassain managed to laugh. 'You will never catch him, never.'

Duncan got up and walked behind Hassain, who couldn't turn.

'I promise you this one thing; you will never, ever

leave prison. So, that gives you about forty years. A lifetime. Forty years as a guest in Her Majesty's Prison Belmarsh.' He stayed behind him and waited for that to sink in, and then continued, 'Who's going to protect your daughters from all the boys? Arabs, whites, and the big-cock-black-boys who will want to take their virginity? Perhaps one of the boys at school has fucked Adeena already? What do you think?'

Bolts secured the chair to the floor. Hassain tried, desperately, to pull himself free and attack Duncan but could hardly move an inch. 'You will die in the fires of hell. Oh, Allah help me to kill this blasphemous bastard.' Globules of spit flew in all directions to no avail.

Duncan stared into Hassain's eyes. 'When Adeena arrives, she will have to be strip searched. We're short on staff, so I might have to do that myself, and if I like what I see, I might even stick my cock in her mouth so she can give it a good sucking.'

'You bastard. You will roast in hellfire for eternity.'

Duncan moved so that he stood extremely close to the back of Hassain's head and screamed into his ear, '*Where is Aashif Jamal? Where is he, you terrorist bastard?*'

Hassain, about to scream more abuse, stopped when the door opened, and Richard entered.

'Out,' was all he said. Duncan made for the door. Richard turned and winked when he passed.

***

'I've just arrived, Mr Hassain. What on earth is

going on here? How are you?'

Hassain broke down into tears. 'That bastard. He says he's going to do things to my daughter. She's only fifteen. He's an animal. Help me, please. Don't let him touch her.'

Richard pulled the chair up close to Hassain.

'I would like to help you, but you have to help me first. I can make sure your daughter stays safe in the care of your wife. Think about it. No worry about your daughter.' Richard shook his head and proceeded with a classic interrogation technique, 'Abdul, I know how you feel. I have two teenage daughters of my own, and they're so precious to us, aren't they? I could help you even more. You didn't plant that bomb. I mean, you didn't really kill and maim all those people. It was your friend Aashif. What you have to think about is this: while you're going to spend the rest of your life in prison, he's out drinking Arak and enjoying life. For all I know, he could already be back in Syria.'

'He's not ...' Hassain didn't finish.

Richard pushed on. He leant forward. 'Help us, and I'll get your sentence reduced dramatically. When you're older, you will still have time with your children and the little grandchildren.'

Hassain cried at the mention of his children. 'I will need protection in prison. They will kill me.'

'I can protect you. You'll do your sentence in a special segregation facility. I can arrange it all. Don't worry. It will all work out. Now, Aashif Jamal? All I need is an address. Just those few words, and I will look after you.'

Hassain took a deep breath. 'As far as I know, he

is still here. We made the bomb in a flat above a newsagents in East Ham High Street.'

'The name of the shop?'

'It just says "Groceries." The window is full of special offers and stickers. I think it's number forty-three. And, if he's not there, then I can't help you any more.'

'The shopkeeper is involved?'

'Yes.'

'His name?'

'Abbas Mahmood.'

'Are they armed?'

'Yes. Grenades and AK-47 machine guns.'

'I tell you what I'll do, Mr Hassain … one of my colleagues will come back in, he'll give you your painkillers and something to eat and drink, and then we'll have a few more questions. As you're now helping us and yourself, it shouldn't take too long. Okay?'

'Yes, a hot tea and my painkillers, thank you.'

Richard left the room and, in seconds, re-entered the viewing area.

Duncan met him with a smile on his face. 'That worked brilliantly.'

'He's an amateur, who got sucked into something. A bloody fool. I'll organise the visit to East Ham for tonight. We still need all his friends' names and addresses—everything possible … as many contacts as you can get for the three dead men. Also, spend some time on the Central London Mosque. Who are the radical teachers? Who are the next Aashif Jamal's?' He paused, thinking, and then said, 'And, last, I want to know what the keys are for? I'd guess it's some sort of storage facility for bomb making equipment. Find out and send me a full report. Good job, Duncan, and so quick.'

'As you said, a beginner. I almost feel sorry for him.'

'I know what you mean, but I just think about the two hundred dead and wounded from the tube. He'll rot in prison along with the other so-called glorious Martyrs.'

CHAPTER 8

Very much a typical January day, cold and overcast with heavy, grey clouds, they'd forecast snow for later in the week. Yousef hoped that it *did* snow. He felt desperate to see the white stuff and touch it for the first time in his life. Today, he wore his new cream-coloured Chino trousers with an expensive brown leather belt. Also, he had on a new plain white tee shirt and, on top of that, a new blue, size sixteen collar shirt. Two other new items turned him into a fashionable, smartly dressed tourist: brown brogues and a hundred-pound, dark-blue long wool coat.

Yousef felt good, walked with a new confidence, and felt that he belonged in the tourist attractions of central London. Currently, he stood outside Westminster tube station, taking in the sights. He knew not to stand in one place too long because of the massive CCTV coverage, which saturated the entire area. Above him lay Portcullis House, home to many of the Country's Members of Parliament not senior enough for an office in the actual House of Commons.

From his vantage point, he looked over at Big Ben and the House of Commons, the home of democracy and mother of so many parliaments, and which had been copied by so many nations. A wonderful building with such history. Slowly, he walked ten yards and waited at the traffic lights, busy with hundreds of tourists. The little man went to green, and the crowd rushed for the other side. Yousef got across and joined the crowd moving toward the parliament building entrance. After a further ten yards, he got there and walked past four police officers, who stood chatting amongst themselves. They looked rather elderly and didn't appear to carry weapons.

Just past the entrance, he stopped and looked through the black-painted railings at the driveway, which contained vehicle obstacles and a further security hut. Also, two police officers, armed with German-made Heckler and Koch MP5SFA3 semi-automatic carbines (one of the best machine guns in the world) stood just off the road. And what security lay beyond that, he could not tell.

Not wishing to draw undue attention, he walked on and traversed Parliament Square, stopping to admire the Winston Churchill Statue. His next objective stood nearby, as he strolled up Whitehall. A sign pointed to the Churchill War Rooms, another tourist attraction from World War 2. Then, slowly, he moved past the cenotaph. More would die soon.

Then he reached his target. Downing Street, home of the British Prime Minister, puppy-dog to the greatest Kafir on the Earth, the American President, Barack Obama. Yousef stopped and mingled with the crowd, which pushed up against the massive black security gates, trying to get a glimpse of number ten. Security looked tight; six police officers patrolled, two of them armed (again) with Heckler and Koch machine guns. Everybody had a good time, and tourists from all over the world crowded Whitehall, Parliament Square, and Westminster Abbey.

They wouldn't be so happy when he'd finished with them. Yousef chuckled and continued sightseeing, strolling up to Trafalgar Square, and then cutting up the Mall for a look at Buckingham Palace. He loved the soldiers in their red jackets and black bearskins. While strolling, he reflected that life in rich London was so far removed from what he'd grown used to in Syria and Iraq that it felt like being on another planet. The decadent Western ideology would continue to be attacked by bombs as long as their indiscriminate killing of men, women, and children continued in Syria and Iraq.

During his stay in the UK, Yousef had begun reading the papers and felt amazed that British and Western cultures thought a bomb in a bus terminal was so much more barbaric than a Typhoon Fighter dropping laser-guided Tomcat missiles and killing numerous civilians as collateral damage.

At five pm, he called it a day, though he'd wanted to walk past Scotland Yard and take a selfie. In the event, he decided that it might not be a good idea. Instead, he got back on the tube at Hyde Park Corner, but not before noticing the huge luxury hotels and houses in Park Lane, one of the most expensive addresses in London. Hard to believe that so much wealth stood on show while his whole country languished as a bombed ruin.

By six-thirty, he got back to White City tube station, came out, and turned right to stroll up Wood Lane. The evening had grown dark and cold, and he gave thanks for his new coat. When he got back to the flat, he should pray; he needed to settle his head, having seen so much obscene wealth and decadence during the day. His next turn took him left, down South Africa Road. At the Springbok pub, he felt tempted to pop in and try some beer but walked past, not looking at the establishment.

Low and behold, just up the road, another pub had exactly the same name. It seemed a big pub with a car park, and on a sign outside it said that it had a large-screen Sky Sports television, snooker tables, a darts team, and Tuesdays were quiz nights. He shouldn't go in but had to understand the British mentality, and a visit to a pub (just once) was essential intelligence gathering.

Yousef pushed open the door and walked into a large bar area. Such drinking bars in Syria seemed tiny in comparison. Three or four older men sat at the bar. The night being young suited him. He sauntered to the bar and looked at the beer pumps. Then the bottles behind the bar caught his attention. The young Asian recognized BECKS, and then he saw the Guinness pump. A young, big breasted lady came over to him, wearing tight jeans and a black jumper, and asked what he would like. Her accent sounded strong, and he thought it might be Irish.

'Guinness, please.'

'Pint?'

'Yes, a pint, thanks.'

The barmaid placed the long Guinness glass under the pump and pulled. Murky, horrible-looking stuff poured into the glass. Yousef didn't feel overly impressed.

'That'll be four-pounds-fifty, please.'

The price shocked him. He thought it expensive but handed over a five-pound note.

The lady laughed and waved the note in the air. 'Shall I keep the change, then?' She wasn't backward in coming forward.

Yousef felt unsure what was happening, and then it hit him. 'Of course. What's fifty pence between friends?'

'Thank you, kind Sir,' she replied.

All this proved an education and well worth the visit. Yousef glanced back to the beer. The glass now stood full of a deep-black velvety-looking thick liquid. The barwoman did something on top of the lather head and handed it to him.

'You can't beat a good pint of the black stuff,' she said.

'That's what I always say myself.' Yousef nodded and smiled. 'Thank you.' Then he turned and went to sit by the window.

He looked around. A workingman's pub, bit dirty, threadbare carpet, but probably good beer. He held the glass up, and it looked magical, so he took a sip. Never had he tasted anything quite like it. The liquid went down smoothly. Yousef held the glass to his lips and drank; he loved the feeling as it flowed down his throat. When he took the glass away, it shocked him that he had drunk over half already. Drinking in England was an expensive hobby. He couldn't resist it, and five minutes later, he went back to the bar. The barwoman sauntered over and, before she could say anything, he waved the glass.

'Another pint of the delicious black stuff, please.'

'Coming right up, Sir.'

He handed over the five-pound note. 'And keep the change.'

'Thank you, Sir. You may come again.'

'Yes, I may well do that. I've just moved into the area, and you're my local, so see you later.'

Seated once more, he knocked back the Guinness, and then felt ready for home. He left, happy to have chalked up another experience. Cold and hungry, he walked at speed back toward the flat. As he entered Canada Way, he stopped. He could never understand it but had a sixth sense. Something felt different. Something had happened, and he didn't know what. However, instantly he went on alert. If only he had a pistol tucked away in his coat.

Cautious, he continued walking, scanning the area in front and to the sides, and then saw the danger. A grey Audi A4 parked at the side of the road, two men sitting in the front seats, both smoking, and windows shut. Not right. He couldn't see their faces, and turned straight around and walked back down the road. Had he somehow been compromised? Yousef walked back to Australia Road, and then cut through so that he now stood on the other side of the car. From there, he looked closely at the driver and passenger. With a nod, he recognised Adhan. Why hadn't he called to say he was coming? Yousef took out his mobile, needing to know what was going on. He rang the number, and Adhan answered. Yousef cut off. He waited the two minutes and rang again. Adhan answered the phone. Yousef said, 'Beacon,' and a second later, Adhan spoke.

'Yes?'

'Report.'

'Yes, Master. I am in a car near your flat, waiting for you to return. I have a visitor with me that you will be interested in meeting.'

'Who is the man who smokes so much?'

'You can see us?' Adhan and the man looked around to see where he hid.

'I do not want you seen coming to the flat. In one minute, I will get in the back of the car on the kerb side, so make sure the door is open. You will pull away immediately and drive. Do you understand?'

'Yes, Master.'

The car engine started, Yousef walked quickly toward the vehicle, pulled the back-passenger-door handle, and slid into the seat. 'Go.'

The car pulled out and sped around the corner, away from the flat.

'Who are you?'

Before the man could speak, Adhan blurted out, 'Beacon, meet the Kensington tube station bomber, Aashif Jamal.'

'Adhan, how many times do I have to tell you not to use fucking names?'

'Sorry, Master. I forget.'

Yousef looked at the man; he looked between forty-five and fifty, had a full head of hair, and a rascally face.

'Aashif Jamal, all the praise goes to Allah, but I

61

give you praise for your work. A masterstroke of defiance against the cowardly British, who hide like women in the cockpits of their multi-million-pound fighter planes. You will be rewarded now and in the afterlife for your effort. Congratulations.'

Aashif turned around. 'Thank you, Beacon, and now we must get some hot food. I am starving.'

Yousef smiled at the man—a lot older than himself—and felt that he had so much he wanted to talk to him about. 'You have trained in Syria?'

'No. I answered the call with three of my closest friends from the Mosque. They raided the houses. Three killed, and another badly injured.'

'So, the security services will have interrogated the live one?'

'Yes.'

'They will have your name, address, everything?'

'Yes, they will.'

'What else will they have?'

'I don't understand?'

'Is there any connection to Adhan?'

'No, none at all. This is the first time I have had contact from Adhan.'

'Good. My mission here is of the utmost importance and cannot be compromised by either of you. What is your plan, now, Aashif-the-bomber?'

'I want to go to Syria, but Adhan says I must lay low here for some weeks.'

'Where will you stay?'

Adhan butted in, 'We have friends up north. He will go to a safe house.'

'Good. You seem to be on top of things.'

'I am following instructions, Master.'

Yousef chuckled. 'Did I tell you that I like you, Adhan?'

Adhan smiled. 'No, but everybody likes me, so why should you be any different?' All three laughed. 'It is one of my great strengths, meeting new people and being liked.'

Twenty minutes later, the three men parked up in a quiet council car park and sat eating a selection of delicious takeaway Kebabs.

Yousef asked Adhan, 'Have you tried the delicious black stuff?'

Adhan laughed. 'Of course. I have been here ten years, but I prefer premium lager to Guinness.'

All three laughed again. Yousef enjoyed himself, and it felt good to be amongst friends and laughing for a change.

CHAPTER 9

Richard checked his Glock pistol; the weight and touch of it gave him a comfortable feeling. Loaded, he slipped the weapon back into his shoulder holster. Richard hadn't wanted any slip ups and so only MI5 people comprised the team. Neither Atallah nor Siddique had been included, as it might have blown their covers. If at all possible, he wanted Aashif Jamal and Abbas Mahmood taken alive.

The two blacked-out Range Rovers had parked up in Masterman Road, just off East Ham High Street, opposite the Tesco Express. At seven o'clock, the pitch-black area remained reasonably busy with people shopping at Argos, Primark, Specsavers, and numerous other big brands all along the high street. One of the cars had driven past the grocery shop twice, which stood between Bairstow Eves the Estate Agents and a branch of Superdrug. A man had been seen serving at the shop counter who fitted the age and description of Abbas Mahmood. No lights burned in the dingy-looking flat above the shop. Following the drive past, one of the team had gone on foot to buy cigarettes in the shop, and another to explore the area behind it.

***

Veteran MI5 agent, Barry Gunn, pushed open the glass door and strolled up and joined the small queue. Immediately, he noticed the high counter.

The suspected Abbas Mahmood, in his flowing white robes and long black beard, looked down on him, and Barry could imagine he had an AK-47 under the counter, which would take only a second to grab and fire. He clocked where the back door lay, and then his turn came. He purchased twenty Benson and Hedges, paid with a ten-pound note, took his change, and wandered back out of the store.

***

Tony Green had recced the rear of the shop. The back entrance looked like it had a reinforced metal security door. At each end of the parade of shops were steel steps leading up to the flats. It would be possible to get a team outside the flat door prior to them attacking and taking Abbas Mahmood. The store would stay open until eleven pm, and Richard decided to wait a while. He planned the action for eight o'clock. The teams split in two. Four men would attack the flat and four the shop, and it would take precision timing to ensure success.

At seven-forty-five, the agents had their last cigarettes and got ready for action. Four agents made for the back of the shop, left one man covering the back door, and the three others climbed the stairs quietly and positioned themselves outside the flat door. Through the dirty back windows it looked pitch-black and didn't appear as though anybody was at home, but you never knew.

***

The four men at the front, including Richard, got

ready. Andy Clegg would go into the store and pretend to look at the chiller cabinet drinks, and twenty seconds later, Richard would go in. Everybody looked at their watches. One minute to go. Andy walked into the shop, he glanced around, found no one else present, and took station by the chiller.

***

One of the team outside the flat lifted the battering ram and got ready. The countdown began at both locations: five, four, three, two, one, go. The battering ram hit the door, which crashed open, and Richard walked into the shop and approached the counter.

***

Above, the three agents entered the flat, guns held out in front, ready to combat any danger. The team moved through the property, alert and with torch light now crisscrossing the rooms. Sporadic shouts of 'Clear!' came as they checked each room.

***

In the shop, Andy moved to the side of the counter and lifted his Glock pistol at exactly the same time as Richard, who shouted at the man behind the counter. Andy aimed his pistol at the man's head, ready to fire.

'Put your hands in the air. Put your hands in the air.'

The man, at first shocked, stood and stared, and then ducked under the counter. Andy and Richard froze, waiting for him to reappear firing.

'Come out, or we will open fire. You have one more chance. Come out with your hands in the air, or we will commence firing.'

'Okay. Okay, I'm coming out now, please don't shoot, don't shoot.'

Richard and Tony braced themselves, weapons ready.

The hands appeared first, shaking violently, followed by his arms.

Richard screamed at the man, *'Keep your hands in the air, high in the air.'*

The man appeared, and when Richard looked at him, he knew straight away. 'Put your hands on your head and stand still.'

Richard signalled Andy to move in, who went forward grabbed the man's arms and pinned them behind his back, securing them with a plastic tie.

Richard strode forward. 'Your name? What's your fucking name?'

The man shook. 'Abdul Fattah Abdulla.'

'So where the fuck is Abbas Mahmood? Talk.'

The man was almost shitting himself. 'Gone.'

'What?'

'He took a phone call about two hours ago and said there was an emergency at home, and he rushed out the door. That's all I know. I work part-time, looking after the shop.'

Richard couldn't speak but just stared at the man, wanting to smash his face in with the weapon.

Five minutes later, the teams tore apart the shop and the flat as they searched for clues as to the whereabouts of the two fugitives.

They took away the hapless Abdul Fattah Abdulla for questioning amidst a hail of protest.

Richard sat in one of the cars, wondering who the

mole could be. What bastard had made the phone call to Abbas Mahmood warning him of the raid?

CHAPTER 10

Richard Carpenter sat in Charlie's Café on Whitton Road in Twickenham, West London. Small, it had old fashioned wooden tables and chairs, and red-and-white-checked plastic cloths covered the tables. Salt, pepper, and sugar dispensers topped the covers, and what Richard thought was watered down tomato ketchup. He had his back to the counter, seated in the corner so that he could see who came in and out. Dressed in scruffy jeans, shirt, jumper, and a dirty, short blue donkey jacket, a flat cap finished off his appearance. Far removed from his normal work clothes.

His wife didn't know about this guilty secret; at least once a week, he liked to have a café full English Breakfast. Just then, he tucked into sausage, egg, beans, mushrooms, bacon, and black pudding, and to the side of the large, white plate lay a side plate with two doorstop slices of buttered white bread. Richard sipped at the huge mug of indeterminate-coloured tea that came with the *all-in* price of five pounds. He had asked the man to meet him at the café, as it lay on the opposite side of London to where he would be based and working, and it gave him the opportunity to have his beloved full English.

Now ten-thirty-five, the man was due in five minutes, and Richard didn't like agents being late. He took a mouthful of fried egg and black pudding, the yoke ran down his chin, and he caught it with his tongue. He picked up the paper napkin just as a tall, well-built Arab man in a brown Thobe entered the café. Richard put his right hand in his jacket pocket and brought out a folded copy of the Sun newspaper, which he unfolded and laid on the table. The man ordered a cup of tea, and then approached Richard.

'Can I borrow your paper, please?'

'Keep it. I've already read it. Sit down.' Their passwords exchanged and correct, Badi al Zaman Siddique had arrived in London.

Richard glanced around the café. Two other customers sat on the opposite side, near the front door. Richard and Siddique could not be overheard.

'So, how was your trip?'

Siddique replied in good English, 'Good, no issues. How are you?'

Richard took an immediate disliking to the man, too cocksure and arrogant, and he ignored the question. He stared at him.

'You have settled into the house?'

'Yes, it's very nice. I was hoping that —'

Richard cut him off, 'Quiet.'

'Sorry, I'll keep quiet.' Siddique smiled, showing his rotting yellow teeth.

That was better, Richard thought. He took a large brown envelope out of his inside jacket pocket and placed it on the table.

'These are your instructions, which you need to follow until I tell you otherwise. There are contact details, passwords, and methods of work, and most importantly, your cover story. Memorise it all and then destroy the paper.'

'Yes, Sir.'

'Why did the Americans sack you?'

'All a misunderstanding. They are fools. I did nothing.'

'Shut up.' Siddique went quiet. 'You do realise that we work closely with the Americans?'

'I say what I think. You want me to lie?'

'If you think that all Americans are fools, then you are the fool. We will meet here every Thursday at eleven am until further notice. You may go.'

'I really wanted to ...'

Richard leant across the table, 'When I give you an instruction, carry it out immediately or you will be going back to Syria quickly. Have I made myself clear?'

'I was only ... yes.' Then he got up, turned, and walked out of the café.

Richard felt beyond anger; he couldn't stand the man. He took out his mobile and pressed a speed dial.

'It's Spitfire. Is Bunny in today?'

A second later, the unmistakable voice of Bunny came down the line, 'Yes?'

'I just met up with Norma. She could well be finishing earlier than anticipated.'

'Oh really? Why's that?'

'Not surprised her other friends dropped her; she's a difficult sort, could be an issue.'

'Watch her closely then. We don't want any problems. Goodbye.'

Richard finished his cup of tea and was about to

71

get up when his phone buzzed. A message had come in from Thames House. He opened it and read:

TALIBAN ATTACK BACHAKHAN UNIVERSITY IN PAKISTAN 21 KILLED 4 TALIBAN EXTREMISTS DEAD

Richard sighed. It seemed never ending. He rose from his chair, thanked the lady behind the counter, and sauntered out into the sunny but freezing January day. Then he walked toward his car. All of a sudden, he halted, took out his phone, went through his contacts, and found who he was after. Then he pressed the green button.

'Laurie? It's Richard. I have a priority job for you.'

...

'Yes, direct surveillance.'

...

'Never mind who it is. I'll send over the info later today.'

...

'Yes, twenty-four-seven. I want to know when he farts.'

—

CHAPTER 11

Yousef stretched his arms and rolled over. Then he pulled his new, white thirteen-and-a-half-Tog-rated duvet up around his neck and shut his eyes. It had been a late night. How had Adhan and Aashif gotten on, driving up north? It had felt good to meet up and enjoy their company, and the Kebabs had tasted delicious. He had praised Aashif and thought that if a home-grown could bomb a tube train, then he would have to achieve even more. Apparently, Aashif was headed for somewhere called Bradford, which had the largest Muslim community in the country. Adhan would get back at about four pm. Yousef would phone him to make sure that everything had gone according to plan. Already, he had planned out the next week. Four days would be spent as a London tourist, with one day at home in the flat to clean and rest. He felt worried about something and needed to pray. Again, he had dreamt about the girl in flat eighteen. Sin always lay only a heartbeat away, and even to dream it meant damnation.

Yousef showered and dressed and got ready for his trip into London. He put on different coloured clothes to his last visit. The security services monitored the tube, and he didn't want to leave any chance of one of them recognising him as a frequent traveller of interest. He set off, as before, from White City station on the central line, but this time changed at Notting Hill Gate and transferred onto the District and Circle line.

The train rumbled at speed through the black tunnels and, this time, he got out at Victoria mainline station. He ascended the escalators and went through the ticket barrier, remembering to pick up his ticket when it emerged from the slit in the machine. Then he strolled through the busy ticket machine area and climbed the steep steps to the exit two at a time. When he reached the top, he emerged into the sunny but chilly daylight.

Victoria seemed a huge station, with masses of people hurrying in every direction. Yousef walked the twenty yards to the front entrance. Long lines of black taxis drove off in every direction, huge bright-red double-decker buses passed everywhere, and then—siren blaring—a police car screeched around a corner, lights flashing, and sped away. He set off walking down Victoria Street, nervous but also incredibly excited. His heart pounded, and he kept imagining that people stared at him.

To calm himself, he took a few deep breaths. People weren't looking at him, specifically; it was just nerves. Everywhere he walked, he saw CCTV cameras. They seemed to be on every wall and at every set of traffic lights. He knew all about the vehicle number plate recognition systems—one of many reasons he'd decided not to hire a car, plus the tube being so quick and comprehensive meant that he didn't need one.

Not far now, he stood on the other side of the street to the building he wanted. The blue sign read: NEW SCOTLAND YARD. Yousef almost burst out laughing. While he stood and watched, an armed police officer sauntered down the pavement on the opposite side of the road, going back to the Scotland Yard building.

Yousef set off again, strolling casually as though he didn't have a care in the world. With so many people, so many cars, and very few police officers, today he did allow himself a little chuckle and truly believed himself almost invisible. He continued down Victoria Street, noting the old and beautiful Westminster Abbey on his right-hand side. When he reached Parliament Square, he again crossed the roads and headed for the entrance to the House of Commons.

Similar to the previous occasion, four or five much older, and probably unfit officers, stood guard on the gate, and inside, next to the security box, stood another two officers armed with machine guns. He felt sure that more security would be elsewhere, but in truth, that didn't overly concern him. Next, he strolled past and turned right at the end of the road, headed toward Westminster Bridge. Yousef noted the steps down to the embankment, where leisure boats picked up customers.

When he got to the bridge, he stopped and leant on the wall, looking down at the river. He loved the water, and it brought memories of the river Euphrates at home; this seemed another world. Yousef walked across the bridge, loving every step, as he smelt the water and heard the waves lapping on the bridge supports. It took a few minutes to get all the way across, and again, he stopped and looked down at the river. This time, he got a surprise. When he leant over, a police launch appeared from under the bridge and motored off up the river.

Yousef reflected that the British police and security seemed understated. Not to call it unprofessional and unready for any attack, but compared to the Americans' big, brash 'We've got more and bigger guns than you, so watch out' style, it would be easy to assume such. However, he knew for a fact, having read history, that the British were just as (if not more) ruthless than most. You didn't build an empire by being nice to everybody.

Yousef turned around and looked back across the bridge. Police cars travelled both ways on the road. So much for understated security. He crossed over to the other side and sauntered back over the bridge. When he got to the end, he spent a minute looking at the Union Jack flags and memorabilia in the small and expensive wooden kiosk. Then he turned right and walked down a flight of stone steps and onto the embankment. A glance to his left revealed Westminster tube station and Portcullis House.

Yousef scanned the area, taking in distances and studying the layout of benches, trees, traffic lights, rubbish bins, and parking spaces. He wanted the area to feel like his second home. All done, he strolled along the embankment, stopping at Westminster Pier to get a closer look at the long leisure boats that ferried tourists up and down the river. How great it would be to transport one of them back home with him to the village. The thought brought a smile. The sight would leave the villagers speechless. Nostalgic, he turned and walked back up the embankment and retraced his steps to Parliament Square. He had two locations that he couldn't wait to visit. After crossing the road, he made for the station. Alongside which, and therefore underneath Portcullis House, stood a branch of Café Caesar.

Yousef got to the entrance, jam packed with tourists, and walked in and joined the queue. He looked around and did a quick count. There must have been close on a hundred people enjoying morning coffee and pastries. From the end of the long queue, it appeared that most people ordered takeaway coffees. After a glance at his watch, he waited and waited. It seemed like an age but, in fact, had only taken six minutes when a server asked what he would like. He ordered an Americana and a chocolate muffin. Then he paid the four pounds sixty and went to the end of the counter to wait for his coffee.

Another long wait followed; this time, five minutes. The queue seemed non-stop. People kept coming in. Did it stay busy like that all day? Yousef carried his coffee and muffin and managed to squeeze into a seat by the window that somebody had just vacated. As soon as he sat down, a middle-aged man in a smart suit opposite him said, 'Good Morning.' Yousef replied with a smile and a nod and took a sip of his coffee. A woman occupied the place next to him, and he picked up her scent — pleasantly musky and, for some reason, it reminded him of Syria. Surreptitiously, he took a look at her. When he saw her to be a beautiful, well-dressed Arab woman, it left him surprised and shocked. He turned fully to her and said good morning in Syrian. She turned and looked at him, and her huge almond-shaped eyes struck him. She said good morning in return and turned away. The man in the smart suit stood and left the table. Yousef felt more confident with him gone.

'Where are you from?'

Their eyes met, and then she also stood, walked to the door, and left the café. Beneath her long and beautiful multi-coloured dress, she wore leggings, and above her shoulders, a pink scarf for modesty. Her abrupt departure shocked Yousef. Perhaps he should have spoken to her in English? He drank his coffee and enjoyed his chocolate muffin, and then left the café.

He emerged into the sunlight and took a deep breath, and then coughed when the cold air penetrated down to his lungs. He looked for the woman, but she had gone, and he would probably never set eyes on her again. Perturbed, he walked fifty yards and turned right into Canon Row, where he then crossed the road. At the St Thomas' Tavern Pub, he opened the door and walked in. Then he stopped and looked around. Though not lunchtime yet, about twenty people sat having coffees and conducting what he thought must be breakfast business meetings.

Yousef ordered another coffee and sat in a corner, watching the door. He imagined the scene at lunchtime. Most likely, it would be incredibly busy. Then he got another shock: who had just walked in but the mysterious woman from Café Caesar. He pulled his collar up and slunk back into the shadows. The woman ordered a Soya milk Latte and sat on the opposite side of the bar so that she, too, could watch the door.

What the hell was she up to? Yousef wanted to talk to her but felt scared that she would just run away again. He looked at her more closely. She looked about thirty and, for the first time, he noticed four solid gold bracelets dangling on her wrist, which meant she had money, and those eyes … big, beautiful eyes that trapped you so you couldn't look away. Unsure what to do, he opted for watching and waiting. Nobody joined her; she just sat and sipped her coffee and minded her business.

Fifteen minutes later, she stood and made for the door. As she left the pub, Yousef stood and followed. The woman walked briskly across Parliament Square and headed up Broad Sanctuary toward Victoria Street. Yousef kept his distance; he had received training in surveillance and noted that she never turned or looked once to see if anyone followed her. Soon, she reached Victoria Street, and then she took the first right into Storey's Gate, and then a quick left into Broadway. Yousef saw what he thought must be her destination, The Broadway House Hotel. It had lovely, pub-like double wooden entrance doors, and you could see into a well-lit bar and reception area.

The woman strode in through the doors, and he lost her when she walked through the reception area. Yousef looked at the sign above the entrance. A three-star hotel; somewhere you might stay to keep a reasonably low profile. Yousef felt intrigued. Who was she? What was she doing in London? All very mysterious, and he remained uncertain what to do next, if anything. He decided to do nothing. He didn't need the distraction, and his superiors would frown upon any idea of him meeting with her; not that he had any intention of telling Adhan about the woman.

***

Durriyah Kassab walked through the reception area to the lifts. She pressed the button, and one of the doors opened instantly. Seven seconds later, she got out on the fourth floor and walked down the long grey-carpeted corridor to room forty-seven. At the door, she swiped the lock with her key-card and pushed open the door, which she then closed and locked behind her. Durriyah threw her handbag onto the desk chair and collapsed onto the bed. Then the tears began to flow.

CHAPTER 12

Francis Matthews, codename Bunny, a career professional, had reached the dizzy heights of controller of Counter-Terrorism at MI5. She did nothing in her life other than practice her Russian language skills and work for MI5 from the minute she woke to the minute she retired; a little like Margaret Thatcher in that she only had five hours of sleep a night. She arrived in her office at seven am and left at eight or nine pm. At weekends, she either worked from home or could be found in the office. Her staff thought her boring, dull, and one-dimensional. The MI5 Director General loved her; after all, who else would commit their whole life to a cause twenty-four hours, seven days a week?

Francis was born to Geoffrey, a Church of England vicar, and Mavis, who had stayed at home and brought up the children. Both parents remained alive and well and lived in Witney in Oxfordshire. They had three children: Francis, the eldest, followed by Christopher, forty, and Samuel, thirty-eight. They had all gone to Oxford on scholarships and done well for themselves. Christopher worked in the City as a hedge fund manager, and Samuel had followed in his father's footsteps and joined the church. They all met up once a year at Christmas and, apart from that, didn't keep in contact unless a family emergency arose.

MI5 had recruited Francis from Oxford because

of her Russian language skills. She still holidayed in Moscow, St Petersburg, and other cities every summer for two weeks, topping up her fluency. The Russian cold war threat had diminished, and MI5 had scaled back its Russian operations. Then they invaded Crimea and started the war in Eastern Ukraine. Russia came back on the agenda, but nowhere near the top of the list; Al Qaeda and Isil now proved, by far, the most dangerous threat to British citizens at home and abroad.

Francis had had one great love affair in her life when she spent a year in Russia learning the language for her degree. It happened with Aleksei Semyonov, a history student at Lomonosov Moscow State University. She informed MI5 that she had met a young Russian man, and they ordered her to drop him. It had been a heart breaking decision at the time and one that she sometimes looked back on with massive regret. They had said it was too dangerous for her to continue the relationship, and that he could well be a plant working for the KGB. Francis then started eating to forget the pain and ended up piling on the pounds, which she also blamed on MI5.

As for her life now, MI5 *was* her life. Though overweight, she didn't care, as she had no interest in men, or women, for that matter. Operatives like Richard Carpenter liked her. They always knew where they stood with Bunny, good or bad. They trusted her with their lives, which on occasion, they'd had to do.

She lived in a lovely two-bedroom flat in a converted house in Hampstead. Francis loved her flat. It provided her haven, although she loved her office at Thames House just as much.

If you saw her in Waitrose, you'd think her a tea-and-scone spinster.

CHAPTER 13

'David? It's Richard. Just a quick chat before the meeting with Bunny. How's your man getting on?'

'His codename is Desert. I'm happy; he hardly speaks, and when he does, he says something sensible. What could be better than that?'

Richard let out a sigh of exasperation. 'Wish mine was the same. He's a pain in the arse, opinionated, talkative, and has rotten teeth.'

David laughed. 'No wonder the Americans dropped him, then.'

Silence fell for a second, and then Richard asked, 'How did you know that?'

Another second of silence ensued. 'Come on, old boy; office gossip. You know how it is?'

'Well, people should stop it. It's highly unprofessional and could be dangerous.'

David grew serious, 'Yes, you're right. I'll have a quiet word with the person who told me.'

'What's your man up to?'

'Can't tell you, old boy; classified.'

'Yeah, all right. I'll see you shortly, then.'

'Oh, Richard?'

'What?'

'I know I shouldn't gossip but, apparently, Bunny is in a foul mood. Just giving you a heads up.'

'Thanks, David.'

I'll be about half an hour.'

'Okay.' Richard cut off the call.

At lunch time, Richard went to the canteen. Though not particularly hungry, he picked up a bowl of chicken soup and a small French Bread stick. He had an hour, as his meeting with Bunny was scheduled for two o'clock.

At five-to-two, Richard made his way to Bunny's office. He didn't have any good news, so didn't look forward to it.

'Come in.'

Richard entered to see David Morgan already seated at the conference table, coffee in hand.

'Good afternoon, Richard,' David said, as though he hadn't seen or spoken to him for months.

Richard nodded at David and turned to Bunny, 'Good afternoon, Ma'am.'

'It might be for you, Mr Carpenter, but not for me. Sit down, and let's get on.'

'Coffee, Ma'am?' Richard used this politeness to mask asking for a cup for himself.

Bunny said, 'No, thank you. I have one.'

Richard wasn't having that, so he went to the coffee machine and poured his own. He took it back to the table, placed it in front of himself, and then looked up and smiled at Bunny, who returned the smile.

'Quite ready, are we?'

'Yes, Ma'am, ready.' Richard took a noisy slurp of his coffee.

Bunny burst out laughing. 'Richard, you are so annoying but, occasionally, you make me laugh, which I don't do much of these days. Now, let's get on with it.'

The controller turned to David, 'What is Atallah up to?'

'He's visiting Mosques to get his face known.' He looked down at his notes. 'So far, he's been to King's Cross, Suleymaniye, Brick Lane, and Baitul-Aziz. He says it would be normal for a newcomer to look around, but that he should go to his local mosque, which would be Central London in Whitechapel Road.'

'Do we want him and Siddique at the same Mosque?' Richard asked.

Bunny said, 'Good question. The answer has to be no. I want Siddique to attend Forest Lane Mosque. Apparently, it has new members of interest to us. Our current sleepers aren't aware of the two new arrivals and shouldn't be told.'

'Yes, Ma'am.'

'So, onto our friend, Aashif Jamal. Any news?'

Richard and David both remained silent. Finally, Richard spoke up, 'All our agents, snitches, and friends are trying to find out where he might be. Word at the moment is that he has probably gone north.'

Bunny looked horrified. 'Probably?' She shook her head. 'Probably? I detest that word, Richard, as you well know. Do not use it again. Our weakest point; why couldn't he have behaved and stayed in London? So, let's assume he's in Luton or Leeds or Bradford—how will we find him?'

David spoke this time, 'With extreme difficulty, Ma'am. We have people of interest under surveillance in those three areas plus Manchester, Derby, Huddersfield, Wigan, Liverpool, and

Sheffield. If he should contact any of those, then we could get lucky.'

'Get lucky? We are talking about the defence of our country, and you dare to say to me *we could get lucky?*' Bunny closed her eyes, took a deep breath, and continued, 'What about Abbas Mahmood, the shopkeeper? What about Ibrahim Muhammad, the late-night visitor to Hassain?'

Neither of them spoke. Bunny raised her brows. 'I take it from your silence that there is no news on either of those murdering terrorist scum?'

'That's correct, Ma'am,' David said, trying to hide his bluster behind his cup.

'I think I may have to review your roles somewhat sooner than I had anticipated. The supposed professional British MI5 secret service cannot locate a bloody shopkeeper. I want answers, and not in a week or a month, but now. Do you understand me?' She looked them both squarely in the eyes. 'Push Atallah and Siddique hard. They can help us enormously.'

Richard spoke calmly, 'Yes, but you know, this is a difficult area for us. Once Atallah and Siddique are in place, intelligence will improve. Hassain, Mahmood, and probably Muhammad, are home grown. They will make mistakes.'

'True, but the problem is when they will make the mistake. Aashif Jamal has already proven he is a capable bomber, and how long before he decides to strike again?'

David spoke, 'We can push them, but it will increase their danger to being compromised; their cover stories are not perfect.'

Bunny just looked at him. David got the message—push them hard and don't worry about the consequences.

Bunny clasped her hands together and rested her chin on them. 'So, in summary, I want Atallah and Siddique working in the mosques tomorrow. I want all our resources made use of in locating Jamal, Mahmood, and Muhammad. Is that clear?'

Richard and David both said 'Yes' at the same time.

'Good, and before you go, any news on possible new arrivals?'

Both men shook their heads, and Bunny looked about to lose her temper again but restrained herself.

'Keep everybody alert. I'm off to GCHQ; apparently, they have some news. Let's hope it's something positive.' Bunny lifted her hand in an almost royal wave to inform Richard and David the meeting was over.

'Good day, gentlemen.'

CHAPTER 14

It pleased Yousef that he had learnt so much in only two weeks. Seated at his small kitchen table, he ate lightly browned toast with masses of thickly spread fig jam. Today made the last Friday in January, and he'd spent the day at the flat cleaning, cooking, and resting.

He reflected on the past week, Aashif Jamal had arrived safely in Bradford and would leave for Syria in about a month's time. Adhan had told him everything and that he was looking for Abbas Mahmood and Ibrahim Muhammad, who had both disappeared into the community. Adhan wanted to find them before the security services did, as they could prove highly useful in future attacks.

Yousef had gotten his Glock G30S; he had particularly wanted that model because it was slimmer and easier to carry or wear than some of the other heavier Glock pistols. As he shoved another delicious piece of toast and jam into his mouth, he laughed. He'd overspent, money seemed just to disappear, but he didn't care. He was the sword that would punish the Kafirs, and so he wasn't bothered. Isil had so much oil money that they didn't know what to do with it all.

Yousef had stocked the cupboards with all sorts of tasty luxurious foods, and as well as fig jam, he now had Blackberry, Strawberry, Apricot, Blueberry, and Raspberry. Again, he laughed aloud. So many jams. If only his friends from the village could see them. At ten am he had planned the day. The morning would be spent cleaning the kitchen, he would eat lunch at one pm, and in the afternoon, he would sleep for an hour, then some planning, and later, he would cook himself a lovely lamb kebab dinner and drink whisky.

Now, he watched BBC1 and 2, as he hated turning the commercial channels on. It seemed that every five minutes an appeal came on for Syria, either for blankets or coats or to pay for fresh water. He still thought it strange that on the one hand the British bombed his people and on the other, collected blankets for refugees.

At seven-fifteen, his chores done for the day, Yousef sat down to eat his kebab dinner. He'd cooked pilaff rice and a spicy tomato sauce to go with the lamb kebab, and now he tucked in. In no time, he polished off the delicious food and retired to the lounge with a good tumbler of whisky. Life seemed good. He drank the whisky, and then a refill, and finally fell asleep in his comfy chair.

With a start, Yousef awoke and took a second to understand what time of day it was. A glance at his watch showed the time at ten pm; he had slept longer than he'd wanted to, and then he heard the banging. That must have woken him in the first place. Then screaming accompanied yet more banging on the front door. He jumped up and fetched his Glock from on top of one of the kitchen cupboards. Then he shook his head. It must be time; they must have found him. He would kill as many as he could. Resolved, he walked to the front door, ready to fire straight through it. There, he stopped; the banging had ceased. Sobs and cries came from the hallway. Through the peephole, he saw a girl on the floor outside the front door. He didn't need the distraction or attention, but then the girl stood and started battering the door again, shouting for help. Yousef tucked the Glock into the back of his trousers and opened the door.

The girl from number eighteen stood there crying with her make-up running down her cheeks; she looked rough.

'Help. Help, my stepdad, he's drunk, he's beating my mum, he's going to kill her.'

Yousef had to think quickly; he could just slam the door, but if the police had been called, then they would — without question — interview the neighbours, including him.

'What's his name?'

'Ted.'

'Have you called the police?'

Through the sobs, Mandy said, 'No. Hurry, please.'

'Don't call them. I'll sort it.' He grabbed Mandy's hand and strode toward number eighteen. The door hung open, and he walked into the hall. Immediately, he heard sobbing and the dull thumps of someone getting slapped and punched.

Mandy pointed toward what Yousef thought must almost certainly be the lounge. 'In there. He's in there.'

Yousef pushed open the door. A woman lay on the floor on her back. Blood covered her face and her eyes looked bruised and had swollen closed. A tall, fat man kicked her repeatedly in the face and stomach.

'You fucking slag. When I tell you to go and buy me whisky, fucking well do it.' He kicked her head like a football. 'Fucking slag. Dunno why I waste my time with you.'

Yousef looked at the man in his string vest and filthy tracksuit bottoms. 'Ted, stop right now.'

The big man stopped, shock dropped his jaw, and then he turned around and saw Yousef.

'Who the fucking hell are you, wop?' He looked at Mandy, who cowered behind Yousef.

'You'll be fucking next; another slag who needs something big shoved 'tween her fucking legs.' He looked back at Yousef.

'Fuck off out of it, wop, before I fucking have you as well, cunt.'

Yousef took three steps. The man put his arms in front of his face and swung a right hook at him, but Yousef moved to the side and smashed his fist into the side of the man's face. He went down like an elephant, hitting the carpet with a crashing thud. Slowly, Ted sat up and looked around. Yousef hit him plumb on the jaw with a sledgehammer of a punch. Ted swooned, out of it. Yousef grabbed his right leg and pulled him toward the door.

Mandy rushed to her mum and helped her up onto the old brown sofa. Yousef dragged Ted to the lifts and, a minute later, pulled him out onto the concrete steps at the front of the flats. Then he yanked him to the side, behind a pillar, and left him. A little out of breath, he ran back into the flats and got in the same lift, which he took back up to his flat. Once in his kitchen, he took the biscuit tin down from the top of the cupboard and retrieved two bundles of cash. Money in hand, he ran back to the lift and soon stood outside, shaking Ted back to life. The man appeared groggy, and Yousef continued to shake him until he thought he could understand simple instructions.

'Listen, Ted. I'm giving you one hundred pounds.' He stuffed the notes into Ted's hand. 'Don't come back here. If you do, I will kill you, do you understand that?'

Ted smiled, looking at his fistful of notes. First stop for him would be the off Licence.

'I said, do you understand?' Yousef slapped him around the face.

'I understand. What the fuck would I come back for? Not for that sour-faced bitch, that's for sure.'

He stumbled to his feet and limped off into the night. Yousef pushed his hair from his face and strolled back into the flats. He didn't want any fuss and just wanted to be left alone. He arrived on his landing, glanced at number eighteen, and found the door shut. Thank goodness, all seemed quiet. With a sigh, he opened his door and went in. Yousef made straight for the kitchen and poured himself a large vodka, which he chucked down his throat and then refilled and did the same again. He filled the glass one more time and went and sat in his comfy chair. One of the golden rules of a sleeper was to join and interact with the community, but he thought he could have done without Ted and his drunken attack on the girl's mum.

When Yousef awoke next, the clock read eleven-thirty pm. He yawned. A gentle knocking sounded on the front door; people seemed to like knocking on his door. Under his breath, he swore, rubbed his eyes, and decided that he wouldn't answer. The knocking continued. 'Fuck.' Still cursing, he made his way to the door and opened it. He would tell whoever it was to fuck off.

'Hello. I just came to say thank you.'

'That's okay. Anytime.'

'My name's Mandy.'

Yousef cursed. Why did people like telling him their names that he didn't want to know?

'You saved my mum's life.'

'Well, I'm not sure about that.'

'No, truly, you did. Here, this is for you.' Mandy held out a bottle of whisky.

'There's no need. Your mum might like that. Is she all right?'

'No, but she'll be fine in a couple of days. Aren't you going to invite me in?'

'It's too late, Mandy, I have to ...' Before he could finish, she brushed past him.

'Quick nightcap, and then I'll leave, I promise.'

She went straight to the kitchen, grabbed a couple of glasses, and poured two good measures.

Then she looked around. 'You live on your own, and it's very clean; I'm surprised.'

'Why would I want to live in a pigsty?'

'What's the bedroom like?' The girl winked at him.

Yousef almost panicked. He didn't know how to talk to a woman, especially a young white English woman.

Mandy knocked back her whisky like a seasoned campaigner.

'If you're not going to show me the bedroom, I better go then. I need to look after my mum anyway.'

Mandy strolled out into the hall. Yousef squeezed past her and opened the door.

As she passed him, she kissed him on the cheek.

'Thanks again … oh God, what's your name?' She looked him in the eye.

'Stephen.'

'Well, Stephen, thanks again, and if you like, you can take me to the pub for a drink one night. What do you say?'

Yousef smiled. 'Yes, let's do that. I'll knock for you sometime.'

'Just make sure you do, okay?'

'I will. Now, goodnight.' He eased shut the door.

Safely concealed in his flat, he jumped and whisper-shouted, 'What the fuck are you doing? Prat.' Then he shook his head. He would *not* knock for her, no way. In fact, it was impossible that he would knock for her. Dismayed, he walked to the bedroom and lay on the bed, where he started to cry. Alas, he knew he *would* knock for her because he kept having that dream. Her image filled his head while he moved his hand down inside the front of his jeans.

CHAPTER 15

Hesam Atallah wore a traditional long-sleeved pale-blue Dishdasha Thobe with a red-and-white checked Shemagh wrapped around his neck. Still cold, he had on a slightly shabby dark wool coat. He drove a beat-up old silver Ford Escort, provided by MI5 from their collection of surveillance vehicles. It looked old and decrepit but, in reality, had an excellent engine and proved extremely reliable. He kept at a steady twenty-nine-miles-per-hour; not wanting to draw attention to himself from any quarter.

Atallah, married to Qudsiyah, had been blessed with two daughters, Abia (six) and Rahiq (four). He doted on his two girls, and his children's future made for one of the main reasons he worked for the British. The work in Syria and Iraq had been dangerous; anyone even suspected of working for the enemy would be killed by beheading, stoning, or fire. The opportunity to come and work in the UK had come as a true blessing for him, and he'd jumped at the chance, mainly because of the promise that he could bring his family over after six months' service. A new life for his wife and children was a dream for him, and he, of course, wanted it for himself as well. However, his family was the priority. His family stayed in a city called Al Tabqah, on the shores of Lake Assad, fifty-five kilometres from Ar-Raqqah, the well-known Isil stronghold.

Just then, he drove along the Mile End Road, heading up toward the Central London Mosque in Whitechapel. As he drove sedately on his way, he scanned the shops and attractions. When he passed the School of Mathematical Sciences, he wondered what, exactly, the students learnt. On he came, past Stepney Green tube station, and the traffic stayed light at two pm. Next, he passed into Whitechapel Road; he must be near.

To his right stood Whitechapel train station, and then came the Royal London Hospital on his left. Another minute and there it was: a vast, wonderful Mosque. The entrance looked huge and — traditional and beautiful — the minarets rose skyward in all their glory. Hesam took a deep breath, and then passed the London Muslim Centre, itself an impressive and large building, and drove on, looking for Whitechapel High Street. In another minute, he got there and saw the striking yellow-and-blue NCP Car Park sign. He pulled into Spreadeagle Yard and parked in one of the many white-lined spaces. He didn't care how much it cost, as MI5 had given him five hundred pounds for expenses, most of which he intended to send home to his wife.

He walked back up the road, looking for somewhere to have a late lunch and begin asking questions. Whitechapel Road seemed full of Arab clothes shops and, nestled in between two of them, hung a dirty sign that read 'Arab Café'. Hesam pushed open the door, and lovely quiet Arab string music and glorious smells of home cooking welcomed him. The space felt small. He counted

97

eight square tables, and so the place could seat around forty covers. A glance around showed that most people had eaten and left, and a couple of stragglers looked as though they wouldn't be going anywhere anytime soon. A forty-odd-year-old man came from behind the bar and ushered him into a seat by the window.

'I will bring you the menu.'

'Do not bother, my friend. Just bring me whatever is good. I trust you.' Atallah couldn't help but notice the jagged scar that ran halfway down the man's left cheek from his eye. The waiter smiled; he liked the new customer already and could see a substantial tip on the way.

'Of course, we will start with Mezza, including delicious Tabouli Salad, Makdous stuffed Aubergines, Safiha mini meat pies, and Mutabal Shawandar Beetroot Salad, and following that, we give you Kufta Kebabs with Red Burgul Pilaff. How does that sound?'

'Stop talking and bring it. I'm starving.' Hesam laughed loudly.

Two men sitting across the café turned and lifted their hands in acknowledgement, and one of them shouted across, 'The food is excellent. This is your first visit?'

'Yes, I am trying to forget this country that I find myself living in.'

'What is wrong, brother?'

'I don't know you, and so must be circumspect in my conversation.'

'Suffering is a gift. In it is hidden mercy. Do not worry about us. This country is a cesspit of disgusting culture. We don't care who hears us. Do not worry; we are taking over the world. It will take a bit of time but will happen. You cannot change your religion and would not want to. Every Muslim should be a Jihadi terrorist.'

Atallah felt shocked but pleased. These two young men, in their matching grey Thobes and leather sandals, were brash and loud and didn't care who heard them.

'You say what you think very loudly. I am always scared of the police.'

Both men rocked with laughter. 'The stupid, ignorant police are on our side; they protect us and discriminate against the amusing Britain's First and English Defence League morons. Come, share a bottle with us.' They motioned for him to join them.

Atallah stood and moved across to sit at their table. 'May the mercy, peace, and blessings of Allah be upon you.'

'And may the peace, mercy, and blessings of Allah be upon you.'

The taller of the two men introduced them, 'Brother, I am Ami Nejam and my friend is Ayoub Tawfeet. We are pleased to meet you.'

'And I am pleased to meet you. Do you work around here?'

Ayoub replied, 'Yes, we have a clothes shop up the road, but it's really a front for a terrorist organisation.'

Atallah laughed, and then he stopped, as he realised that the two men hadn't joined in and watched him closely.

Atallah pretended to be shocked, and then the men burst out laughing.

'We got you then, brother.' They continued laughing, and Atallah joined in.

The food arrived with a bottle of Al Mimas Arak and a Domaine de Bargylus Grand Vin de Syrie red wine. It should be a lively meal. Though they had just met, Syrian hospitality abounded while the three men continued into the early evening, ordering more food and wine. The waiter had already added an extra bottle of wine to their bill, and they hadn't finished yet.

Finally, at six-thirty, Nejam and Tawfeet said that they had homes to go to. It had been an enjoyable education for Atallah, and he shook hands with the two men. All three said that they hoped to meet again in the café one day. The two men paid the whole bill, which pleased Atallah even more. As he rose to leave the café, the waiter approached him and took his arm.

'Thank you for coming to the café. I hope we will see you again.'

'For sure. The food is excellent. I will be attending the Mosque up the road, and so will definitely be in again. Thank you for the good service.' He slipped the man a ten-pound note.

When he made to turn and leave, the waiter held onto his arm. 'They are noisy, your two new friends, they talk a lot, but that is all they do.'

Atallah felt unsure where the conversation was going but interested. 'They are generous, good people and, yes, you're right, sometimes it is someone who has little to say, but when he speaks, it is worth waiting for.'

The waiter took a piece of paper out of his pocket and slipped it into Atallah's hand. 'Call this man. You can meet him for coffee. You may be able to help each other.'

'I don't understand. Who is he?'

'Do not ask questions. If you want to call him, do so. If not ...' He shrugged and turned to go back behind the bar.

Atallah called after him, 'What's your name?'

Without an answer, the man disappeared behind the bar.

Atallah felt pleased; he had his first lead, and MI5 would be delighted. He left the café and immediately called David Morgan, explained the situation, and they agreed that a recording machine and tracer would be put into the house at Gadwell Close, Custom House.

***

On the morning of Tuesday, the third of February, the small terraced house at Gadwell Close was full. Technicians had installed trace and recording equipment to the BT system. David Morgan and Richard Carpenter had arrived in the very early morning. They stood in the small kitchen, drinking coffee and looking out into the small, unkempt back garden.

'This could be a good break.'

Richard laughed. 'Well, we need a break for two reasons, one so we can make progress and two, to keep Bunny off our backs.'

'Yeah, I know what you mean.'

One of the techies came in and said they were

ready.

Richard and David went through to the lounge/dining room. Atallah, seated at the large oak dining table, looked tense.

'Don't worry, Hesam; you'll be fine. You ready?'

'Ready as I'll ever be. Let's do it.'

It went quieter than quiet. Everybody sat down and tried to relax.

David was the last to speak; he nodded at Atallah. 'Over to you, Hesam.'

Hesam picked up the piece of paper and lifted the phone off the cradle, then he typed in the mobile number. The atmosphere felt electric.

Everybody could hear the ringtone as it rang and rang, and then it stopped.

'Hello?'

'Yeah, hi, I … urm … was given this number.'

'Who, exactly, gave you the number?'

'In the café on Whitechapel Road. The waiter.'

'So, what can I do for you?'

Richard did a thumbs-up at the trace technician, who replied with a nod. With the trace working, he just needed time.

'He thought it would be a good idea if we got together for a coffee.'

'What is your name?'

'Atallah, Hesam Atallah.'

'Always good to talk, brother. Meet me tomorrow in the Library at the Muslim Centre, Whitechapel.'

'How will I know you?'

'I will know you. Ten am.' The line went dead.

Richard and David both looked at the trace techie, who shook his head.

'Sorry, not enough time.'

'Don't worry,' Richard said.

David stood, 'We need more surveillance on the Muslim Centre.' Already, they filmed everybody who went in and out of the front entrance twenty-four hours a day. 'I want the back covered from six o'clock tonight. I don't care how you guys do it, just organise it, okay?'

Terry, the lead techie, said, 'We'll get on it straight away.'

'Good. Let me know the details, and I'll join you there about five.' He turned to Richard. 'Are you coming?'

Richard, though tired, said, 'Yes, I'll be there.'

David said, 'Also, I want the voice prints put through the system. If we don't have anything, send it over to the CIA and see if they have.'

'Will do.'

Richard said to Atallah, 'Let's go through some different scenarios.' He, David, and Atallah headed back into the kitchen.

When they informed Bunny of the good news, all she could say was don't fuck it up.

Richard and David went through procedures with Atallah. It would be a casual chat where the man would ask pertinent questions, and if he felt happy, then he would meet with Atallah again, where he would be interrogated in detail. When he left the Muslim Centre, he should assume he was being followed, and so should come back to Gadwell Close and act as normally as possible. The techies would remove all the equipment and return the house to its original dirty state.

CHAPTER 16

Yousef stood just around the corner of Dartmouth Street, across from the Broadway Hotel. From there, he had a clear view of the entrance. The sun shone, but the morning still dawned freezing, and he had stood there as though waiting for someone since seven-thirty. He looked at his watch. Nine-twenty. The cold had gotten through to his bones. Yousef smacked his hands together and rubbed them to get the circulation back. He would leave it ten minutes and, if the mysterious almond-eyed woman hadn't appeared, he would enter the hotel.

Yousef wanted to learn her identity and the reason for her presence in London. Nine-thirty arrived, and he took a step toward the hotel. Just then, he caught sight of her and turned away. He stood back and half-turned to see which way she headed. The woman turned left out of the hotel and, two minutes later, walked into the Pret A Manger in Tothill Street. Strange behaviour. If she'd had breakfast in the hotel, why on earth had she entered a restaurant? Deep in thought, he shook his head. Perhaps she didn't like the hotel coffee, which sounded more than a bit feeble.

Perturbed, he walked past the huge front window of the Pret A Manger and glanced in. The woman sat at the back and, yes, she sipped at a cup. Yousef felt unsure what to do next but also desperate to speak to her. The straightforward approach would be best. He turned and marched into the Pret, strode up to the counter, and ordered an Americana coffee. Two minutes later, beverage ready, he collected two sugar portions and extra milk, and then plonked himself down, sitting opposite the woman.

'Good morning. I think we met yesterday in Café Caesar?'

The woman looked up. Sadness darkened her eyes. 'Yes, I was rude to you. I'm sorry.'

'No, it was me, chatting to a complete stranger. I'm the one who should apologise. It would be very frowned upon at home.'

'And where is home?'

'A small village in Syria with a river and olive groves and rich farming land. And you, mysterious woman?'

She smiled and laughed. Beautiful white teeth showed. 'I am from Iraq. A town called Qu'im.'

'I believe that's close to the Syrian border, near Al Bukamal.'

His companion smiled again. 'That's right. You know your geography.'

'I've travelled all over Syria and Iraq.'

'You dress well but look and smell like a fighter?'

Her forwardness surprised Yousef. 'I was but not anymore.' He laughed. 'I have escaped.'

The woman looked at him closely. 'What is your name? I will know if you lie.'

Again, he felt in a quandary and had to think quickly. 'Akeem Hassain. And you?'

'Durriyah Kassab.'

'Pleased to meet you, Durriyah. I confess that I'm

desperate to ask you a question. May I?'

'You may ask, but I do not promise to answer.'

Yousef smiled. 'So, the question is this, what are you doing in London?' And with a small wink, he said, 'And I will know if you lie.'

Durriyah returned the smile, but it turned to a frown all too quickly. 'I am on holiday, of course. My family is wealthy, and I am travelling throughout Europe for a month. And you?'

'The same. On holiday.'

The two of them sat there, staring at each other, both knowing the other was lying but not sure what to say next.

Durriyah drank the last of her coffee and placed the cup back onto the saucer. 'It is time for me to go.'

'Where are you going for your next coffee?'

She gave him a cautious look. 'I like to wander and, yes, I pop into various places for coffee. I sincerely hope that you have not been following me?'

'No, just that if you tell me where that will be, I will go ahead and wait for you. I think you are beautiful.' Yousef gave her his best smile.

'You are sweet, Akeem.' Durriyah took a deep breath. 'You are so young but ...'

'Yes?'

'I was going to say I like you.' She stood, and Yousef thought that he had failed, then she spoke again, 'Come to the hotel at nine o'clock tonight. You will buy dinner, and then you will tell me your real name.' Then she marched off into the cold, sunny morning.

***

Durriyah hadn't wanted to meet anyone and hadn't said the name of the hotel. Akeem hadn't asked, and so she knew that he had followed her, and also that Akeem wasn't his true name. Though a mystery, he had something about him that she liked. At a guess, he must be in his mid-twenties. With Durriyah at thirty-three, it made a relatively small age gap. Already, she looked forward to seeing him. It had been a year since … she walked down the road, not knowing where she was headed and not caring.

CHAPTER 17

MI5 had prepared a new observation post in the master bedroom at 156 Field Street, which looked over the back of the London Muslim Centre in Whitechapel Road. Both the Muslim Centre and the Central London Mosque had high walls surrounding the properties, but could still be overlooked from the top-floor of houses and flats in Field Street. A friend of a friend, only too happy to help MI5, owned the house.

Richard and David arrived at five am in the cold, pitch-black morning and they both felt worn out. A high-tech camera waited in place for filming, and listening headphones would catch any speech on the covert listening devices that they'd planted all over the building months before. The back entrance was rarely used, but they hoped for a lucky break.

After passing around steaming mugs of coffee, another (possibly) long and monotonous wait began. Hesam Atallah was due to arrive at the front entrance at nine-forty-five. All visitors to the front and back would be photographed, so even if they didn't recognise anyone, Atallah would be able to pick out the contact. At six am, a white van drove into the back of the premises, and everybody became instantly alert.

Three men in Thobes got out of the van and opened the back door. Then they took out buckets, mops, brushes, and cleaning materials. A false alarm. The team consumed yet more coffee and chocolate croissants. The morning grew lighter. Then came the break that they desperately needed. David and Richard stood at the back of the room chatting, and then the spotter shouted:

'Red Ford Escort pulling into the centre.'

David and Richard both knew the significance. Could it be the same car driven to meet Abdul Muta'al Hassain in his house? They rushed to the window.

'Get the reg' and as many pictures as possible of the occupants.'

The vehicle contained only a driver, who exited the Escort. While he locked the door, he glanced back to the gate, and the spotter got a perfect image. The man strolled to the back entrance and entered the building.

Richard looked at David and smiled. 'So, that's Ibrahim Muhammad. How many surveillance drivers do we have?'

David frowned. 'One.'

'Not enough. We have to be sure. I'll go as well.' Ibrahim had to be followed when he left the centre so that they could discover his home address. They could then plant bugs and tap his phone.

Slaps on the back showed everybody's happiness at getting a result for a change. The team sent through images of Muhammad to Thames House. Another piece could be placed in the jigsaw. Time dragged on but, eventually, it got to nine-forty, and the room went quiet and tense again. Two minutes later, a radio message came in: Atallah had arrived and now approached the front entrance. He went in, and then came more waiting. Richard left the house and sat in his Audi outside, ready to move at a moment's notice.

***

Hesam Atallah pulled open the front doors and entered the Muslim Centre. Three Thobe-wearing Arabs with traditional, long shaggy beards manned a reception desk. Atallah approached the desk.

'Good morning. I am here to study in the library.'

All three men just looked at him, and then, finally, one of them spoke, 'Are you a cleric?'

'No. My name is Hesam Atallah. I am writing a thesis.'

One of the men nodded to the others. 'Please, follow the sign to the lifts. The library is on the first floor.'

Atallah's heart pounded when he got to the lift and pressed the button. With the lift there already, the door slid open. The car arrived at the first floor, the door opened again, and he stepped out into a small corridor. Then he approached the door to the library and entered.

The space looked large and must have held thousands of books. A desk sat in the middle of the room with two more bearded, Thobe-wearing staff. Hesam walked down the centre of the aisle, reading the signs. When he came to Geography, he turned into the small recess, studied the book titles, and took out three reference books about Syria and Iraq. Next, he sat at the tiny desk and began to read the first book. It proved fascinating, and he soon sat immersed in the contents.

Someone said good morning to him from the

aisle. He turned to see a middle-aged, traditionally dressed man.

'Good morning. The Library is wonderful. So many books.'

'Yes, we have a marvellous collection and are adding to it every week. So, eventually, it will become the greatest reference library in the world.' The man paused. 'Hesam Atallah?'

'Yes. And you are?'

'You do not need to know at the present time. Come, let us go and find refreshment.'

Atallah followed the man out of the library and down a long corridor. They stopped outside a door, and a large young man took Atallah and placed him against the wall gently. The young man searched him thoroughly, even feeling around his genitals.

'He is clean,' the man said.

'Come in, Atallah. Sorry about that but we have to be careful.'

'I understand fully.'

The man sat behind his desk, and Atallah seated himself in a hard-backed wooden chair, already placed right in front of the table.

Then the man lifted his mobile and aimed it at Atallah. 'Smile for the camera. Just another security measure.'

Hesam nodded.

The man asked, 'So, you enjoyed the food in the café?'

'Delicious. Just like at home.' Atallah smiled.

'Where, exactly, is home?'

'Al Tabqah.'

111

The man raised his hands and smiled too. 'I know it well. Which street do you live in?'

'The main road, just around the corner from the First Quarter Market.'

'You are almost in the lake, then?'

'Assad Lake is beautiful and the water as clear as good Arak.'

The man burst into laughter. 'Well put, Atallah, well put indeed. I think we will get on well. Would you like some coffee?'

'I'm sure it will be strong, thick, and incredibly sweet, so yes, I would love some.'

His unknown companion picked up the phone and asked the person on the other end to bring coffee.

'So, Hesam Atallah, what are you doing in the UK?'

'I have come for a gallstones operation. It seems that, without too much difficulty, I can get it done free on the NHS.' MI5 had fabricated a whole cover story with St Thomas' Hospital in London.

'You mean, you'll have it done and then leave without paying?'

'Well, I ...'

'Do not worry. The NHS is full of foreign patients who never pay for anything. It shows you the stupidity of the British. Do you think you could turn up in Aleppo and get a free MRI scan? It would never happen.' He roared with laughter.

Atallah thought the man strange and that, perhaps at some time, he had suffered some sort of mental disorder.

Coffee arrived. It tasted delicious.

'So, you want to leave this country as soon as you can, then?'

'I am here for three months minimum. It is choking me. Breathing the air makes me sick, and seeing the drunkenness and the women with their breasts hanging out, it is almost unbearable. But I must have the operation, and so I am stuck here for the time being.'

'I know how you feel. The culture here is beyond repair, which is why we must take the country from them. Already, we have Sharia law in many areas of London and the north. Make no mistake; one day this will be a Muslim country. Remember Allah at all times.'

'Of course, you are right. The waiter at the café said that I might be of use to you. Well, I'm not sure what I can do but am at your disposal.'

The man took a deep breath and leant back in his chair. 'That is comforting to hear. We need good men for various work, and you must leave it with me for now. Give me your card, and I will contact you again in the not-too-distant future.'

Hesam did as asked. 'May Allah reward you with good, and I wait to hear from you. All the praises are due to Allah.'

The man who had searched him opened the door, and Atallah left the office. Then the man escorted him to the front door and watched him leave. Atallah stopped outside the door, both to collect his thoughts and to make sure that the observation post saw him leaving. He looked up and down the road, pulled up his collar, and then walked back toward the NCP car park.

Atallah walked at a leisurely pace, stopping on occasion to look in a shop window or at a car for sale. His stop-start stroll gave the observers plenty of opportunity to detect whether anyone followed him or not.

***

On this occasion, they sent word back to David and Richard that he had no tail. Richard remained seated in his car, waiting to see if Ibrahim Muhammad would leave after the meeting. He sat for an hour, and then decided to go back into the house for a hot drink. After a hot coffee, he asked the team to wake him the second they saw any movement, and then promptly fell asleep in one of the lounge chairs. At one o'clock, someone shook his shoulder and spoke into his ear, 'He's on the move.'

Richard jumped up, rubbed his face, and made for the door. Seconds later, he turned the key in his Audi, all ready to go. His radio sparkled into life.

'Red Escort is leaving the premises and heading down Whitechapel Road East toward Bow.'

Richard roared out of Fieldgate Street and turned on Whitechapel Road. Within five seconds, he searched for the red Escort, and then saw it turn right into Sidney Street. He followed at a safe distance. A glance in his mirror showed him that George—in a white transit van—followed two vehicles behind him.

'George? Are you patched in?'

'Confirm.'

'Stay where you are for the moment.'

'Confirm.'

The red Escort turned left into Stepney Way, drove for two minutes, and then indicated left and pulled into a metered parking space in front of Stepney Green Park. The driver got out just as Richard drove past. He drove on for ten yards, and then shouted out loudly, 'FUCK.' The driver, a young man, certainly wasn't Ibrahim Muhammad.

CHAPTER 18

Never before had Yousef prepared himself like this, he had showered for ten minutes, had sprayed and poured and powdered himself with all the new male grooming products that he'd bought from Superdrug. Dressed for smart casual, he wore a new dark-blue Yves St Laurent shirt and an expensive matching blue cashmere jumper. Every time he spent money on luxuries, he felt so guilty that he could have killed himself. Thankfully, that feeling only lasted for a minute or two. If Abd Al-Ala Hashemi saw him now, he would—without question—think that Yousef had turned Western and order him back to Syria for a hard session of re-education.

By seven o'clock, all ready to go, he felt excited beyond reason. He had never had a relationship with a woman and didn't understand them at all. What he did know was that Muslim men were all powerful where women were concerned; wives and mistresses made the only exception to this as they travelled the world with their husbands and lived financially independent.

From where did Durriyah Kassab get her money? Obviously, she had to be financially well off, or she wouldn't be staying in a London hotel, but what he desperately wanted to know was why she had come? He looked in the cracked but clean mirror and thought he looked handsome; in fact, almost the Muslim James Bond. Satisfied, he put on his new coat and went to the kitchen, where he opened the biscuit tin and got the shock of his life. Only two bundles of notes remained, a hundred pounds from the thousand that Adhan had given him. Yousef shook his head; he would have to ask for more, and serious questions would get asked. However, he didn't care; money just poured through your fingers like sand, and they would know the cost of staying in the UK, so let them ask.

With a small frown, he took the hundred and slipped it into his pocket. Then, ready, he left the flat and—curses upon curses—the Mandy girl stood on the landing, talking to another young girl. He nodded at her.

'You look nice, Stephen. Are you taking me out, then?'

Yousef chuckled. 'Not tonight, Mandy. I have another engagement, but don't worry; I haven't forgotten you.'

'That's a shame.' The girl mock-pouted, then grinned and said, 'Got any smokes?'

He took a nearly full packet of Marlboro's out of his coat and gave them to her.

'Oh, thanks. You're the best.'

'Maybe I am.' He smiled. 'See you soon.'

'I hope so.'

Yousef skipped down the stairs to get away quickly and soon walked outside, heading toward White City tube station. The whole situation had him worried: the good clothes felt so natural on him, the woman Durriyah, the young Mandy, and the good food and plenty of booze, he liked it all too much. He swore to himself that, after this night,

117

he would revert to being a good Muslim, and then he remembered that he hadn't prayed for days, which plunged him into even more guilt.

Young people going out filled the tube trains; they all seemed so relaxed, chatting and laughing loudly, and appeared so confident in their skins, unlike Muslims who stayed mostly introverted. Even though cold, some of the girls wore skimpy outfits that left nothing to the imagination. Why did they flaunt their bodies like prostitutes? Or was it simply because they had the choice and they chose to exercise that right when and how they wished? Regardless, it wasn't as though they were naked, and what was *really* wrong with showing a bare leg?

Yousef sat and asked himself so many questions, and then the tannoy's announcement awoke him: THE NEXT STATION IS WESTMINSTER. He jumped up and just got through the door in time. Early, he walked slowly past Café Caesar and looked in; there were a few diehards left. The sign by the door indicated that it would close at eight-thirty. His watch read eight-twenty-five. Still strolling and taking his time, he walked around Parliament Square. Busy traffic jammed the roads, and tourists scurrying to and fro filled the pavements.

The evening felt beautiful if slightly cold and a clear sky held stars that shone brightly. All of a sudden, he had a terrible thought; he hadn't brought a present to give Durriyah. With a curse, Yousef looked around. The newsagents next to the station remained open, and he rushed toward it.

Once inside, he looked around, wondering what he could get for her. The shop sold a few London memorabilia statues, and he decided to get one — the small House of Commons building, featuring Big Ben, looked good and, guiltily, he paid eight pounds for it. When he glanced at his watch again, it showed eight-forty-five. Time to go. A little more buoyant, he walked at speed to the hotel and entered the large double glass doors. Unsure of what to do next, he went to the reception.

'Could you please inform Miss Durriyah Kassab that her visitor has arrived.'

The receptionist studied her computer for a second, and then lifted the phone and pressed three numbers.

'Hello, Miss Kassab, your visitor has arrived and is in reception.'

She turned back to Yousef. 'Miss Kassab will be down shortly. Please, take a seat. Can I get you anything?'

Yousef felt sure that she was flirting with him. 'No, thank you.' Instead of engaging, he turned and took a seat that faced the lifts. Ten minutes later, one of the doors opened, and Yousef's heart missed a beat. Durriyah Kassab came out of the lift, wearing the most beautiful long flowing ivory-coloured silk dress that he had ever seen in his life. The woman looked absolutely stunning and had taken great care to prepare herself for dinner with him. A great compliment. As she approached and smiled, Yousef stood.

He bowed his head slightly. 'Durriyah, you look so amazing. You are the most beautiful woman in the hotel, and I feel so fortunate to be having dinner with you.'

'So, whoever you are, you look nice as well. Shall we go to the dining room? I am so hungry.'

They strolled to the restaurant area, and Yousef noticed men turning to look at Durriyah as they passed. He considered himself the luckiest man on planet Earth, and goodness only knew where the night would take him. Yousef chose to sit in one of the corners, away from other diners, so they would not be overheard.

'So, have you had a good day, mystery man?'

'Every day I am alive is a good day.' He slid the carrier bag with the present across the table.

'What is this?'

'A small present. In fact, tiny.'

Durriyah took out the ornament. 'It's lovely, thank you. No one has given me a present for some time.' She ran her fingers over it, and then put it back in the bag. 'I do not want to play around; what is your real name?'

Yousef just stared at her. The waiter arrived to deliver menus, thus saving him from having to answer, and asked if they would like a drink.

Durriyah spoke before he could respond, 'Bring a bottle of Pernod and a good quality claret.'

This gave him a touch of worry; Durriyah spoke as though used to giving orders and not having them questioned.

'So, handsome young man, what is your real name? And I will know if you are lying.'

Choices, choices. He could stick to the name he'd given her before. He could invent something new.

He could tell her the truth.

'I am happy to tell you my real name, but you must tell me what you are doing in London?'

Now Durriyah resorted to sitting and staring at him. Eventually, she spoke, 'Agreed. So, your name?'

'Yousef El-Sayed.'

She continued to look at him. 'I believe you. Good, it is a start.'

The drinks arrived, and Durriyah poured a large measure of Pernod for Yousef and a red wine for herself.

Yousef put the glass to his lips and drank half. 'Delicious. Thank you for ordering it.'

Durriyah sipped at her red wine, and then topped up Yousef's glass.

He pressed, 'So, what are you doing in London?'

'I am not doing anything, which is what I am doing in London. If that makes sense?'

'Not really.'

'I am travelling and trying to heal. You cannot see the wounds, but they are here, deep wounds that will take a lifetime to mend if ever. Do you understand now?'

'I'm beginning to understand. Does it …?' He stopped and gathered his thoughts. 'Does it involve your family?'

Her eyes filled, and a tear rolled down her cheek. 'Yes.' Durriyah wiped her eyes with the linen napkin. 'You are perceptive.'

'Do you want to tell me more?'

'I will try, but I will cry, so you must forgive my softness. My husband and two children, I cannot tell you their names, it upsets me too much, an apparent mistake, American planes in the wrong place. They dropped bombs. I'd gone out shopping …' She broke into sobs and took a deep breath. 'They were blown to pieces. Nothing left.' Slowly, she pulled herself together. 'That was over a year ago. I can't get over it. I never will. So I travel, looking for something. I don't know what but hope one day to find it.'

Yousef touched her hand, and she smiled at him.

'I expect people have said to you before, you are young, marry again, have a new family, it will fill your heart, the memories will not go away, and that is good, but the pain will. Your husband would have wanted you to be happy, and you cannot be that while you are still in mourning. Harsh words, but you need to get on with your life.'

'Yousef El-Sayed, you are of course, right.'

The waiter reappeared, and they placed identical orders for well-done racks of lamb.

Yousef poured himself another glass of Pernod and drank with gusto.

'So, it is your turn, Yousef. What are you doing in London?'

'I'm not sure why I'm telling you this, but I am, and you will be shocked beyond belief.' He looked into her eyes.

'Nothing can shock me,' she said.

'I stole money. Not just any money. Isil money. Oil money.'

Sure enough, she sat there unable to speak. Then, at last, she said, 'You realise what you have done?

Do they know it was you?'

'Unfortunately, they do.' He drank heavily from his glass and had already finished over half the bottle of Pernod.

Neither of them spoke further. The waiter arrived with their dinner, and they tucked in. Between mouthfuls, they would make eye contact but still didn't speak.

'You understand you are talking to a dead man?'

'You can hide; there are places where you could start a new life.'

'You know as well as I that they will never give up looking for me, never. It's like a life sentence, and every second, I expect a knife or bullet in the back.'

'How much did you take?'

'A million dollars.'

'I don't know what to say. Where are you staying?'

'I cannot tell you. Just sitting here with me puts you in extreme danger, and the less you know about me, the better.'

'We are both in a mess, then. Are you staying in the UK?'

'Not for long; they know I am here somewhere. The UK is full of Isil sympathisers, deep cover agents, and eventually, someone somewhere will see me. I must move on, but where to, I am not sure.'

'Go to America; it is a huge place where you can disappear and start a new life.' Durriyah laughed. 'Maybe we should go together.'

He smiled. 'Any man would be lucky to be with

you.'

She took a gulp of her red wine. 'Let's go.' Then she half-rose from her chair.

'Where are we going?'

'To my room, Yousef the thief.' She flashed her beautiful white teeth in a glorious smile.

He protested, 'I have to pay.'

The waiter appeared, evidently wondering what was happening.

'Put it on my room tab,' Durriyah said, showing her key-card.

Then she strode toward the exit, and Yousef rushed to catch her up. Soon, they stood in the lift. Yousef felt scared stiff, and his heart pounded. Durriyah was a mature woman who had been married and had children—a woman of the world—yet he was still a virgin.

She stood opposite him in the lift. 'Why don't you come closer and kiss me?'

He swallowed and, hesitantly, took two steps until he stood right in front of her. The perfume that she wore smelt musky and intoxicating. All at once eager, he almost lunged for her, kissing her on the cheek, and then just as quickly drew back.

'What was that?' She raised her brows.

He didn't answer straight away, as he felt confused. What to say? What to do?

'I ...'

'Yes?'

'I am inexperienced with ...'

'Ah, I see. You have seen death and fought on battlefields and stolen money, but you have not had time to learn about women?'

'Well put.' Yousef fidgeted.

The lift stopped, and the door slid open. Durriyah took his hand and pulled him toward her room. He felt the happiest he ever had in his life. They got to the room, which they entered, and she closed and locked the door. When Durriyah switched on the light, Yousef looked around the lovely modern room, which held a super-king bed, a luxurious bathroom, a solid wood desk with chair, a comfy chair, and stylish cupboards.

Durriyah took charge. 'Take off your shoes and sit on the bed with your back against the headboard.'

Yousef did as instructed. What would happen next? In the event, he didn't have long to wait. Durriyah stood at the end of the bed, smiled at him, and lowered the zip at the side of her long dress. Then she pushed the garment down, revealing a black bra and matching panties. Yousef's eyes popped out of his head, and he grew excited.

'Do you like what you see, Yousef the thief?'

'Yes.' He found it difficult to breathe.

Then she reached behind her and undid her bra, which she pulled off to reveal full, ripe breasts, and then she bent down and slipped out of her knickers. Yousef now felt in such a state that sweat covered him, and he had to be about to split his trousers. Durriyah climbed onto the bed and crawled toward him. Then, gently, pushed his legs apart and nestled into his body, kissing him on the lips.

'We have plenty of time. No rush. And we must

make sure that you enjoy your first woman.'

The first time finished in seconds, the second in a few minutes, and the third with a bit of DIY long enough for Durriyah to have her first orgasm in just over a year.

CHAPTER 19

'So, what has he been up to?'

'Not much. He stays in the house most of the time, listening to music and chain smoking. He visited Forest Lane Mosque yesterday, and he entered on his own and left on his own.'

'Anything from the phones?'

'No, do you want us to continue? We have urgent jobs stacking up.'

Richard cursed; he wanted to continue but knew the pressure on the surveillance teams was immense. Plus the fact that he hadn't told Bunny that he'd authorised a team to monitor Siddique twenty-four hours a day.

'Fuck it. Break off. If needs be, we can always start again.'

Richard pressed the red button on his mobile and swore even more.

At home in Camden, sitting in his small study at the back of the house at ten am, Richard felt exhausted. He'd had to drag himself out of bed, and felt as though he could have slept for a week. He'd seen Andrew and Harry, briefly, before they set off for school—a bonus. Unbelievably stiff and achy, he stretched his shoulders back, trying to get rid of the aches. More coffee was in order. With that goal in mind, he left his comfy leather swivel chair and headed to the kitchen, from where he could hear Serena washing dishes.

'Any coffee?'

Serena didn't turn around. 'You know where it is and how to make it.'

Shit. He'd best be careful what he said. 'Would you like one, hun?'

'I'll make my own when I've finished the chores.'

'Okay.' He went to the cupboard, deciding that instant would be quicker than putting on a proper brew.

'What time are you home?'

The dreaded question that Richard always hated. 'Don't know. It's crazy busy at the moment.'

A moment's silence fell, but Richard knew it was coming.

'So, shall I cook a dinner for you or not?'

'That would be great. If I'm late, I can microwave it.'

'Well, I've thrown away three dinners in the last week, so maybe we'll miss this one, eh?'

'Yes, okay then.' Another silence. 'Look, the job's got to be done. There are people out there seeking to destroy our way of life, and I have to try and stop them.'

'Well, it's obviously far more important than your marriage, so get on with it, but don't be surprised when you come home one day and we're all gone.'

'What am I meant to do? You knew what I did when we married.'

'When did we last go out as a couple? Go on, tell me. This is *not* the life I wanted, Richard. I think I'll find myself a nice plumber or electrician.'

'It won't always be like this, once we have —'

Serena erupted, yelling, 'Yes, it fucking well will

be. Nothing will change. When did you last do something with your two sons? *When*, Richard? Do you even remember their fucking names?'

She stopped washing up and grabbed a tea towel to wipe her hands. 'Why don't you move into one of the company flats, or go and live with that dried-up excuse for a woman, Francis Matthews?'

She made for the door and turned as she grabbed the handle. 'Seriously, Richard, I've had enough. Don't bother coming home tonight. I need a break. I'm going into town. Don't be here when I get back, or I won't be responsible for my actions.'

Richard stood and looked at her with nothing to say. He loved her and the boys, but the job had to be done, and the truth was that he loved every minute of it. The front door slammed. He stood in the kitchen, reeling from the attack and the truth. The kettle boiling interrupted his thoughts and, mechanically, he made coffee. Still numb, he strolled back to his office. Short-term, he needed to give Serena space. Then he roused himself and set about packing up essentials. Next, he headed upstairs to fill a holdall with clothes. Finally, he rang Andrea Houlihan, one of the admin team at Thames House.

'Hi, Andrea, the flat in Knightsbridge? Is it vacant?'

'Yes. How long do you want it for?'

'At least a month.'

'I'll book it for you from today?'

'Yes, thanks. How's Bunny today?'

Andrea laughed. 'Same as always. Do you want to speak with her?'

'No, I'm not—'

'Hold on, please.'

Richard waited.

'I'm putting you through now.'

'Richard, why are you moving into the Knightsbridge flat?'

Richard cursed under his breath. 'Serena needs some space. It won't be for long.'

'I hope any problems at home won't affect your work?'

'No, Ma'am, not at all.' No concern. No fucking appreciation of what partners went through.

'Good, now let's talk about important issues.'

Richard cursed again; family life and marriage were of no concern to Bunny.

'GCHQ have intercepted some more interesting chatter about a new man having arrived here; have you heard anything?'

'Nothing, Ma'am.'

'I see. Well, keep your eyes on the ball. Now, you lost this Ibrahim Muhammad character at the Mosque?'

'I'm afraid so, Ma'am, but we're on the case.'

'For some reason, that's all I ever hear from you and, frankly, it's just not good enough. When is Atallah meeting with him?'

'He's waiting for contact.'

'And Siddique? Why have you had him under surveillance?'

'Just a hunch, Ma'am. Best to be on the safe side.'

She took a deep breath. 'Yes, Richard, but resources are tight. Did you find anything?'

'No, and I've put the job on hold.'

'Very sensible. We should be watching the enemy, not our team. Now, any news on Aashif Jamal?'

'No.'

'Perhaps you would like to expand on that?'

'Word is, he's still in the north, and every available asset has been mobilised to find him.'

'If he were to get away, I would be most upset. You do understand me, Richard?'

He had an urge just to tell her … to tell her to fuck off and leave him alone. 'Of course, Ma'am. We'll find him. … A quick question, Ma'am?'

'Yes?'

'Did you tell David Morgan that the Americans had dropped Siddique?'

'No, why?'

'Doesn't matter. Not important.'

'Aashif Jamal, find him.' The phone went dead.

Richard shook his head; working for that woman was not easy, never had been, and probably never would be.

He collected all his bits and pieces and opened the front door, then took a step out and turned and locked up. Then he took six more steps and pressed the key opener for the Audi. The comforting click accompanied the doors opening, and he turned back and looked at the house. Thoughts of the boys assailed him. Probably, they wouldn't even notice he'd gone for about a week. His mobile beeped, and he pressed for messages: Terrorist bomb attacks in Brussels, Belgium; thirty-five dead; two hundred injured. Tears welled in his eyes for his boys and the dead; he shook his head, got in the

car, started her up, and drove out of the drive,
headed for central London.

CHAPTER 20

Seated at the small Formica table in the kitchen, Yousef picked up the silver Lorient digital watch and, carefully, unscrewed the back. Then he disconnected the buzzer, picked up the especially small, hot soldering iron and some wire, and—one at a time—soldered wire to the buzzer leads. The smell of burning reached him when the wire melted.

Yousef worked with precise and methodical care. He liked his work to be perfect and, thus, took his time. Next, he took the constructed timer and soldered the buzzer leads to the coil of the relay, then he put the soldering iron down and relaxed. After moving over to the kitchen worktop, he took a swig of his now cold instant coffee. Then, with a deep breath, he went back to work. Next, he wire-connected the 12-volt battery to the coil relay and solar igniter.

The solar igniter was the type used in powerful firework rockets. Yousef went to the drawer and took out the four packs of brick-red Semtex plastic explosive. Then he cut several lengths of brown masking tape and, again carefully, taped all four packs together. Next up, he connected the solar igniter to the semtex and laid it on the table.

The young man then retrieved the standard black briefcase from the floor, opened it, and placed it on the table. Already, he'd fitted out the case to hold the bomb. In the cut-out channels provided, he positioned the device, closed the lid, and picked up the case by the handle. It felt light. He would place papers in there, which would act as a distraction should anyone enquire while he set the timer at the target.

All done, he went back to finishing his coffee, pleased with his work and life. The mission remained on time, he felt ready, and that—coupled with his relationship with Durriyah—had changed him. Yousef couldn't get enough of the beautiful woman with the almond eyes, and every time they met, he just wanted to rip off her clothes. In fact, he had taken to sex like a duck to water. Satisfied, he hid the briefcase in the airing cupboard, went back to the kitchen, and made himself another coffee, which he took to the lounge, where he sat in his comfy chair and relaxed. All he had to do now was pick a date. It would not be long away.

***

Richard Carpenter parked his Audi in the reserved space in the underground car park, two-hundred yards from the MI5 flat in Knightsbridge. He felt lonely, like never before; he may have got home late on many occasions, but he (usually) crawled into his own bed, warm from Serena's naked, firm body. However little he saw of the two boys, he *did* see them, hear them, and even smell them in the house.

He got out, grabbed his bags from the boot, and locked the car. On many occasions, he'd stayed in the flat, but only during operations and only for one or two nights before going home. The old-style Victorian block of flats had seen better days, but stood in a striking location, literally just around the corner from Harrods.

Richard entered the main foyer and pulled open the old-fashioned lift door. As usual, it made one hell of a noise, and Richard cursed while he pressed for floor one. The two-person lift took an age to travel even one floor; eventually, it arrived, and he got out and walked down the badly lit corridor to flat twelve. As he leant down and lifted the door mat to reveal a key, he laughed to himself; MI5 were, undoubtedly, a high-tech organisation, but Mavis from number fourteen would have slipped the key under the mat probably an hour before his arrival.

While he opened the door, Richard made a mental note to check with Thames House to find out if they had any information on the two keys found in the ceiling coving at the Hassain house. Though tiny, the flat proved adequate with a small kitchen containing both old and new utensils, a lounge-dining room, and bathroom. After he'd taken the holdall into the bedroom and thrown it on the double bed, he came out and made for the lounge, where he stood looking out of the large windows across London. Such a great view and, probably, it made the flat worth a few million.

Cold, he returned to the kitchen and clicked on the heating. A roar sounded as the burner lit in the boiler on the wall. Richard opened the cupboards, which held a few tins of tomato soup (the one soup he hated and, it seemed, everybody else did as well). Before he left, he would drop in to see Mavis to tell her what groceries he wanted her to buy and to arrange a convenient time for her to come in and clean. Though not his home, it would do until he and Serena had sorted out their issues. If they could sort them out.

The pressure on all the security services was immense, and London remained at a state of red alert, which meant bombings and attacks could happen at any time. Whether you worked at Heathrow in border control, the Metropolitan Police, MI5, or MI6, you worked your butt off to safeguard London from terrorist attacks. Subdued, Richard thought that another year was about all he could take. Most probably, in a flat somewhere in London, a person or persons would be planning an attack even now, and he had to find them before rather than after the event. He looked at his watch: midday. He would go and see Mavis, and then pop over to Thames House.

***

Aashif Jamal had arrived in Bradford at three am, and Adhan had taken him to a typical Bradford terraced house in Arran Street, right in the middle of Little Worton, a predominantly Muslim area. They'd delivered him to the back door and, to all intents and purposes, nobody saw him enter the property and, therefore, he remained invisible. Someone showed Jamal to an upstairs room, which pleasantly shocked him. The two bedrooms had been turned into a single large room. It held a single bed, a sofa, a small coffee table, a desk, and office swivel chair, and the bathroom stood next door. Far better than he had imagined, especially as he would be staying in the room and not going out for maybe one or two months. The net curtains hung drawn, and his companion explained to him — along with a host of other rules — that he should not open the curtains under any circumstances. One other man lived at the address and occupied the downstairs. This man would provide all Jamal's meals and, if he needed anything, he had only to ask.

**

Durriyah Kassab had enjoyed the night with Yousef. She had given herself to him and, at the same time, shown him how to make love to a woman. He had been a quick learner and now couldn't keep his hands off her. She wanted to persuade him to move to America and, if he asked, she would go with him. She felt she had met someone she could trust even though he had stolen a huge amount of money from Isil. Though a few years younger than her, it seemed a minor issue. Durriyah now worried that Isil agents were scouring London looking for him, and if they found him, he would end up getting thrown off a tall building roof or shot in the head. She wanted a new life and hoped that, having met Yousef, she would get that opportunity of happiness again.

**

David Morgan stormed out of Ladbrokes, screwed up his betting slips, and threw them in the bin. He had lost again, which had become a habit, and he had to get it under control. Married to Cathy, he lived in Bexley Heath on the outskirts of London and had a single daughter, Annabel, who had left school in September and attended college,

doing her A-levels. David, at thirty-seven, had
been with MI5 since leaving university. Over the
years, he had grown tired of the endless intrigue,
the relatively poor pay, the endless hours, and
working for the bitch of all bitches, Bunny. He had
discussed with Cathy leaving the service and going
to work in the private sector; the money would be
considerably better, but it would be the same old
security work and, probably, even more boring
than MI5. For now, he did just enough to keep
people off his back.

***

Kaashif Bashara, codenamed by Yousef as
Adhan, had dropped Aashif Jamal to a safe house
in Bradford. He stayed with sympathisers and
drove back the next day, arriving in London at
three pm. His handler contacted him to check that
the mission had gone well, and he confirmed it
had. Adhan had been a sleeper in the UK for ten
years and had worked live for the past twelve
months. Still learning his agent tradecraft, looking
after Yousef formed part of that education. By now,
he had grown all too used to Western ways and
doubted if he could survive back in Syria if sent; in
fact, it had been mooted that he should go back for
training, but he had managed to wriggle out of it.
He had a lovely flat and went to fancy restaurants
and nightclubs—all part of his cover as the
university-attending son of a wealthy Arab Prince.
He liked Yousef but thought him naïve like most of
the fanatics he met.

The plan to turn the UK into a Muslim state was
taking shape, but the Kafirs would, eventually, rise

up and fight, and millions of Muslims would die for the cause. Marriage loomed on the horizon as the next big issue for Adhan. His family pestered him to go back to Syria to find a wife; or even worse, they suggested sending a wife to the UK for him. He'd had sexual relationships with English girls and found them more attractive and worldly than a typical Syrian girl. Though he'd put marriage on the back burner, it would not go away.

CHAPTER 21

Number-plate-recognition cameras on the A12 at Newbury Park, and on the A406 North Circular Road, near Ilford, photographed the old red Ford Escort on a Saturday and Sunday during the second week in February. MI5 had put the false registration number on the system, hoping to get an idea of the possible location of Ibrahim Muhammad. They felt that he could well be in the Newbury Park, Ilford area, and so applied resources to find him. Richard had sent two teams of spotters to Ilford; he had a hunch and, sometimes, they paid off; sometimes not. Following the meeting at the Muslim Centre library, Atallah still waited for the contact that could also lead them to Muhammad. MI5 had also informed the Metropolitan Police that they were interested in locating the car and, this time, luck ran on their side.

The car had been seen being driven into a garage at the back of a row of terraced houses in Hampton Street, Ilford, and the driver had been reported as Arab-looking. The spotter team rushed to the location, recced the area, and set up an observation post in a blue Ford Transit van that had (apparently) broken down, to see just which house he lived in. An Arab man left number fourteen on foot, and a three-strong surveillance team went live and followed. MI5 compared his photograph to the one from the Muslim Centre and identified him as

Ibrahim Muhammad. The news flashed through to Richard, who immediately authorised an offensive penetration operation to plant covert listening devices all over the house, as well as asking for the BT line to be tapped.

Richard felt happy, as did Bunny, when told the news. Richard felt that things were beginning to look up. They had Muhammad under surveillance, Atallah still had to be contacted, they knew Aashif Jamal was in the north, and Abdul Muta'al Hassain — much to his chagrin — was still being debriefed and providing nuggets of quality intelligence.

Richard remained mightily concerned about the phone call that Abbas Mahmood had received at his shop in East Ham High Street two hours before the raid. It was possible that there had been a family emergency, and that MI5 had just been unlucky; however, Richard knew that was extremely unlikely and would put his money on someone having warned Mahmood of the raid. A mole in MI5 seemed unthinkable, but it had happened before and probably would again. Richard felt in a quandary. Should he go to Bunny? Could Bunny be the mole? No. Crazy. Then he thought about Philby, McClean, and Burgess in 1977. Anything could be possible. He felt isolated and didn't even trust his friend, David Morgan. Also, over a thousand people worked at Thames House, but not many had the necessary security clearance to know about Abbas Mahmood.

On Thursday night, Hesam Atallah got a call

from Ibrahim Muhammad, inviting him to visit the café on Whitechapel Road at eleven the next morning. The news of the call elated Richard because Atallah would meet another contact and not Muhammad. Slowly, the jigsaw puzzle took shape.

***

Atallah drove up Whitechapel Road on a typical February day with dark cloudy skies and a continual downpour of rain. His windscreen wipers swished on full and made an irritating scraping noise against the glass. Eventually, he arrived and parked in the same NCP car park that he had used on his last visit. Nervous and tired, he tried hard to act nonchalantly while he walked down Whitechapel Road toward the café. The freezing cold, wet weather had him covering his mouth when he started to cough.

***

Terribly important, the meeting had to go well. Richard had surveillance teams all over Whitechapel: taxis, road sweepers, mothers with prams, traffic wardens, young, old, fat, and thin. He had cars driving up and down Whitechapel Road, ready to follow the new target. Richard himself sat in a communications ambulance parked outside The Royal London Hospital on the other side of Whitechapel Road. From the ambulance, he could control all the teams, and it provided the perfect disguise. Atallah glanced at his watch: ten to eleven. Not wanting to be late, he increased his pace and arrived at the café with two minutes to spare. His heart pounded, and he felt clammy.

When he entered, he smiled at the waiter, who didn't seem to recognise him, and then took a seat in the corner, from where he ordered a traditional coffee. Atallah glanced around the café but didn't see anybody he thought could be his contact. Five minutes later, a man of about fifty entered, wearing a traditional white Thobe and a coat that stopped at his knees. He sat, and the waiter brought him a coffee without asking what he wanted; he must be a regular. The man sipped his coffee, and soon the café emptied except for the man and Atallah.

Atallah looked across at the man and said, 'Allah be praised.'

The man stared at him, and then motioned him to join him at his table. Atallah's heart skipped a beat. He stood and moved across to the man's table.

'Have a seat, Atallah.'

'Thank you, Sir.'

'Your wife, Qudsiyah, sends her regards to you and, of course, your two beautiful daughters, Abia and Rahiq.'

They had been to Al Tabqah to check on his background just as expected.

'Allah blessed me with a wonderful family.'

'All the praise goes to Allah.' The man raised his hands. 'You have not asked who I am. That is good. You are learning.'

'I am trying, Sir. I am a real beginner.'

'And how are your gallstones?'

Atallah had been to see an MI5 Doctor to get a complete rundown on how he should feel and the hospital process. 'They give me terrible pain in the tummy, not all the time but enough to make life difficult.'

'And what treatment are you having?'

'I had an X-ray and an ultrasound scan, and now they have decided to remove my gallbladder. They say I don't need it, but it does make me wonder why we have it in the first place? I'm not a great fan of operations or hospitals.' He put on a worried face.

'Do not worry; nowadays, it is a minor operation. You will get out of hospital the same day. What are you doing with your time?'

'One problem is that my operation won't happen for two months. I could go home, but that would cost me a fair amount of money. I am lucky to be staying with a friend at no cost.'

'You are, indeed, lucky to live in this Kafir country. You need lots of money to pay all the bills. They come through the letterbox every day.'

The two men shared a laugh.

'You are going to the Mosque?'

'Yes, Sir, to Central London Mosque.'

'Good. What do you want to do for us?'

'I have no experience in anything but am a quick learner. Something simple would be for the best.'

The older man smiled. 'Good. You want to start at the bottom, and that is only right. I think we can use you. It will be basic work but rewarding.'

'Thank you. Is there any pay for the work?'

The old man's face turned dark, and he raised his voice, 'No, we do not do this for money. You will deliver items in London and, occasionally, to other locations. If you incur travel expenses, then of course, we will pay you for that upon production of a receipt.'

'A courier? That is a good, worthwhile job, Sir.'

'Yes, it is. Just remember one thing: never ask questions. It does not concern you who sends the item, who receives it, or what the parcel contains. All you do is deliver it to the location you are told, on the correct day and at the right time.'

'I understand.'

From his pocket, the man retrieved a brown envelope and handed it to Atallah.

'Inside is a key to box 33 in the Mail Box Shop in Whitechapel High Street. You have access twenty-four-seven. You will receive a phone call, and someone will just say, "Ready." When you get that message, you go to the Box Shop and open 33. Inside, will be a parcel, envelope, whatever. Also, you will find a piece of paper with the location the package is to go to and when. Very simple. When you leave the shop, memorise the delivery address and destroy the paper.'

'It is an honour to be helping. I am so happy with the simplicity of the task.'

'It may be a simple task, but also important.' He paused. 'Certain people would be interested in what you will be carrying, so you must stay alert at all times. If you believe you are being followed, your priority is to get rid of the item and the key. You understand?'

'Yes, I understand.'

'If you were to get arrested, you know nothing. Understood?'

'Yes, Sir.'

'Good. We will be in touch.' The man stood and

left the café.

***

Nine different surveillance agents followed him, keeping in touch by radio earpieces. They took eighty-seven photos of the man from every angle imaginable. Richard stayed in contact with the surveillance team as they tracked him to the Muslim Centre, and gave him the codename, Bow. The team stayed in place for when he left. Things were beginning to hot up in the communications ambulance.

CHAPTER 22

Yousef had a big breakfast, which entailed a huge bowl of Frosties cereal with cold milk followed by two fried eggs on toast, and coffee. On the day of a mission, he always had a big breakfast. The last thing he needed was to have hunger pangs at a critical time.

That morning, he'd woken late (at eight-thirty) and immediately fallen to his knees, praying for Allah to bless the operation. A glance through the bedroom window showed that, as usual, it drizzled with rain, and the day looked overcast and grey-skied. Yousef didn't care but could have done without the rain. It had poured throughout most of January and February, so he'd grown well used to it. He finished his breakfast, even licking the last of the egg yolk from the plate. Then he washed up the cutlery and dishes and left them to dry in the grey plastic rack.

Calm and methodical in everything he did, next up was a shower. The young man spent longer than usual soaking in the steaming-hot cascading water. Soon, ten o'clock arrived, and he returned once again to the kitchen, where he made himself a small yet strong coffee and piled in three heaped teaspoons of sugar. Cup in hand, he sat at the small table, going over the plan of action again and again. They'd trained him to make things as simple as possible. If you did that, you had less chance that things could go wrong, and Yousef didn't want anything to go wrong on this day. While he sipped at his drink, he glanced at his watch. Ten past ten. This had become a bad habit that he had to stop.

A little amused at his skittishness, he finished his coffee and went to the bedroom, where he opened the cupboard and took out a dark-blue suit, white shirt, and light-blue tie. Dressed, he looked in the mirror and felt pleased; he looked like a successful business person or politician. Finally, he put on his black brogue lace-up shoes, which he had worn around the house to break in. They felt comfortable. At the airing cupboard, he collected the briefcase, took it to the kitchen, and opened it up on the table. From the worktop, he took the four sheets of A4 and placed them on top of the bomb. Then he shut the case and stood still, ready.

Once he'd taken his coat from the peg on the back of the kitchen door and put it on, he picked up the case and went to the front door, where he listened for any talking or noise on the landing. Upon hearing none, he opened the door and walked out. Outside, he strolled to White City tube station, still completely calm. His training had taught him that to remain calm, you had to control your breathing, and so he paid special attention to taking long, slow, careful breaths. Soon, he waited on the platform at White City, sitting on the same bench in the same space as always. An elderly lady came hobbling down the steps and, as she reached the bench, she nearly collapsed onto it. Yousef bolted up in a second and held out his arms in case she fell onto the concrete platform.

'Thank you so much, young man. It's what happens when you get a bit old.' The lady gave him a broad smile.

Though he returned the smile, his mind roamed elsewhere. The night before, he'd spent with Durriyah, and they had talked about moving abroad. She felt convinced that America was the place to be, but he'd spent his whole life hating the American Kafirs. He'd fallen in love, and so felt desperate to stay with Durriyah. If asked, he'd follow her to the ends of the Earth.

The noisy arrival of the train broke his thoughts, and he strolled on and sat where he always did: the first seat on the right-hand side. Settled in place, he glanced about the carriage. Elderly, young, a pram with a baby crying ... a mixed bag of commuters. Yousef imagined a bomb going off in such a confined space and grimaced when he thought of a packed carriage exploding into blood and limbs and screaming in the inky darkness. Disturbed, he shifted the briefcase on his lap, and sweat slicked his palms. He'd taken the Central line into the city centre, and this time, he got off the tube at Bond Street. At road level, he turned right and walked twenty yards down Davies Street; his timing proved perfect, as a black cab appeared as if by magic. When he waved his arm, the cab pulled up right next to him.

'Horseguards Avenue, please.'

'All right, guv.' The taxi pulled away.

Ten minutes later, it dropped him in the Avenue next to Whitehall Gardens; he paid the cabby and walked the hundred yards down to the river

Thames until he reached Victoria Embankment. There, he turned right and strolled past the Royal Air Force Memorial statue and headed on.

Yousef loved the sound and smell of the river and, for a second, it took him home yet again. At Westminster Pier, close to his destination, he slowed down. His heart pounded. His hands grew clammy. His brow beaded with sweat. At the corner of Parliament Square, he stopped and looked around. The square heaved with tourists. The cold and miserable day seemed perfect on which to kill Kafirs. With a deep breath, he walked around the corner, keeping his head low as though avoiding the slight drizzle. Nearly there — another few steps, and he pushed open the Café Caesar door and walked in. The café looked full and noisy, and sounds of laughter and people chatting in languages from around the world reached him.

At the counter, Yousef ordered an Americana and had to wait for a full five minutes for it to be ready. His palms grew slicker, and his breathing became shorter and more laboured. He took his coffee to the side of the café and hovered, waiting for a spare seat. When a Chinese woman got up to leave, he rushed for the seat and sat with his back to the wall. After placing the briefcase on the floor, he took the deepest of breaths and let it out slowly, regaining control. Then, wiping his palms on his trousers, he looked around the packed establishment. A quick head count tallied about a hundred people. He needed to get on with it.

Nonchalantly, Yousef squeezed the briefcase onto his lap. The woman next to him smiled and made extra room for him. He lifted one of the papers, apparently reading something, and slipped his left hand under the other sheets to the bomb. Earlier, he'd set the timer for five minutes, and he now clicked the start button. Task done, he placed the papers back on top and shut the case, locking it by spinning the number dials on either side. Then he pushed the case tight against the wall, drank his coffee down, and slipped out of the chair and made for the door.

As more people traipsed in to escape the rain and have something hot to eat and drink, Yousef stood to one side. Time was going, and he needed to get moving. The crowd coming into the café thinned, and he stepped out to squeeze through. In the doorway, he bumped into a large American woman, who turned to him and said in a loud voice, *'Please.'* Yousef carried on and made it through. Out on the street, he turned right and took two steps. For some reason, he glanced back into the café, and his body went into shock. Yousef stopped, and his body wouldn't, couldn't do anything. Durriyah had just come out of the ladies toilet and now stood at the counter.

The young man tried to move his feet, then stumbled, nearly falling over. Hardly able to breathe, he looked more closely. Yes, definitely her. His eyes welled with tears, and then something else caught his attention. The woman who'd been seated next to him approached the counter, holding the briefcase. Distressed yet resolute, he turned and quickened his pace, almost running.

Tears streamed down his cheeks as he ducked

into Westminster tube station and slowed. Once through the ticket barrier, he got onto the escalator, taking two steps at a time and descending deep into the ultra-modern steel-and-chrome-finished station. He listened. Nothing. Was it faulty? At the platform, the train sat there, doors open, and he sprinted and just made it. The doors closed, the train pulled away, and then there came a rumble while the very ground around them shook. They had moved off; the timing had been perfect. Yousef tried to pull himself together; he didn't want to draw attention to himself. Not now. Vigorously, he rubbed his face and sat back.

Someone said, *'What the hell was that?'*

Relaxed, free and clear, he shut his eyes. Why had she been there? Durriyah, Durriyah, Durriyah. What a punishment. It could be nothing other than a punishment. Then another thought struck him: maybe she'd walked out. Maybe she'd just been wounded. No, she'd queued at the counter, so she must have been blown to pieces.

The next stop would be Victoria. Yousef stood. The plan had gone perfectly. After disembarking, he followed the exit signs to the mainline station. At the left luggage boxes, he took a key from his pocket, opened number 27, and grabbed the backpack. A minute later, he entered the men's toilets; he had come prepared and slipped the two twenty pence pieces into the barrier and went through. In just three seconds, he stood in the locked cubicle. Two minutes after that, he re-emerged. Now, Yousef stood in jeans, scruffy tee shirt, trainers, woolly hat, and dirty anorak. His suit and shoes, he'd stashed in the backpack.

Next, he retraced his steps down the stairs to the tube station and again descended on the escalators two steps at a time. He travelled the two stops to Oxford Circus, changed back onto the Central line, and walked out of White City station twenty-three minutes later. When he emerged into the fresh air, it still felt cold, but the sun shone; surely a message that all was well? He didn't want to hang about and stretched his legs to get back to the flat and a large glass of Arak.

After the short journey, he entered the tower block, confident of his escape. Shattered and on a high at the same time, he took the lift, but as the doors opened, he cursed.

'Mandy, how are you?'

'Much the better for seeing you, Stephen. Or can I call you Steve? It's so much friendlier.'

'Steve it is, then.'

'What you up to?'

Yousef felt strong, invincible, and wanted a drink. Mandy stood there in her mini-skirt and cropped top, which showed her firm breasts jutting out. 'Fancy a drink?'

'Your place? Or going out?'

Yousef answered by taking his key and opening his front door and then standing to the side. As Mandy sauntered through, he grabbed her arse and squeezed.

She didn't mind at all and backed up against the hall wall. He shut the door, and she smiled. Like an animal, he pulled up her top, lifted her pink bra, squeezed her ample breasts, and then sucked the nipples. In moments, she had her hands on his jeans, undoing the buttons. Once she had them undone, she pushed them down. His huge erect cock erupted, and she grabbed it and stroked up and down. Yousef ripped her skirt open and pushed his hand into her knickers. A few seconds later, she lay on the floor, legs apart, and Yousef thrust into her at a frantic pace. It all finished quickly but had felt incredible.

'I'll get that drink. Whisky or vodka? Or how about some Arak?'

Mandy gasped for breath. 'That was good. I'll have vodka.'

Yousef grinned. 'That was only the beginning.' Durriyah had slipped his mind rather quickly.

The pair fucked three times more, and then he'd had enough. He cited tiredness and said he needed to sleep, then he gave her the half bottle of vodka and promised that they would do it again real soon. At the door, he kissed her goodbye and felt better that she had gone. The second she'd left, he rushed into the lounge and turned on the television.

***

Durriyah had also gotten up late and planned on a lazy day, spoiling herself in the hotel spa. Seated in the hotel restaurant at a two-person table, she gazed out of the window. The day looked its typical overcast and miserable, but having been in London some time, she'd become used to that by now. After a light breakfast of toast and honey with her normal strong sweet coffee, she went back to her room and got ready for the spa, packing a green one-piece swimsuit and also changing her clothes. Donning, instead, a comfortable beige trouser and top combination.

A little while later, she sauntered to the lifts and descended to the basement, where she booked in with the receptionist and changed into her swimsuit. Sauna first — she loved the heat and the way her skin cleansed while she sweated profusely. After thirty minutes in the sauna, she took a swim in the small pool. The water felt warm, and she swam ten lengths, feeling fit and clean and horny for more good sex with Yousef. Showered and cleaned off once more, she then picked up a newspaper from reception on her way to her room.

With the glorious view from her room, the cold and wet February day didn't matter; she loved London so much. Durriyah felt the urge to go for one of her wanders and spent the next thirty minutes fixing her hair. She loved to people watch, which was why she spent so much time sitting in coffee shops. Her hair finished and tied back, she put on warm underwear and a tailored trouser suit, and then slipped on a short coat, grabbed her large green handbag, and stood all ready to go. Where to? Mmm, Parliament Square. One of her favourite spots, mainly because it had so many tourists. Durriyah played a game, trying to guess where in the world they came from.

In no hurry, she sauntered toward the square. As usual, thousands of tourists thronged the streets. Durriyah headed for Café Caesar, one of her best people-spotting locations, and she'd met Yousef there as well. As ever, she found it packed. After queuing, she ordered a Latte and got lucky when a family left just as the barista handed her the coffee. Not long after she'd seated herself at the four-person table, other patrons took the other three seats.

Relaxed, she looked around and found it easy to pick out the oriental Japanese or Chinese; she always seemed able to spot French and Italian women because they always dressed so well. Durriyah sipped her coffee, content with her life for the first time in months, and that mainly came down to meeting Yousef.

Coffee finished, she needed a pee before heading out, and so she made for the ladies and, luckily, found it free. When she slipped in, the horrible smell and terrible mess shocked her. Disgusted, she layered tissue paper around the seat and, three minutes later, on her way out, she passed the counter and noticed her left hand remained damp from washing. She almost turned to go back for another tissue from the cubicle, but someone beat her to it. With the queue at the counter so small, she joined it. While waiting, she glanced around. A man caught her eye, standing outside the café, wearing a business suit. It shocked her at how much he looked like Yousef. Durriyah turned back to the counter. A few seconds later, about to ask for a napkin, she paused when a lady lifted a briefcase in the air next to her and passed it over the counter.

'A nice young man left it at my table. There're just papers in it,' she told the counter girl.

'Can I have a napkin, please?' Durriyah asked.

The girl behind the counter took the briefcase and

put it on the floor, pushing it against the counter with her leg, and almost in the same instant, handed Durriyah a paper napkin. She took a step back from the counter and wiped her hands. All done, she put the napkin in her trouser pocket and walked at a brisk pace to the door, where she let two people enter and then left. After just two steps, a massive rush of heat and wind drove her to the floor and pushed her twenty yards into the road. It all happened incredibly quickly, and she fell to the tarmac, unconscious.

***

The serving girl had pushed the briefcase against the well-built and strong counter. The bomb went off and vaporised the poor girl in the massive explosion. The roof caved in, and bricks and thick black smoke erupted through the windows, showering the pavement and road with deadly shards of razor-sharp glass. People screamed when they looked and saw their limbs had torn from their bodies. Heads and other body parts blew onto the pavement, the road, and even as far as the green. Fifty-seven lay dead in mangled heaps of flesh and bone and blood. Dead and dying bodies covered some of the injured living. A scene from hell.

Passers-by rushed to help as best they could, even if only to comfort the dying. The explosion could be heard all over London, and nowhere louder than in New Scotland Yard, a stone's throw from the square. Police officers closed off the roads, and ambulances and fire engines arrived three minutes later. With the café on fire in a few places, fire crews rushed to put out each blaze. It proved a race against time to get the injured out and to hospitals across London.

The Prime Minister, holding a cabinet meeting in Downing Street at the time, had also heard the bomb explode. Though he wanted to rush to help, security told him — in no uncertain terms — it would be impossible as there could be other devices still to go off. Police firearms teams poured into the area, closed the roads, and checked cars. Armed police officers also poured onto the tube and bus networks, but with no idea of whom they should look for, it was an almost worthless knee-jerk reaction.

***

Yousef rushed to the kitchen and grabbed the bottle of Arak, which he swigged while he ran back to the lounge, then pushed the button on the TV remote. The set flickered to life, and the scene at Parliament Square materialised. Emergency paramedics had covered the dead bodies with white sheets, and there seemed to be dozens of them. Other workers still worked at pulling the wounded out of the wreckage and either carried or led them into ambulances. The seriously injured, the paramedics treated on the spot. Doctors and nurses from a nearby hospital (probably St Thomas') worked alongside the emergency teams. Yousef couldn't take his eyes off the television and continued swigging the Arak. The next scene showed the Prime Minister getting interviewed outside Downing Street.

'This outrageous act of terrorism against

Londoners and tourists from many countries of the world will only strengthen our resolve to defeat the barbaric people who commit these heinous crimes. No one has claimed responsibility yet, but intelligence sources believe it is the work of Isil. I send a message to them, loud and clear: You cannot win; you must know that a country, which stood against Nazi tyranny on its own for two long years during World War Two, will never surrender to a group of cowardly terrorists.'

The Prime Minister looked directly into the camera and pointed. 'Whoever is responsible for this outrage will be hunted down and found, it doesn't matter how long it takes or where you hide, when you are captured, you will face the full force of the law and be incarcerated for the rest of your lives. We pray for the dead, the injured, and the families of all involved in this cowardly attack.'

***

Richard Carpenter, seated at a desk in the main operations office at Thames House, heard a loud bang and rumble. Everybody knew instinctively that it came from a bomb and from not that far away. As soon as word came that it had happened in Parliament Square, he rode in a pool car with two agents, hurtling along Southwark Street toward Westminster Bridge. Although the Metropolitan Police had charge of the overall area, MI5 officers would take over control of the crime scene, with Home Office Crime Scene Officers taking charge of the hunt for clues as to who was responsible.

Police stopped the car at Westminster Bridge, and

Richard flashed his Secret Service Identification. The officers let them through and, ten seconds later, the occupants saw the devastation as they parked as close as possible without causing obstruction. Richard and the two agents jumped from the vehicle, looking for the person in charge. Bodies, some dead, some moaning in agony, lay all over the pavement and road outside the destroyed café. Richard's mobile rang.

'It's Bunny. How does it look?'

Richard had to report in a calm and detached way as much as possible. 'Fifty dead. Same again injured. Badly wounded are being treated here by paramedics and doctors who ran over from St Thomas'. It's too early to assess anything except that a large bomb has detonated, Café Caesar is destroyed, and a couple of offices of Portcullis House have collapsed as well.'

'Any MPs dead or hurt?'

'Too early to know. Send more staff. It's going to be a mammoth job, and the sooner we get information, the sooner we can start looking for this bastard.'

'Aashif Jamal?'

'I honestly don't think so, Ma'am. It's too soon after the Kensington bomb.'

'That's bad news. So, we have another bomber on the loose. Could be tied in with the chatter from GCHQ.'

'I agree.'

'I very much want to know who the Atallah contact is. Has he picked up a parcel yet?'

'No, and I'm sure the first two or three will be

empty to test him.'

'It doesn't matter, Richard. You have the man under solid surveillance?'

'Tighter than a ducks arse.' He regretted that instantly.

'Yes, well, do *not* lose him. Has he made any other contacts?'

'Not that we know of, Ma'am, but it's early days.'

'I'm sending you admin help: Andrea Houlihan, Carla Westburgh, and Debbie Bowditch. Do them good to see a bit of blood and guts. I want all available CCTV film back here yesterday.'

'Top of the list, Ma'am.'

'Good. Carry on.' The line went dead.

Richard and the two men tried to remain detached from the death, screaming, and rivers of blood as they walked through the carnage. Richard noticed a striking woman lying in the road, receiving no assistance. He couldn't help himself and went to her. At her side, he knelt. Alive, her breathing came laboured. Her hair had burnt off, and her clothes had ripped to pieces in the explosion. Tenderly, he touched her face. She had lovely almond-shaped eyes.

'Can you hear me?'

A faint whisper came, 'Yes.'

'Are you in pain?'

'No. I can't feel anything.' She started to cry. 'Do I, do I still have all my limbs?'

'Yes. What's your name?'

'Durriyah. What happened?'

Richard didn't see the point in lying. 'A bomb went off in the café. You got lucky.'

'What is your name, please?'

'Richard. Look, I'm going to leave you for a second to get help. I'll be back.'

'Thank you, Richard.'

Richard looked around for medical assistance. An ambulance drew up close by, and two crew members jumped out. He shouted and beckoned them over, flashing his badge. 'MI5. I want this woman taken care of immediately. She is of interest to us.'

The ambulance crew rushed over to Durriyah, who had again fallen unconscious. They assessed her and inserted a drip, and then loaded her onto a stretcher and carried her back to the ambulance, which left at high speed, siren blaring, toward St Thomas' Hospital.

Richard stopped. The woman—something about her. He shook his head and went to look for the senior police officer.

***

Yousef had not moved from his comfy chair for three hours. He flicked between channels, catching up on every shred of news. He had finished the Arak and nearly all the whisky. A knock came at the door. Most likely Adhan. Yousef just managed to stand without falling over and stumbled to the door. After he'd opened it, Adhan stepped in and shut it quickly. The man grabbed Yousef and hugged him.

'All the glory goes to Allah.' He squeezed him tighter and tighter until Yousef pushed him away.

'Are you trying to crush the life out of me?'

Adhan fell to the floor on his knees. 'Master, you

have shown the way, you are an inspiration, and your memory will be a benediction. Allahu Akbar, Allahu Akbar.'

'Quiet, you fool. Do you want the neighbours to hear?' As he spoke, he swayed. 'Did you bring it?'

'Of course, Master, and more than you asked for.' Adhan passed him a Co-op carrier bag.

Yousef took it, looked inside, and smiled. 'Adhan, did I tell you I like you? Come, get the glasses. We need to celebrate.'

He carried the bag to the kitchen, took the bottles out one at a time, and placed them on the table. The bag empty, he stood and looked at the bottles, happy. Whisky, Pernod, vodka, brandy, and Stones Ginger Wine. He picked up the green bottle of Ginger Wine and turned to Adhan. 'What the fuck is this?'

'A present from me, Master. You must drink it chilled with ice.'

'Bollocks to that.' Yousef opened the screw cap and smelt it, then pulled back. 'It's strong.'

'Try it, Master. It's delicious.'

Yousef lifted the bottle and drank. After a second, he stopped and looked at Adhan, who stood, eyes wide, hoping he liked it.

He tipped the bottle up again and drank heartily. 'I love this. You must get me more.'

'I'm so happy that you like it, Master. The chief sends his thanks for doing such a good job.'

Yousef slurred his words, 'Good. Now, look, I'm going back to the lounge with one or even two of these bottles. You will stay in here and cook dinner. I'm starving, so make it a big meal.'

163

Yousef held onto the wall while he made his slow way back to the comfy chair.

CHAPTER 23

'That's the second parcel of blank paper he's delivered; it won't be long now, Ma'am.'

'Where, exactly, is Atallah delivering these useless parcels?'

'A dead drop in East Ham; nobody even picks them up, but they do follow him. We now have one more man under surveillance; codename, Cover. We don't know his name yet. Seems to live at Forest Lane Mosque.'

'Aashif Jamal?'

'Nothing.'

Bunny stood. 'Right, let's go and see what the Parliament Square CCTV tells us.'

Bunny and Richard made their way to the fourth-floor film and photographic studio. The specialist studio where all CCTV was held, evaluated, and presented to the operational teams. They entered and, immediately, felt the tense atmosphere. Already seated were David Morgan, Hesam Atallah, Badi al Zaman Siddique, Sir Terence Brady, Jack Taylor, administrative staff, and two other senior Field Agents.

Head of Department, Philip Sayers, stood and moved to the front. 'Good afternoon. You all know what's going on. We've had teams studying the Parliament Square CCTV all night and are ready to present our initial findings. The camera in the café, unfortunately, blew to pieces, so that is unavailable to us.'

Richard would like to have said, *We all know that; get on with it.*

'I must emphasise that we still have a long way to go. Film from outside the square and Westminster tube station hasn't been looked at, as yet. So, we have to start with the cameras that give us a view of the entrance to the café and the pavement on either side of it. The bomb went off at eleven-thirty-six. We've studied the door and pavements for fifteen minutes prior to that time. The bomb had to be of a sizable nature to cause the explosion and damage that occurred. As a matter of interest, Semtex is the explosive used. Now, where was I? Yes, the bomb must have been in a container of some sort, so the usual suspects: backpack, briefcase, or holdall. The bomber had to leave the bag for as little time as possible to avoid someone finding it, and the staff becoming suspicious. So, fifteen minutes would seem more than enough time. We've decided to play you the full fifteen minutes of film from the camera outside the station, pointing down toward the entrance to the café. Draw the curtains, please.'

The curtains swished closed, and the room became dark. The film played onto a huge screen at the front of the room. Richard adjusted his eyes and studied the images. People, so many people, pouring out of the tube station and many heading left toward the café. It proved difficult to see people's faces. He looked for Arab-type men or women, carrying a bag of some sort. Business men and women, carrying an assortment of bags, flowed from the station, and some entered the café.

The film stopped, and the light came on.

Philip stood again. 'So, we are now at the critical time, eleven-thirty. Eight minutes to detonation. Keep focussed. Something interesting happens.'

The lights went off, and the film started. The atmosphere grew electric, as they all hoped to see the bomber.

Richard leant forward, rubbed his eyes, and re-focussed. He couldn't be sure but thought he saw the woman called Durriyah walk down to the café entrance and enter. She had a large handbag with her and, clearly, came from the Middle-east somewhere. Could she be the bomber? He kept watching. Then a young Arab-looking man in a smart suit, carrying a briefcase, came from the opposite direction and entered the establishment too. People went in and came out seemingly every second. With nothing happening, Richard searched for the young man, and then he came out. Without the briefcase.

Richard jumped up. 'That's him.'

Philip also stood. 'Yes, without question, he is of great interest. Now, keep watching.'

The young Arab man turned toward the station, and the camera got a classic, perfect full-face image. Then he stopped and looked back into the café, stumbled, and looked shocked. After a further second or two, he rushed toward the station, and that — as they say — was that.

Philip said, 'There is no doubt that the young Arab male is the prime suspect. Any questions?'

'Any idea why he looked shocked when he glanced back into the café?' David Morgan asked.

'We don't know. Maybe he recognised someone, or maybe he had an accomplice who couldn't leave, it's pure guesswork.'

Richard asked, 'What about the Arab woman with the large green handbag?'

'Well spotted. We're not sure, but she came out of the café just as the bomb went off. We need to look more closely at her movements.'

Bunny spoke next, 'What do you plan now?'

'We'll check all the other cameras, with particular reference to the young man and the woman with the green handbag. Image stills will be available soonest, and we'll get those to you as early as possible. We've asked for all tube train and station film, but it will take days to check for our new friends. Rest assured, however, that it will be done. It would prove helpful to know exactly how he travelled to Parliament Square.'

Everybody seemed delighted. It had become obvious that the young man must be the bomber and maybe, but only a maybe, the woman with the handbag an accomplice. The Director General, MI5, had already decided that, as soon as a good image was available, it would be given to the press for the next day's front page '*HAVE YOU SEEN THIS MAN?*' Meanwhile, life would go on, and that meant finding Aashif Jamal.

***

Oh dear, raining yet again. Richard felt lucky and thankful to find a parking space in the small St Thomas' Hospital car park at the east side of the building. He jumped out of the Audi, walked to the double glass doors, and as he got close, they opened automatically. All the information so far had him confused; there had been talk of the woman being a possible accomplice to the bomber, but no evidence to support that. Also, she just had something about her. Had he fallen for her that moment he found her bleeding and unconscious in the road? The thought brought a smile; she'd had no hair and hardly any clothes left.

Bemused, he entered a large hallway, which held a smattering of mostly older men and women, standing around. Richard took the stairs up to the ground floor two at a time. His phone enquiry had proven helpful. The hospital said that the woman was recovering well and that her name was Durriyah Kassab. They'd also given her address in London as the Sanctuary Hotel. For some reason, he couldn't wait to see her, those almond eyes, so large, so beautiful.

The main hospital reception area held a huge restaurant. Richard thought about getting a takeaway coffee but then decided not to and looked for a sign to the wards. Eventually, he found one and got into a lift to the eighth floor, looking for the Alan Apley Ward in the north wing, which had been taken over short-term for the wounded from the bombing. When he left the lift, he found himself in front of a small reception desk manned by a middle-aged brunette nurse in light-blue uniform.

'Good morning. I'm here to see a Ms Durriyah Kassab.'

The nurse smiled. 'Good morning, Sir.' She keyed in the name, and then looked at her computer screen, and after what seemed an age, glanced up. 'Miss Kassab booked out this morning at eight o' clock. I'm sorry. Are you a relative?'

Richard felt incandescent with rage. 'Who the hell let that woman out of here? Who?'

'Please, Sir, there's no need ...'

Richard took out his MI5 identification. 'What idiot let her leave this hospital?' He shook his head in frustration.

'Miss Kassab left the hospital of her own volition against our advice, she—'

'And where the hell are the guards? The police were meant to be guarding her room.'

For a second, the nurse flushed in shock and surprise, and then her expression cleared. 'Oh, you mean the officers outside room twenty-seven? Guarding one of the patients from the bombing?'

Now Richard felt flustered. Did they still have her or not?

The nurse said, 'Mrs Patricia Aldershot—'

'Asian? Arab?' Richard snapped.

The nurse flinched back. 'N-no. Chinese. British Chinese.'

'For fuck's sake!' Spittle flew from his mouth. Richard got on the move, running for the lift, and pressed the button.

'Come on, Come on.' Every second seemed an eternity, and he kicked the lift in annoyance. Finally, it arrived, and he pressed for the ground floor. How the hell had they made such a monumental fuck up? He waited and waited, the lift slowed, and the doors opened. He ran from the lift, knocking aside a couple as he hurtled toward the steps down to the car park.

Ten seconds later, he screeched left and onto Lambeth Palace Road, narrowly avoiding a double-decker bus. He took the next left and flew toward Westminster Bridge, which stood closed. Richard seldom used it but needed to get through quickly. He pressed a button on the dash, and blue lights flashed over the front and back of the Audi.

He got onto the bridge, went past the Houses of Parliament, and hurtled round the square at eighty-miles-per-hour. Not far away, he prayed he reached the hotel in time. At Broad Sanctuary, he'd made it, just ten seconds away. Outside the front of the hotel, he screeched to a halt, not worrying about parking restrictions, and then he jumped out of the car and strode into the hotel. Just inside the door, he stopped. The reception desk stood just ahead, surrounded by people booking out. One of them … yes, he felt sure it was her. She wore a green-checked trouser suit. Though he couldn't see her face, and she wore a headscarf, he approached her. When he got closer, she turned. He saw her eyes, big and beautiful and almond shaped. Next to her, he took her arm in a soft grip.

'Miss Durriyah Kassab? I need to speak to you in private. Please, come through to the lounge with me.'

'I-I'm booking out. You have no — '

Richard whispered in her ear, 'I am from MI5, secret service, and need to speak with you about the bombing. It won't take long, please.'

As she had received injuries in the attack, Richard walked her slowly to the lounge. In fact, she had suffered superficial wounds but nothing serious. He guided her to a two-seater table at the far end, where they could not possibly be overheard. They sat down, and a second later, a waiter appeared. Before he had time to speak, Richard ordered two Americanas.

'I'm sorry, I didn't ask what you would like.'

'It is not a problem. I like any coffee.' Miss Kassab fidgeted in her seat.

They sat for a moment, just looking at each other.

'I hope you are recovered? Although the hospital told me that you shouldn't have left so early.'

'I am fine. Are you not going to introduce yourself?'

Richard held up his hands. 'I'm sorry. Richard Carpenter, MI5.'

'Ah, the famous British Secret Service. And what do you want with me?'

'You know that we've met before?'

She looked at Richard. 'No, I don't know you, and I never forget a face.'

'After the bombing. I found you in the road and tried to comfort you. I called the medics, who took you to the hospital. I felt so worried about you and am happy to see you again and looking so well.'

Durriyah burst into tears, 'You saved my life. Oh God, thank you, thank you.' She must still feel in an emotional state following the bombing. Richard nodded, and she said, 'You must think me such a fool, I'm so sorry.'

'Not at all.' Richard wanted to put his arm around her but held back. This should be a professional interview, for crying out loud. Instead, he asked, 'Where are you going?'

'Paris. I need to get a break from London. I'm sure you can understand that?'

'Why were you in the café at that specific time?'

'So, Richard, am I being interrogated as a suspected bomber?'

Richard didn't answer.

Durriyah shuddered.

He leant forward. 'No, so tell me the story.'

'I'm on holiday. I love just wandering around, and Parliament Square is one of my favourite places. I had breakfast, spent some time in the spa, and then decided to go for a stroll. I popped into Café Caesar for a coffee, and then, apparently, you found me in the road. That's the story, nothing more.'

'I believe you. Tell me about the inside of the café before the bomb went off.'

'What can I tell you? People sat around chatting and drinking coffee.'

Richard took a sip of his Americana. 'It may sound strange, but sometimes people don't understand just what they've seen. The devil's in the detail.'

'I saw nothing of any interest. I bought a coffee, sat down, and drank it. Then I went to the toilet and left. That's it.'

'Okay, let's start again. You walked into the café. Who was in front of you?'

'I don't remember. I *do* remember that it was so busy. When I went to the counter and ordered a Latte, there were no spare seats, and then a family at a table for four got up, I rushed over and grabbed one of the seats, and ten seconds later, the other three seats also got taken.'

'Who sat at the table with you?'

'I don't remember, maybe two women and a man, but I don't know.'

'Don't worry. You are doing well. Continue.'

'I finished my coffee and needed to go to the toilet. I remember being pleased because it was empty, and I also remember being disgusted by the smell and mess.' She took a breather and a sip of coffee. 'I came out and, on my way out, noticed my hands were still wet. I took a paper napkin from the girl behind the counter, dried my hands, and left. I'm sorry, that's all I can tell you.'

'The girl behind the counter—you remember her?'

'She was nice. And quick. She handled the ... oh my God. I see it.' Durriyah, agitated, stood and began shaking. Richard got up and put his arm around her shoulder and, gently, put her back into her seat. Durriyah burst into tears again. 'I know what happened. I saw the bomb.'

Richard couldn't believe his luck. 'Tell me, what happened?'

Between sobs, she managed to speak and told him all about the customer finding the case.

Richard chewed his bottom lip, then said, 'I think, almost certainly, it was the bomb, and we have an image of the young man who took it into the café.'

'I didn't see the man. The girl behind the counter, she ...'

Richard shook his head. 'She didn't make it.'

Neither of them spoke for a minute, and then

Richard broke the bad news. He put on his professional hat, 'Miss Kassab, I'm afraid that you are not able to go to Paris. As a material witness to the bombing, you must, therefore, stay in the UK.'

'I thought you were going to say that. For how long?'

'It could be months.'

'I can't afford to stay in a hotel. What will I do?'

'Don't worry. You will go onto a witness protection plan and will be given accommodation in a safe house.'

'Where?'

'I don't know. It's too early to say. Look, let's go back to the bombing. One more thing, I have a picture of the suspected bomber, and it may jog your memory.'

'Yes, let me see the animal that killed all those poor, innocent people.'

Richard took a small, grainy image out of his jacket inside pocket and placed it on the table in front of Durriyah.

She looked down and went ashen-faced.

At first, she couldn't speak, and then mumbled, 'I know him. I saw him outside the window as he left. I didn't think it was him because of the suit.' She breathed quickly, sucking the air in, which proved too shallow and she hyperventilated. In a panic, she shouted, 'Help me, help me, I can't breathe.' Then, as she tried to suck air into her lungs, a rasping, frightening, high-pitched screeching came from her. The woman rocked on the chair, toppled to the side, and fell onto the carpeted floor.

Richard took control. A designated first aider member of staff rushed over with a brown paper bag, which he placed over her mouth and nose until her breathing settled and she calmed. Nothing more than a serious panic attack, and if it had continued, Durriyah would have become unconscious but would have suffered no lasting damage. Five minutes later, she sat sipping another coffee, this one heavily sweetened.

'Thank you, Richard. You keep saving me.'

'You've been to hell and back. It's been my pleasure. I have to ask, how do you know this man?'

A tear rolled down her cheek. 'He is — was — my lover. I met him in that same café some days ago. He lied to me. All lies just for sex.' She closed her eyes.

'There will be many, many more questions, but three serious ones I need to ask you right away. Do you know his name?'

'Yes. Well, he told me his name is Yousef El-Sayed.'

'And where is he from?'

'I only know that he is Syrian.'

'And do you know where he has been staying in London?'

'I wish I did, so that I could tell you, but I don't. I'm so sorry.'

'Listen, Durriyah, you must pack all your belongings; you are coming with me.'

'You're going to save me again?' A small smile lifted the corners of her mouth.

'I promise you; I will not let anybody hurt you

ever again.'

As Richard stood, he looked at the picture of Yousef El-Sayed the bomber, and felt intense hatred towards him.

CHAPTER 24

'So, not only do we have a picture of the man but, now, we know his name is Yousef El-Sayed. Are we sure that he gave her his real name? Why would he do that? This is a serious development, Richard. We've been lucky, but does it help us in finding him?'

Richard took his time answering and chose his words with care, 'I think he may have been in love with her. Apparently, he was a virgin, and you know what young men are like about their first real love. So, every scrap of information could be useful, and his name, if that was his real name, has to be helpful.'

'Anything from the newspaper pictures?'

'Yes, hundreds of calls. We're checking anything of interest.'

'Keep me up to date with developments, and I understand that Atallah, at last, has a serious drop? Blank passports, I understand? What time is he due in Bradford?'

'That's correct, Ma'am. The drop should be made at three pm. He's taking the train from King's Cross. Should get there at two-thirty-five; so, plenty of time.'

'Good. I'm taking it as read that he has full support.'

'Absolutely. More than required so there'll be no slip-ups.'

'Are we in Bradford already at the drop?'

'Yes, the pick-up is at a café on the station. He sits in the corner, reading the Times newspaper, and the envelope has to be on the table. Someone will just walk past and take it.'

'So, hopefully, another piece to the jigsaw and a step closer to finding our friend Aashif Jamal.'

'We hope so, Ma'am.'

'Well, make sure nothing goes wrong. Now, onto Durriyah Kassab. She is safely delivered?'

'Yes, she's at the safe house on Epsom Downs. I wouldn't mind staying there; it's lovely. Jim Matthews and Mrs Evans are looking after her, so she's in good hands.'

'We could still ask her to go back to him, double-cross him?'

'I had thought of that but believe he would kill her. She's a liability he could do without. And she might have to be intimate with him, which she couldn't do.'

'Yes, I suppose you're right, pity. Atallah is doing a good job, but I never hear about Siddique — what's he up to?'

'Surveillance.'

'On whom?'

'He's with the team watching the Muslim Centre in Whitechapel.'

'I seem to remember that I asked you to get him involved inside the Mosques? That's where he can get information and make a difference.'

'I just don't trust him, but if you insist.'

She gave him a hard look and took a deep breath. 'I listen to you, Richard, because — over the years — I have come to trust your judgement. However, you have to understand that there is no time, not a second to spare. Aashif Jamal and this new bastard Yousef El-Sayed could strike again at any time. Hundreds more dead. We must throw caution to the wind in the search for them. Do you see that?'

'I do, Ma'am, but ...'

'Spit it out, man.'

'I think there could be a mole in the camp ...'

'What? Mole? Why have you not come to me before? Explain yourself.'

'The phone call to Abbas Mahmood at the grocery shop, supposedly a family emergency, but my instinct tells me it was a warning call from an insider. I think we have a mole, Ma'am.'

'That's all we need.' She couldn't speak for a few seconds. 'You think we have a mole yet you have let Atallah go to Bradford? Everybody could end up compromised, and we may even have to shut down and start the operations again. What about Siddique?'

'Everybody is expendable for the cause.'

'You're getting more like me every day. So, you didn't tell me of your concerns because you thought it could be me?'

Richard smiled. 'No, Ma'am, impossible.'

'Well, it's not impossible, but it's not me. Let's keep this between the two of us for the moment, okay?'

'Yes, Ma'am.'

Bunny looked Richard in the eye, and then lowered them to look at her notes. She turned a few pages over, and then glanced up again. 'The keys found at Hassain's house ... what's happening with them?'

Richard cursed; she never forgot anything. 'No luck as yet, Ma'am.'

'I don't like the word luck. Luck is usually a result of hard work, don't you agree?'

'Of course, Ma'am, but I have to prioritise.'

Bunny looked at him while fiddling with her papers. Richard waited for the broadside but got something else.

'I trust your judgement, so let's hope one of them isn't the key to the Semtex store.'

CHAPTER 25

Yousef opened his bleary eyes; he lay on the bed, fully clothed, and smelt urine. Must have peed himself while in his drunken stupor. His body felt like death warmed up, his head throbbed, and his mouth was like the bottom of a bird cage, dry as a bone, gritty, and tasting disgusting. In this hung-over state, he knew neither the time of day nor the day. He knew he'd drunk a lot, but from the way he felt, it must have been a huge amount. A glance around the room revealed an empty whisky bottle lying on the floor.

The first attempt to lift his head failed, and immediately, he let it fall back onto the pillow, as the slight movement had caused a splitting headache. Best to stay in bed until he felt a little better. Instead, he closed his eyes and remembered the bombing. He was a star, had done his job, and everybody felt happy with him. Durriyah flashed into his head, and he imagined her body getting torn to pieces in the explosion. Maybe they wouldn't even know she existed, which would be best. And then he thought of Mandy, so young, so fresh, so horny, and felt his excitement and determined to see her as soon as possible for some more pleasure.

By three pm on Thursday, he wondered what had happened to Adhan and when he'd left the flat. In one fluid movement, he got up and managed to sit on the side of the bed. A sharp pain shot through his head; he needed Paracetamol, but that would mean a trip to the corner shop, and he wouldn't leave the flat for anything. Slowly, he stood and took measured steps toward the kitchen—he had to have at least four mugs of coffee.

Dirty dishes filled the sink. He just managed to fill the kettle and turned it on, then looked around. Empty vodka and Pernod bottles littered the worktops. Yousef swore under his breath and went to see what the lounge looked like. When he stepped in, it shocked him to see yet more bottles on the floor. His head continued to throb. He rubbed his face, scraping the gritty sleep from his eyes, and then he heard banging on the door. More cursing under his breath—who the hell could that be? He so wasn't ready for Mandy yet. Bollocks. He stumbled to the door, opened it an inch, and looked out. Adhan stood there.

'Why the fuck didn't you phone?'

'I've been phoning all day and wanted to check you weren't in a coma or hadn't died from choking on your vomit.'

'Make yourself useful and do the coffee. I'm completely fucked.'

'That's what happens when you drink yourself into oblivion and start fucking young white English girls.'

Yousef grew more alert, and considering his state, his reaction time was phenomenal. He grabbed Adhan around the throat and squeezed tight.

'You cunt. Did you just kill and maim a hundred Kafirs? Well, did you?'

Adhan's eyes widened in shock, and he put up

his hands to try and defend himself. 'No, Master. Please, Master, I'm sorry.'

Yousef relaxed his grip. 'How did you know about the girl?'

'You got drunk and told me every detail of your drink-fuelled sex.'

Yousef prayed he got the right answer to his next question and took his time asking it, 'Adhan, have …' He stopped and gave the man a fearsome look. 'Have you mentioned this to …?'

Adhan jumped in, genuinely scared for his life, 'I haven't told anyone, Master. I promise. No, no, no, it is between us, I swear.'

Yousef stared at him. 'Good. If it should come to pass that you have lied, I will kill you.'

Adhan fell to his knees. 'Master, I promise.' He sobbed and tears ran down his cheeks.

Yousef ruffled his hair. 'I believe you, so you can relax. Now, tell me all the news. And what's in your carrier bag?'

Adhan stood and put the bag on the chair, then dipped in his hand and retrieved the first item: Paracetamol. 'I thought you might need this.'

Yousef grabbed the packet and rushed to the kitchen, where he filled a mug with water, and then tore open the packet. He ripped the silver foil and took out three tablets, then shoved them into his mouth and gulped the water.

Still groggy, he went back to the lounge. 'You are a life saver. I needed them.'

The next few items turned out to be food.

'Master, you must prepare yourself for a bit of a shock.'

Yousef didn't say anything; he just stared at the bag.

Adhan took out three folded newspapers: The Sun, The Mirror, and The Mail, which he unfolded and handed to Yousef, who took them. The front page of the top paper, The Sun, left him thunderstruck. A large picture of him covered the sheet with a caption beneath it. Shocked to the core, he couldn't understand what had happened.

The caption read:

CAFÉ KILLER YOUSEF EL-SAYED – FIND HIM

He collapsed into his easy chair, unable to take his eyes from the picture.

'How?' He put both hands over his face. 'How did they get my name? I don't understand.'

He looked up at Adhan for an answer.

'I don't know, Master. Do not get annoyed with me, but is it possible you told someone?'

Yousef had told Durriyah, but she had died in the blast; it just didn't make sense.

Again, he looked at Adhan and spoke slowly, 'Am I to be sacrificed? Why would that be? I have done what they asked of me.'

'Alas, I am but a messenger, Master, but I think not. There must be an explanation, and we will soon know.'

'What will we know?'

'How they got your name. We have someone on the inside. Tonight, they will tell us how they discovered your identity. You cannot leave the flat. You've compromised yourself with the Mandy girl. It is up to you, but you understand.'

'Yes, I will take care of the girl.' He paused, and

then said, 'I want to go back as soon as possible.'

'You can go nowhere for some weeks, if not months; the whole country is looking for you. It would not be wise to move anywhere.'

'Shit. What a fucking mess. Are you leaving straight away?'

'Yes, I have much to do.'

'I want more alcohol as soon as possible. The same stuff you brought before.'

'Yes, Master. I will bring it tomorrow morning at ten. And then we will know how they got your name.'

'Goodbye, Adhan.'

After the man had left, Yousef went straight back to the kitchen and ran the tap. Once the water grew icy-cold, he drank at least a pint and felt slightly better. Next, he ran a bath, and once full, he lay there unmoving for half an hour. Now, desperately, he needed a good meal. Back in the kitchen, he opened two cans of lamb stew and heated pitta bread in the toaster. The smells wafting up from the heating food drove him wild.

Seated at the table, he stuffed his face until he couldn't eat any more. After the meal, more coffee, three more Paracetamol, and by then, he felt a lot more human. In the lounge, in his favourite chair, he opened the first page of The Mail. It contained six pages of bomb news, interviews with security specialists, a page of thumbnail images of the dead, and theories and yet more theories. Some said that the bomber had already left the country and gone back to the Middle-east, some said he'd holed up in a one-bedroomed flat somewhere in London, and yet others said he'd gone into hiding in a Muslim community in a northern city.

Disgusted, he put down the paper and leant back, resting his head. From where did they get his name? He must remain on guard from now on. No way would he allow them to sacrifice him to the Kafirs, not for any reason. Better that he go on the run and take his chances. After thinking through all eventualities, he decided he would ask to meet the controller. If he discovered any intrigue going on detrimental to himself, he would kill them all, including Adhan.

The next problem: what to do about Mandy? She had such a sweet, firm body, and the idea of killing her was unwelcome. However, as the only one who had spent time with him, she remained the only person who would surely recognise his picture in the paper. The other major consideration, of course, was that if he did kill her, the police would sniff around; the last thing he wanted. Yousef laughed to himself. Mandy had, probably, never bought or read a paper in her whole life. In truth, he felt unsure of what to do. He would sleep on it.

 Although he'd slept for hours last night, he remained tired. Mouth stretched in a wide yawn, he went to the bathroom, peed, and brushed his teeth, then shuffled to the bedroom and lay on the bed. Within a couple of minutes, he'd fallen into a deep slumber.

He got up early (at seven) on Friday morning, having slept for eleven hours and well rested. As had become his morning ritual, he glanced through the window to see what the weather looked like. The shining sun surprised him; it looked almost like a summer's day. With a smile and a lighter heart, he headed to the kitchen and made coffee and heated a long-life chocolate croissant for breakfast.

His head had cleared, and he felt alert and focussed on the meeting with Adhan, due at ten. Somebody in the organisation had informed on him, but if they had given the Kafirs his name, why didn't they give them his location? It didn't make sense. Yousef did some cleaning and had more coffee.

At nine-thirty, he tucked the Glock into the back of his trousers, always prepared for any eventuality. Then he sat in the comfy chair in the lounge and waited. At one minute to ten, a knock came at the door. Yousef rose and let an as-usual-smartly-dressed Adhan in. Neither of them spoke until they reached the sitting room. Adhan took the comfy chair and Yousef the kitchen chair, which he placed in front of his visitor.

'All the praise goes to Allah.'

Yousef felt in a hurry. 'Report.'

'Yes, Master. The authorities have your identity because you told Durriyah Kassab your name, and she gave it to MI5.'

Yousef ran a hand through his hair. 'She's dead. Killed by the bomb.'

'She survived and is now under the protection of the secret service. The chief says that you are a fool and wants to know about the Kassab woman.'

Yousef took a deep breath. 'Yes, I have been a fool, but a human fool. I met the woman in that exact café. She came from home – such a beautiful woman. I spoke to her, we met, had sex.' Then he lied, 'I realised my mistake and arranged it so that she would be in the café when the bomb went off.' He stopped and took a deep breath. 'She should have been blown to pieces. Do you have any further information?'

'She got injured, and they took her to St Thomas' Hospital. Now they have her in a safe house somewhere.'

'Where?'

'We don't know yet, but have asked for that information.' Adhan smiled at him. 'Beautiful women are intoxicating, are they not?'

'I had never been with a woman. Can you imagine that, Adhan? Fighting and killing and blood and gore? That's all I have ever known my whole life. When I met her, I couldn't stop myself. Oh, those big almond eyes.' At the memory, he shook his head. 'She must have received terrible injuries?'

'Not sure. Listen, don't sweat it. I've had hundreds of white, black, Chinese, and Asian women, and the rest. After all, it's not just for pissing out of.' Adhan laughed.

Yousef didn't speak but gave a weak smile.

'So, Master.' Adhan became serious again, 'The last two parts of the message: Firstly, you will select another target and, secondly, once we find out where she is, you will kill the woman, Durriyah Kassab.'

Yousef sat there for a moment before answering, 'I will need a disguise, but it is possible. All the glory goes to Allah. It will be done.'

CHAPTER 26

The black people-carrier careened into London Bridge Street and screeched to a halt outside the main station entrance. The doors had opened before it stopped, and Richard and three agents, all in black suits and white shirts, hurtled out of the car and charged through the huge, open glass doors. They turned left and sprinted down the steps into the London Bridge underground, where they ran through the crowded retail shopping area, knocking people out the way. Angry shouts and screams met them as they charged into the ticket office and barrier area, and the noise of their shoes smacking on the tiled concourse added to the mayhem.

Richard stopped for one second, and then shouted, 'Move, this way.'

He sprinted, following the black Northern Line sign, and then jumped the ticket barrier. The agents followed, and one overweight, short agent fell as he crashed into it. They got onto the escalator, running down the steps and screaming for people to move out the way, weapons drawn. As quickly as they could, the terrified commuters moved out the way. The agents reached the bottom and jumped off, and Richard checked for the Northern Line going toward King's Cross. He shouted again, 'This way.'

They turned the corner, to be met by a standing train with the last few passengers boarding.

'Hurry, get on,' Richard yelled.

A mad rush ensued. Richard got through the door first and held it open for the others, and the two agents crashed onto the train floor, gasping for breath.

Richard spoke into his earpiece, 'We're on the train, heading north.'

The message came back, 'He's on the train, white Thobe, black coat, and long black beard.'

Richard took one long deep breath and exhaled slowly, and then said in a loud voice, 'He's on this train, let's go.'

As they pushed forward, Commuters rushed for the rear of the train, ready to get off at the next stop. Purposely, the MI5 team strode through the carriages, weapons held out in front, searching for the man. They had gone through four carriages when the tannoy broke into life.

'The next station is Monument. Change here for Bank Central Line and Circle and District Lines.'

'Shit.' Richard stopped and moved toward the doors. He placed his hand on the 'open' button, ready to push it if any delay occurred. Five seconds later, the train pulled into Monument. After it had stopped, the doors opened, and the agents jumped onto the platform, looking toward the front of the train. Hundreds of people disembarked, making it difficult to see.

Richard shouted, 'There he is.'

A man fitting the description walked alongside the train toward the exit. Richard sped up, screaming for people to move and pushing them out the way. Some of them complained, and then saw the guns and screamed instead. Richard could see the man, fleetingly, between the crowds. And then he jumped back onto the train. They only just made it back on before the doors closed. As hard as he could, Richard looked down the train and platform, and then cursed. The man had jumped back onto the platform again, and stood almost at the exit; he had tricked them.

The train jerked forward. Richard lunged for the red emergency stop, and the train lurched to a halt, throwing the people in the carriages off balance. The door didn't open automatically. Richard looked around, saw the emergency axe, broke the glass, and pulled the axe free, which he swung at the door. The glass shattered, and the door slid open. The agents jumped down onto the platform and ran as fast as they could to the exit. They turned and entered a long tunnel, and one of the agents fell back, as the pace proved too much for him. Richard pumped his legs and sprinted down the tunnel, shouting for people to move. Ahead, he saw the man. Most likely, they could catch him. He appeared to be headed for Bank tube station, which had a walking connection to Monument. The man must have heard the shouting, as he broke into a trot.

Richard tried to scare him into stopping, 'Stop, or we will open fire!'

The commuters in the tunnel screamed and either ran or fell to the floor.

'Stop, or we will open fire.'

They closed on him; not far to go. 'Stop, or we will open fire.'

The man turned a corner and rushed down steps onto a central line platform, which went north to Liverpool Street station. He rushed down the lengthy platform. Richard and one agent almost fell when they entered the platform. Ahead, the man headed down the quiet concourse.

Richard sped up, shouting, 'Stop, or we will open fire.' Desperate to take the man alive, if needs be, he would aim for his legs.

The man got halfway down the platform and stopped, exhausted and gasping for breath, and then turned and held his hands in the air. Richard felt ecstatic. They had him alive. The man turned the other way. A train approached. The wind whipped over the platform when the train hurtled into the station. Richard stood, aghast, when the man walked to the edge of the platform and jumped onto the track. Though the driver had, no doubt, seen him, he could do nothing in that short distance and at that high speed. The train ploughed into him and crushed his body beneath the wheels, and flesh and blood squirted in every direction.

Two minutes later, Richard answered his mobile.

'Do you have the parcel?' Bunny asked.

'No. Abbas Mahmood is underneath the wheels of a tube train.' He pressed the red button, and then shouted, 'Fuck.'

CHAPTER 27

Richard felt tired; the job had gotten on top of him. He had so many surveillance teams, so many agents, and so many sleepers to look after, and though he did it all, he only just about kept his head above water.

The man who'd met Atallah in the café on Whitechapel Road, codenamed Bow, had finally been named. Fakhir al Din Shaheen. Aged fifty-three, and married with five children, he lived in Barking, East London. Surveillance had commenced on his house, and the teams photographed all visitors and recorded the number plates of all cars.

Richard had spoken to Bunny, telling her that it had become impossible to watch all the suspected extremists. And, although she didn't like it, she understood and said he had to prioritise.

***

On a Thursday in the first week of March, the weather turned a bit chilly but the sun shone, and the daffodils blossomed. Richard, for a change, dressed smart-casual in cream Chinos and a coffee-coloured roll-neck pullover. While he drove up Old London Road, in the distance, he could see the beautiful white grandstands of Epsom Race Course, home to the world famous Derby. The purpose of his journey, to visit Durriyah Kassab in the safe house near Tattenham Corner. Richard loved the countryside; he looked across the Downs, so green, people walking their dogs, and race horses getting exercised.

Eventually, he turned into the tree-lined Downs Wood Road and stopped outside number three. A year before, he had visited the Epsom safe house — his favourite of them all, the lovely four-bedroom detached house stood in a wealthy area, predominantly white. He got out of the car and took a deep breath, then looked up and down the road. Durriyah could not be in a safer place. Happy, he strode to the bright-red front door and rang the bell. Jim Matthews pulled back a lace curtain to check him out. A minute later, no-nonsense Mrs Evans opened the door, and he entered.

'Mrs Evans. How are you? It's been a long time.'

'Very well, thank you, Mr Carpenter.'

Jim entered the hallway. 'Hey, Richard. Escaped from the smoke, then?'

Richard sighed. 'Something like that. How are you?'

Jim raised his eyebrows and motioned with his hands for Richard to look at the house. 'Couldn't be better. I retire in twelve months, which is why they gave me this cushy number, and I'm loving it.'

Richard turned to Mrs Evans, 'Where is Miss Kassab?'

'I think she's getting dressed.' She lowered her voice, 'A nice, educated young lady. One of the nicest I've had, that's for certain.'

Richard nodded. 'And, in case you didn't know, one of the most valuable as well.'

Mrs Evans shook her hands. 'I have no interest in

what, who, or why. I just like to look after my visitors. After all, it's not easy for them. Now, look, I need to check my baby potatoes. I'm sure she'll be down in a minute.'

Richard and Jim moved to the lounge and talked about old times, of current happenings, and what might lay ahead. After ten minutes, Richard heard movement on the stairs and, a second later, Durriyah Kassab made an entrance. And, oh, what an entrance it was.

Durriyah strode in, smiling that wonderful smile. Richard thought that her eyes had grown bigger and even more beautiful. Some of her hair had grown back, and she wore it cut in a short, modern style. Plain black trousers, a black shirt with rolled up arms, and an elegant gold chunky necklace adorned her lithe form. Simple attire, but she looked fabulous.

'Richard, so good to see you.'

Richard stood. 'Durriyah, you look fantastic.'

She laughed. 'A lot better than last time we met, I'm sure. Mrs Evans and Jim are looking after me too well.'

Jim excused himself.

Richard retook his seat and relaxed. 'So, you're recovering well?'

'I am, although I have to be careful. Mrs Evans is such a good cook that I'm piling on the pounds.'

They shared a chuckle.

'Well, you look pretty good to me, so don't worry.'

Durriyah turned serious. 'Any news on ...' She paused, then said, 'I can hardly say his name.'

197

'Unfortunately, no news. We're working hard to catch him, believe me.'

A shout came from the dining room, 'Lunch is ready.'

Richard raised his brows. 'Shall we eat?'

Durriyah laughed. 'You'll enjoy this.'

'I hope so. I'm living on takeaways at the moment.'

'Poor Richard. You can have some of mine.'

They both laughed while they made their way into the dining room.

An hour later, they returned to the lounge, having had a splendid lunch of cold pork with baby new potatoes, followed by Eton Mess.

Durriyah caught Richard's eye. 'I usually take a walk after lunch. It's quite nice; would you like to accompany me?'

'Of course, it's such a pleasure to get out of London, and I'd love a good stroll.'

Durriyah put on a long black coat and scarf while Richard borrowed a jacket from Jim. They left the house and, for once, Jim could relax as Richard took over the bodyguard responsibility. They strolled down the road, and then turned right. In front of them lay the sprawling Downs.

'I love the peacefulness of it. So unlike central London.'

'Yes, I know. I like the fresh air, the trees.' He laughed. 'And so few people.'

Durriyah chuckled in response. 'I don't know how I've survived so long with so few people to watch, but I do love to see the horses getting exercised in the morning; they're huge beautiful animals, you know.'

'Yes. So strong and graceful. Now, changing the subject, how are you coping? Being on witness protection is tough, you can't go anywhere, and you can't talk to anyone. Is it getting you down?'

She smiled. 'I have my moments; ask Jim and Mrs Evans. Truth is, I'm healing, and from so many traumas. That bastard is just another memory, another problem to get over. An American bomb, dropped in the wrong place, at the wrong time, killed my husband and children. It's been a bad year.'

'I'm so sorry. I wish I could help. If there's anything, just ask, okay?'

'When this is all over, I'm thinking of going to America. If I need help with the visa, perhaps I could ask —'

'Of course. We have an excellent relationship with the Americans.'

They walked on, enjoying the quiet, and then came rain.

'Oh no.' Durriyah screeched and ducked.

Richard grabbed her hand, and they ran for the tea hut. Once they'd made it, they almost fell onto the decking surrounding the hut. Richard placed both arms around Durriyah, and they fell into each other's arms. The moment grew awkward when neither one of them pulled away. Richard wanted to kiss her and made do with a peck on her cheek.

'I'm not meant to start caring for my witnesses; apparently, it makes protecting them more difficult, but I do care about you, Durriyah.'

'Richard, you're a married man.'

He shook his head. 'Separated. The job, you know—never at home, makes for a useless husband and father.'

'What you do is so important; she has to understand.'

'She doesn't. And, truthfully, I don't blame her. We might as well not be married, so …'

'I'm sorry, I'm not ready.'

'I tell you what, when this is all over, let me take you out for dinner, and we'll go from there. What do you say?'

She smiled. 'I would like that very much.'

Elation washed through him. 'That's a deal, then.' He stuck out his hand.

Durriyah took it, and they shook, and then both burst out laughing.

They almost ran back to the house—good job it lay so close. Richard asked Durriyah another hundred questions, and then left at four. He drove back toward London in high spirits. What a marvellous day. They had connected, but whether anything would come of it or not … well, they would have to wait and see. One thing Richard couldn't quite come to terms with was that Durriyah had had intimate relations with that Muslim bombing bastard.

Somewhat refreshed, he arrived back at the flat in Knightsbridge. The day out had provided a wonderful break, and to see Durriyah had put the icing on the cake. Had he fallen in love? Could you fall in love that quickly? Or did it come down to pure lust? The woman came from another world, but they seemed to get on well. Time would tell.

Richard checked his messages. One waited from Bunny. She required his presence at Thames House on Sunday at nine am for a meeting. He re-read it. Yes, it said *Sunday,* and he cursed. Bunny would say to take a day off during the week whenever he liked, but they both knew that that would never happen. He read down the screen. Interesting. Images of Yousef El-Sayed on the tube and getting dropped off near Parliament Square in a black cab had come to light.

That sounded like progress. The meeting, now, didn't seem as onerous as before.

CHAPTER 28

Stood in the bathroom in his underpants, the man looked in the cracked mirror and received a pleasant surprise. He'd shaved his head and now had a black beard and moustache. Because he looked so unlike himself, he believed that nobody could possibly identify him. All he had to do now was change his clothes and he would be unrecognisable from his previous self. Yousef left the bathroom and went back to the kitchen, and though early, he needed a drink. Ten-thirty in the morning wasn't that early anyway.

When he reached for the Bells original whisky, he noticed that his hand shook. Obviously, he'd been hitting the bottle too much. Now, he tried to remember how many bottles Adhan had brought but couldn't. It was a lot though. Not bothering with a glass, he lifted the bottle and held it to his lips. The burning sensation restored him, and the shaking stopped. Yousef wiped his mouth with his cuff and thought about what to wear. He'd asked Adhan to bring a selection of different types of clothes, and now went to the bedroom to choose.

A traditional pale-blue Thobe that he loved, he put to one side. If he went traditional, he would need good leather sandals, a scarf, and an old short coat. Instead, he sifted through the pile and brought out an orange Hare Krishna robe, which he liked but thought that members of that group usually travelled in groups. Next, he discovered some scruffy old clothes, not dissimilar to the ones he'd arrived in, and lastly, running gear. In the end, he decided that, when leaving the flat, he would alternate between traditional, running, and scruffy. Once he'd finished his scrutiny, he wrote down what else he wanted Adhan to provide and, at the bottom of the list, added two bottles of Bells whisky.

Yousef had boxed off the Durriyah woman, and now she'd become nothing but a target. As soon as the informant told them of her whereabouts, he would kill her. He had no more interest in her than he would a goat or a horse and, of course, they had far more value.

He hadn't seen Mandy for days. Had the girl gone cold on him? Some physical pleasure other than self-masturbation would bring a welcome relief. He would call and invite her round for a drink, although he still hadn't decided whether to kill her or not.

Restless, having not been out of the flat for days, he needed fresh air. Given that he still had to decide on his next objective, it would make a good opportunity to stretch his legs while studying the target. He took the tourist-attractions booklet from the bedside drawer and flicked through. It held so many eye-catching possibilities: Westminster Abbey, the London Dungeons, the Tower of London, the Museums, Madame Tussauds, the London Eye, and many more. He wanted it to be spectacular, something that would live in the people's memory for years, and prove even more horrific than the glorious nine-eleven in America.

Tired, he pushed the empty Bells bottle from the bed and lay down, then shut his eyes and fell asleep within seconds.

He awoke at two-thirty with a hard on, having slept for about three hours, and now felt rested. He yawned widely, rubbed his eyes, and jumped up. Ten minutes later, he sat eating lamb and vegetable canned stew with pitta bread. Once he'd finished his meal, he took a quick shower and hoped — no, prayed — that Mandy would be home; he needed a woman up for anything he wanted. Mind full of fantasies, he dried himself off and applied deodorant. He walked around with a permanent hard on and couldn't wait for Mandy to enjoy relieving him of it. Ready, he left the flat, strolled to number eighteen, and rang the bell. Though he listened closely, he couldn't hear any sign of life. And then footsteps approached the door, which then opened.

'Hi, Mandy. How's things?'

She gave him a quizzical look. 'What the fuck have you done to yourself? What's with the disgusting beard?'

He felt shocked; so not the welcome and reaction he'd expected. 'Don't you like it?' He touched his beard, stroking it.

'No, I fucking well don't; it's turning my stomach just looking at it. Go and get rid of it and then come back.'

A shout came from the lounge; the voice of a young girl. 'Who is it, Mand?'

Mandy turned around. 'Friend of mine. Come

and say hello.'

A striking girl of similar age to Mandy appeared from the lounge. Tall, slim, and attractive, she had long blonde hair.

'Hi, I'm Sarah.' She looked closely at Yousef. 'Yeah, go and shave that thing off, and then the three of us can have a good time. That's if you're interested?'

He didn't know what to say and just stood there.

The new girl proved forward just like Mandy, 'Cat got your tongue?'

'Cat?' Unsure what was happening, he decided to retreat. 'I'll go and sort myself out and come back.'

The two oh-so-confident, young and sexy girls stood there, looking at him. He smiled and turned, and behind him, the door shut. Fuck. Two young, gorgeous girls ripe for the taking, and they wanted him to cut his fucking beard off. He felt agitated beyond belief. *Two girls at the same time*, he kept saying to himself. Back in the flat, he rushed to the kitchen and lifted the Bells to his mouth.

***

Adhan felt more than a little concerned. Yousef's drinking had become worrisome. He hadn't mentioned it to his control but, if Yousef didn't keep it in check, he would have to do so to safeguard himself. He had delivered the Semtex and everything else that the man had asked for, and all Yousef had to do now was choose a target. The best thing for the still very young Yousef would be to kill the woman, hit the next target, and then go back to Syria. Adhan had some sympathy for him, stuck in the flat for days on end must be tough, and it was easy to get seduced by the Western way of life. He enjoyed his lifestyle, and no way would he return to Syria to fight in the great Jihad. No, he did his fighting in the restaurants and bars of London, and in his bedroom with countless women of all nationalities.

***

Yousef never returned to see Mandy and Sarah. The next morning, he woke up sweating and clammy. He had no idea of the time and reached for his watch, which showed three o'clock. He remembered coming back from seeing the girls and having a small drink. It couldn't have been that small, though, as he felt sick and rushed to the bathroom and threw up in the toilet bowl. What was happening to him? He felt sick, both physically and mentally, and blamed the British way of life; though down to Western culture, he had proven weak. He made for the kitchen to make coffee; no more drinking, no more womanising. He would deliver death to the Kafirs one more time, and then return to Syria a hero.

***

Hesam Atallah opened the heavy train door and stepped onto the platform. His handlers had told him that he would almost certainly be followed, and they had the photo of him that had been taken at the Whitechapel Muslim Centre. He looked around but saw so many Thobes that his contact could be anybody. Though unsure who was with him from MI5, they had assured him that he had a massive team backing him up. He strolled to the ticket barrier, acting as casually as possible.

Dressed traditionally in a white Thobe and a dark coat, he fitted in well with the local community.

***

The man watching Hesam, a twenty-year-old called Abd Al-Ala Ebrahimi, had the photo in his hand and picked out Atallah when he got off the train. MI5 watched him make the ID. What Ebrahimi didn't know was that an MI5 surveillance team had been in place at the station from the day before. The man pushing the cleaning cart around the concourse was an agent, as was the shelf filler in W H Smith's. They had spotted Ebrahimi as a person of interest earlier in the day while he mooched around the station not actually doing anything. As soon as they spotted him with the photo and obviously waiting for a train, they put him under direct surveillance; another piece of the jigsaw.

***

Atallah, with time to kill, went into Smith's and looked at the book shelves. After that, he strolled to the Station coffee shop and ordered a Latte. Then, as instructed, he sat in the corner. He took his Times newspaper out of his coat pocket and placed it on the table. A glance at his watch showed five-to-three. Then he took the plain brown envelope out of his inside pocket and placed it on the side of the table while he read the broadsheet.

As he sipped his coffee, he felt surprisingly calm and detached. Though he wanted to check his watch again, he resisted the urge, and then the envelope disappeared. Slowly, he lowered the paper and saw the back of a young man opening the door to leave — Ebrahimi.

***

The agent radio traffic burst into life, the shelf filler and the cleaner trailed him to the main entrance, and two more agents in cars spotted him outside. A taxi, which had waited separately from the normal taxi rank, picked up Ebrahimi. The two cars followed and transmitted the number plate to all units. The trailing agents took it in turns to become the lead vehicle following the taxi, which had taken a right turn out of the station and into Croft Street. The taxi turned right again and headed back into the city centre.

Five minutes later, they pulled into City Road and stopped outside Bradford Islam, a multi-purpose Islamic community venue. Ebrahimi jumped out of the taxi and trotted into the centre, and the taxi waited with its engine running. Evidently, he planned to return soon.

The car radio chat now patched into the static observation post already watching the centre. Three minutes later, Ebrahimi jogged out of the centre and got back into the taxi. A blue sign-written builder's van took over the follow, as the taxi moved away and headed left down Tile Street. Two minutes later, the taxi once again slowed, and then stopped outside the Station Road Mosque. Ebrahimi jumped out again and marched into the Mosque.

They weren't, as yet, watching the Mosque but that was about to change, as radios crackled into life. The tailing van broke off, and the original two cars resumed waiting. It took ten minutes, this time, before he returned. The taxi roared away from the Mosque and hit the A6177 ring road a minute later. They drove around the ring road for thirty minutes, and then turned left into the Little Garten Muslim area. Then they wove through the tight streets, finally pulling up outside 67 Arran Street. Ebrahimi left the taxi and looked left and right, up and down the street. He appeared nervous. After he'd knocked on the door, it opened an inch, words got exchanged, and he gave a small passport-sized package to the man inside. The radios went red hot, with the surveillance team convinced that it could be a passport delivery for Aashif Jamal. One of the surveillance cars followed the taxi while the other parked up to watch the house. The team leader received a radio call from Richard, who'd listened to the live mission from the operations room at Thames House.

'Ted? Richard here. Get additional units into the front and back of Arran Street, change them regularly do drive bys, and if anybody leaves the house, arrest them and then go into the property. If Jamal is there, I want him alive. I'll come back to you shortly. No cock ups.'

***

Done on the radio, Richard picked up the phone. 'I need to see you now,' he said, and then listened.

'Yes, it's that urgent. I think we might have Aashif Jamal.'

After hanging up, Richard rushed down to Bunny's office.

'Come in, Richard. Good news?'

'We hope so, Ma'am. The driver who picked up

the passports has visited a Muslim Centre, a Mosque, and a private house. The team feel convinced that's where Jamal is hiding.'

'Was there a delivery to the house?'

'Yes, a passport-sized package.'

'So it adds up. Jamal, if it is him, is looking to leave the country.'

'I think so, Ma'am.'

'So, what do you want to do?'

'I want to take him right now.'

'You think that's the best course of action? What about all the others?'

'Small fish. That bastard is responsible for killing and wounding hundreds.'

'Go back to the ops room. I'll call you in a few minutes.'

***

Bunny felt desperate to take him now as well, but wanted to clear it with Jack Taylor first. Ten minutes later, she put a call through to Richard.

'Yes, Ma'am?'

'It's a go. Bring him down to Dulwich as soon as practical.'

'Thank you, Ma'am.'

***

Richard placed a call through to Ted in Bradford.

'Good news, Ted. Take him tonight, probably best when they're all snug in their beds. I'll be here on live feed and want pictures. Also, arrest the taxi driver and the young man simultaneously. As soon as it's over, bring them separately down to Dulwich. If you need more support, get in touch with the local police.'

'Great news. You've made my day.'

Richard couldn't have felt happier, and then a colleague handed him a briefing paper.

Breaking news — Isil Gunman kills twenty-two holiday-makers on beach in Bali. Dead include fifteen British subjects.

'Bastards.' He screwed up the piece of paper and dropped it in the bin.

***

Ted Philips, at forty-three, a career MI5 agent handler and surveillance expert, sat in his MI5-issue six-year-old Toyota Celica and felt the happiest he had for ages. He wanted to take on the terrorists, extremists, and radicals, and had grown sick of the political correctness and do-gooders in the UK. Action was needed, and now that he had the chance to do something positive, he couldn't wait. First, he arranged for six agents to meet him at the Best Western Hotel on Common Road, Bradford. An agent in the Northern Regional Office in Leeds would take extra firearms and other weapons to the hotel. Finally, he left officers at Arran Road with strict orders that, if anybody tried to leave, they should be arrested.

By seven pm, everybody had arrived at the hotel. To anyone that didn't know any better, they looked like a group of car sales men or teachers or some such. Ted had taken a perfect-sized small meeting room for the night. The team milled around, chatting and drinking the first of many strong coffees. He had told the staff to leave flasks of coffee and that, under no circumstances, were they to be interrupted.

At five minutes past seven, he called the meeting to order. 'Okay, take your seats, please. Good evening. Tonight, we serve our country by taking the bastard that thought it fun to blow up the Kensington tube train and kill and maim hundreds of people. At exactly the same time tonight, teams will arrest the taxi driver—name of Badri Lahan—and one Abd Al-Ala Ebrahimi, who did the pick-up at Bradford station earlier today. Early tomorrow morning, other teams will go into the Bradford Islam Islamic Centre and the Station Road Mosque. Police officers will accompany the teams. What are we looking for? Specifically, a package of blank British passports that were delivered to those locations today.'

Ted glanced at his watch. 'It is now eight minutes past seven, and go time is midnight. We want to hit the property when all the occupants have gone to bed. So, if we detect people up and about, that time may change. However, I will decide that once we are in situ.' He paused for breath, and then said, 'It is not often that we get a chance like this to contribute. We will enter the property front and back with battering rams—'

A hand went up.

'Yes, Steve?'

'Do we know if the doors are reinforced?'

'We looked at that, and think not, but as always, we have to be prepared for all eventualities. So, we create noise by shouting and screaming and stun grenades. The target, Aashif Jamal, has to be taken alive.'

Ted then passed around photos of Jamal, taken from the house.

'We want everybody alive, but if we have to, we kill whoever gets in our way. It's a simple operation, but we all know how things can go wrong. Jamal will have minders, and they could well have orders to kill him if it looks like he'll fall into our hands. So, speed is essential, as is identifying the target. We have a plan of these houses, which we'll look at now, and then we'll decide on who goes where.'

They went through the building plans and came up with a simple idea, assuming that all the occupants would be upstairs. A two-man team would go in the back and clear the ground floor. The stairs lay directly ahead of the front door, so it made sense for the other four men to go in and then straight up the stairs.

After a knock at the door, a man entered.

'Thought you'd got fucking lost,' Ted said loudly. 'Have you got everything?'

'And the rest. Enough gear to fucking blow up Russia.'

Ted laughed, and then addressed the room, 'Everybody, if you don't know him already, this is the provider.' Ted then turned to the newcomer, 'Gary, tell us what goodies you brought for us.'

Gary rubbed his hands together. 'Well, gentlemen, one thing I can assure you is that you will have more firepower than the enemy. In my truck, we have ten Heckler and Koch G36 semi-automatic carbines, eight Glock 17 pistols, two Remington 870 shotguns, one HK417 sniper rifle, ten M84 Stun Grenades, four Tim Smoke Grenades, and of course, two hand-held battering rams.'

Ted grinned. 'Lovely. Music to my ears. We'll sort who has what later. So, any questions?'

Paul, one of the team, shouted, 'I want both the fucking shotguns.'

Everybody laughed.

Ted said, 'Okay, it looks like we're going to war.'

More cheering ensued.

CHAPTER 29

Bunny reeled off the events so far, 'The cab driver, name of Mark Heenen, picked him up in Davies Street, close to Bond Street tube and many bus stops, and of course, he could live close to that location. He doesn't remember the man, not that surprising. He's picked up again, on camera, walking down the embankment toward Parliament Square. I'm so frustrated, seeing him strolling about. I want him.' She paused for a second. 'Not that helpful, Richard, but progress, at least.'

'What about CCTV on the tube, Ma'am?'

Bunny nearly choked. 'I'm annoyed. They haven't made much progress. And with such a huge task, I wouldn't be surprised if we had to wait months for any news. It's not good enough. Something to do with lack of manpower.'

Though he shouldn't say it, Richard couldn't help himself, 'Well, we all know about that, Ma'am.'

Silence fell, and then the phone clicked off.

***

A man, with a pronounced limp, stumbled onto the dirty red double-decker bus at Shepherds Bush Green and bought a ticket to take him to Oxford Circus. He looked as dirty as the bus, and unkempt, with his bushy beard and moustache and bald head. He wore a once-white Thobe and a black-and-white checked Shemagh covered with a thick black coat that ended at his knees. He grabbed a window seat halfway down the bus, on the lower floor.

The journey would cover a fair way and, on this particular morning, he felt happy to sit and look at London life as they made their way up Holland Park Avenue. Though tired, happiness lightened his heart. One more mission and he could go home. Something caught his eye and interrupted his daydreams. Notting Hill tube station came into view, and with it, the Princess Diana Memorial playground. He shook his head. One of the most popular women in history and they built a playground. Astonishing.

They reached the Bayswater Road, and he looked out over Kensington Gardens and Hyde Park; he loved to see the greenery—a stark contrast to Syria, where hardly a blade of grass remained, let alone huge parks. Marble Arch came into view. They were close. The bus passed Bond Street tube, and the man shuffled forward and pressed the bell. The bus pulled into the kerb and stopped. The man limped toward the exit and stepped out onto the pavement. The bus pulled away, leaving a trail of stinking black smoke from its exhaust. So as not to inhale the poisonous fumes, the man limped quickly away.

After looking around to get his bearings, he then shuffled across the road and continued down a side road, into Hanover Square, where he took a sharp left into Princes Street and hobbled on. Then he crossed over Regent Street, turned right, and a quick left, and reached Little Argyll Street. After he'd limped around the corner, he arrived at his destination, Argyll Street—home to the world-famous London Palladium.

Full of anticipation, he strolled on. There stood the iconic building in all its glory. The tall white front had three pillars on each side of the entrance. He looked at the detail of the doors. Three wooden and glass double doors with shiny golden locks and key holes. Already, he'd studied the theatre on his laptop. Built in 1910, she was a grand old lady. He had marvelled at the 2286 plush red seats, including the special private boxes and the strangely named Cinderella and Val Parnell Bars. Also, he researched who would appear, and it seemed the world-famous soul singer, Beverley Cosby, would make the star attraction on the night he had chosen. Slowly, he made his way around the building, mingling with the crowds, some of whom had come to buy tickets, and others just to see the auditorium. After strolling for ten minutes, he felt out of place amidst the tourists, and one or two obviously-British people gave him funny looks. Before he revisited, he would have to think seriously about what he would wear.

Yousef El-Sayed had grown so used to limping now, it came as second nature. Cautious, he retreated from the Palladium and strolled for half an hour. Then he crossed back over Regent Street and headed up Brook Street. He remembered the location from looking at London and Google maps on his laptop. Ten minutes later, he passed the Grosvenor Square Gardens, and then he reached the American Embassy.

Vast gardens and lines of trees hid the building from view. Cameras recorded everywhere: on poles, in the trees, and at the entrance guardhouse. Oh, how he would love to have blown up the Embassy, as well as the Ambassador and his staff with it. Back on track and single-minded about killing as many Kafirs as possible, he made his plans. The BBC news the night before had shown Syrian children killed and maimed by bombs dropped from American, French, and British planes. Oh yes, he would make them pay. In fact, if all went well, he might even stay and kill yet more.

CHAPTER 30

On the phone, Richard said to Ted, 'Just make sure everybody does a professional job. It sounds like the team might be a little gung-ho. All well and great that everybody's up for it, but it's not the Wild West.'

'No, don't worry. They're just looking forward to bringing in a bastard terrorist; that's all.'

'Okay, good. I'll be watching on the live feed. If it's Aashif Jamal, remember that we want him alive.'

'He'll be in Dulwich tomorrow morning; trust me.'

'Good. Speak soon.' Richard clicked off.

To help stay awake and alert, Richard had drunk endless coffee and now sat in one of the ops rooms at Thames House. Jack Taylor and Bunny were present, along with two technicians. A huge screen hung on the wall for live feed. The atmosphere felt tense already, and they still had an hour to go.

***

By eleven pm, the team had gone quiet and prepared themselves mentally for the mission. In the corner of the hotel car park, team members chose their weapons. Ted spoke to each agent separately, giving them encouragement and explaining, yet again, that they wanted the men alive if possible. He split them into back and front teams, and they chatted through who would go through the door first and method of attack. It grew colder, and the smoke from cigarettes drifted into the air. Agents clapped hands and stamped feet to keep warm. At eleven-thirty, two cars pulled out of the hotel car park, and inside both all remained quiet with the agents psyching up for the challenge ahead. In the first people carrier sat Richard Martin, Geoff Higgins, Paul Wilde, and Ted. In the second vehicle sat Barry Gunn and Mark Cooke.

With deep breaths, the men checked and caressed their weapons. Ten minutes from Arran Street, Ted waited, as he didn't want to arrive too early and have to engage in another lengthy wait. Apart from the street lighting, the streets remained velvet black, and hardly any traffic used the roads. Ted felt happy and confident of carrying out a successful mission.

They approached Arran Street, and Ted told the car behind to slow and leave a gap while they drove past the property. The building had no lights on, and he prayed it would give up Aashif Jamal and that he was at home and tucked up in his bed. They turned around at the end of the road and came back, and then stopped thirty yards from the house. You could have cut the atmosphere with a knife.

The team donned their bulletproof vests, helmets, and night-vision goggles. At eleven-fifty, Ted sent Barry Gunn and Mark Cooke to the back of the property. Then he tested the feed with an alert and checked Richard Carpenter was getting the feed . Ted had an infrared night camera on his helmet and would be the first into the property from the broken down front door. After a wait of two minutes, he led the team to the front. One minute to twelve and the two teams stood in place. Richard Martin held the mini battering ram at the front, and Mark Cooke did the same at the back. Ted and Barry Gunn both looked at their watches: five, four, three, two, one, and they touched the shoulders of Martin and Cooke. The bettering rams hit the doors at exactly the same time. Both doors caved in with a shuddering crash, and they were in.

***

The ops room remained silent while the clear images appeared on screen. Richard watched while the front door crashed to the ground when the battering ram smashed it off its hinges. Then came blackness with light flying in all directions from the camera. Shouting and screaming blasted from the speakers.

***

The team charged into the hallway and straight up the stairs. Ted held the Glock pistol in front of him ready to shoot if the need arose. He charged up the stairs and reached the landing in just a second. Martin came right behind him, shotgun in hand. Higgins and Wilde shouted, from right behind the front two men. Ted and Martin ran past the first door and, upon reaching the second bedroom, kicked in the door and went in screaming. Higgins and Wilde smashed the first bedroom door, also shouting and yelling.

***

In the ops room, the tension felt palpable. Not a

word got spoken. Richard almost felt like he was there in the house in person. He wiped his sweating brow; the small ops room was becoming intensely hot.

***

Gunn and Cooke charged into the kitchen and out the other side, where they turned right through the first door, expecting it to be a lounge-dining room and nobody present. They received a shock when they saw two beds and two Arab men jumping up. They screamed for the men to lie down on the floor.

Gunn couldn't see much, but the men certainly hadn't complied and laid down. One of them reached for something on the floor. Gunn caught the glint of a knife or sword and didn't hesitate; he fired his shotgun at the man's head, which disintegrated with bits flying in all directions while blood shot in fountains across the room.

Ted came through the door, momentarily confused, and then turned to his right and saw Higgins and Wilde crash into the room at the same time. He swivelled back. A man moved away from a bed and toward the far side of the large room. Ted yelled, 'Stand still. Hands in the air.'

The man stopped. Ted rushed him and pulled his arms down and put plastic ties around his wrists, and then threw him to the floor.

Cooke concentrated on the second man and rushed him, clubbing him in the face and knocking him to the floor with his carbine handle. He stood over him, ready to strike again if he made any move. The man, dazed, just lay there. Cooke pulled his hands behind his back and secured them with plastic ties.

The room was all clear, someone turned on the lights, and Ted took off his goggles. Then he reached into his pocket and took out the photo of Aashif Jamal, bent down, and looked closely at the prone figure on the floor. They had him.

'We have the package intact.'

The whole house lit up like a Christmas tree, with every light blazing. The police had received phone calls reporting shootings, and three police cars arrived. MI5 technicians turned up to go over the property, looking for evidence. Already, they had Aashif Jamal on his way to London, escorted by Ted, Martin, Higgins, and Wilde.

CHAPTER 31

Bunny said to Richard, 'The gloves are off. I want information and don't care what you have to do to get it. Have I made myself clear enough?'

'You have, Ma'am. There will be no come back on me, job wise or politically?'

'Exactly so.' Bunny laughed. 'But don't ask me to put it in writing.'

Richard just smiled back at her; he could do whatever he wanted with Aashif Jamal to get any information he had. 'Are you staying, Ma'am?'

'I want to see him, and then I'll go straight back to London. What's the news from the raids on Bradford Islam and the Station Road Mosque?'

'We found the passports and some extremist literature but nothing else. The specialist search teams are still there working.'

'Keep me informed of any news.'

'Of course, Ma'am.'

***

Aashif Jamal had slept through most of the journey from Bradford to Dulwich. They now had him in a small holding room at the interrogation centre. It held no furniture, and so it seemed more like a cell than anything else. They'd removed his belt so he couldn't harm himself. Meanwhile, the MI5 team had coffee and croissants and prepared for the coming cross-examination of the prisoner. A whole team of specialist MI5 interrogators had been drafted in. No stone would be left unturned in the pursuit of leads to other extremists and bombers.

It would be a hard interrogation, with no compromise, no promises of leniency, and no worrying about the prisoner's rights. He had killed and maimed hundreds and would yield information or suffer the consequences.

By ten am, the team stood ready. Richard had overall charge, and the senior interrogators would be MI5's Paul Ryman and a six-foot-four mountain-sized American, Chuck Hilton. Various other MI5 intelligence operatives had a presence too, and SAS interrogators from Hereford.

They brought Aashif Jamal to the interrogation room with his head hooded and in leg chains, with his hands secured behind his back. The chains provided a symbol. They told him that his life had changed, and that he would carry a heavy burden for the rest of his life. With small steps, he shuffled in, and the chains rattled when they manhandled him to the same chair that Abdul Muta'al Hassain had occupied recently. After strapping him into the chair, they vacated the room.

The interrogators left him like that for thirty minutes, and then Paul Ryman entered the room and walked around him. As soon as Paul moved behind him, the man tried to move his head but couldn't. Paul then pulled off the hood, and Jamal squinted to get used to the light.

Paul sat at the small table and opened a file. 'Your name?'

Without reply, Jamal kept his eyes down.

Paul stood, moved in front of Jamal, and all of a

sudden, slapped his face hard, twice. 'Your name?'

Again, no reply.

He slapped him three times around the face. A drop of blood blossomed from his nose.

'Your name?'

Still, no reply.

Paul clenched his fist and smashed Jamal in his shoulder, punched him on his chest, and then slapped him again three times around the face. Now, his nose bled heavily.

'Your name?'

No reply.

Paul undid the straps on Jamal's wrists and yanked his arms behind his back, then secured them together with a plastic tie. Jamal moaned in pain.

'Your name?'

No answer.

Paul turned to the viewing room and made a scissor gesture with his left hand. Five seconds later, a man entered and gave Paul a large pair of razor-sharp scissors. Paul then proceeded to cut off Jamal's Thobe and underpants, leaving him naked. He turned and headed to the viewing room, where he spoke to Phil Evans, who had charge of the room equipment and systems.

'We'll start with cold, and then move onto noise.'

Phil went to the control console and flipped a couple of switches. Freezing air pumped into the room, and it didn't take long for Jamal to break into shivers. Soon, the viewers could see his head shaking and his teeth chattering. The cold air pumped into the room for thirty minutes. Jamal shook uncontrollably.

'Turn off. Let's see how he likes a bit of noise.'

Phil once again fiddled with the console and, although they couldn't hear it in the viewing area, they could see the results of the painfully loud white noise that blasted into the room. Jamal turned his face from side to side, trying to cope with the noise. Then he must have decided that there was no point, and he sat still, looking down to the ground. They kept up the noise for thirty minutes, and then turned it off.

Paul returned to the room.

'Your name?'

No reply.

Paul went behind Jamal and smashed his fists into his shoulders and back. Then he moved back in front of him and slapped his face repeatedly. Jamal weakened. The interrogation had only just begun.

'Your name?'

Still, no reply.

***

Afterward, they bundled Aashif Jamal into the vehicle and sat him between two bodyguards. His life was over. He would spend the rest of his life in prison, and that only if he survived prison without meeting some murderous inmate with a hatred of Muslims who killed many countrymen. He didn't care; he'd struck a blow for Isil and felt ready to die, as had his friends, when the authorities raided the house. The journey from Bradford to wherever they ended up proved a long one, and Jamal felt convinced that they'd taken him to London. Upon arrival, they chained and dumped him in a small room. He prayed for strength to combat what he knew was coming. Surely there could be no point in helping the police or secret service. If they wanted to kill him, let them.

He would not talk.

***

Slap.

Jamal's head rocked yet again, as Paul beat him around the face. His eyes closed up, and he felt sure his nose had broken. Then all went black. They'd put the hood on again.

***

Back in the viewing room, at one o'clock, staff laid out sandwiches and tea on a back table. Everybody helped themselves and discussed the best methods of interrogation. Richard, though no expert, had seen enough to suggest that Aashif Jamal was considerably tougher than Abdul Muta'al Hassain and would take some time to break down. Paul could only agree.

***

Throughout the afternoon, Aashif Jamal suffered further cold and noise treatment, and still refused to speak a word. He had now gone about twenty-two hours without food or water, and Richard grew desperate to see progress.

Chuck Hilton took over the interrogation.

He entered the room and removed the hood from Jamal.

'Your name?'

No reply.

Chuck unstrapped Jamal from the chair and

threw him onto the floor, face down. He then tied rope around his ankles and pulled it tight, securing it to Jamal's wrists in an excruciatingly painful position.

Chuck ordered further cold and noise treatment, which took them up to eight pm. Jamal, now suffering deeply, had to be desperate for sleep. Two operatives entered the room, undid the ropes, and carried him back to his room, where they threw him to the floor and told him that he could sleep until the next day. They closed the door and stood outside. Precisely ten minutes later, they re-entered the room, screaming and shouting and kicking him. Then they hooded him and dragged him back to the interrogation room, and put him back in the chair.

Chuck took off the hood and slapped his face. 'Your name?'

No reply.

But then came a murmur, 'Water.'

Chuck stood close to his ear and shouted, 'What did you say?'

The murmur grew slightly louder, 'Water. I need water.'

'Your name?'

Jamal cried in loud sobs. 'Water. Please, some water.'

Chuck slapped him hard around the face. 'Your name?'

Jamal refused to speak. Did he want to die?

Richard strolled over to the other side of the room to speak to Paul.

'What do you think?'

'He'll break maybe tonight, maybe tomorrow.'

'You sure about that?'

Paul looked at him, thoughtfully. 'Yes. He's in a bad way now. Give him a few more hours and he'll beg to talk.'

'What about waterboarding?'

To hear that coming from Richard surprised Paul. 'It could speed up the process. Are you sure? You know it's not legal?'

'Who gives a shit. Go and visit the wounded victims in the hospitals. Visit the families of the dead.'

Paul nodded. 'We can do it anytime you like.'

'It's on the agenda for later; that's for sure, and I have another little surprise for our friend, should he choose not to co-operate.'

Richard grabbed a bit of sleep in one of the bedrooms with the clear instruction that they were to wake him with any news or developments. It took time for him to drop off, but once he had, he slept like the dead. At seven am, he awoke, refreshed, and headed to the bathroom to brush his teeth and shower. Then he returned to the bedroom, where he dressed. What had happened downstairs in his absence? He took the stairs two at a time and made his way to the viewing room, went up the steps, and pushed open the door. Quickly, he took in the scene. Only Paul Ryman and one of the bodyguards remained present. A smell of body odour and sweat permeated the room.

Richard said 'Good morning' and went straight to the window. Aashif Jamal sat slumped in the chair. Chuck Hilton stood slapping his face.

Richard turned to Paul, 'How's it going?'

'Tougher than we thought; he's hallucinating, so he's in a bad way. We've kept him awake all night.'

'Has he said anything at all?'

'Nothing, except to beg for water.'

'What's the plan, going forward?'

'Up to you. Sodium Pentothal is an option. Waterboarding?'

'Or we could try something else.'

'What did you have in mind?'

'You'll see in ten minutes; something that worked not that long ago. Keep him awake. I'll be back shortly.'

Richard and the bodyguard left the room.

***

Chuck continued to beat Jamal and, intermittently, asked for his name.

Fifteen minutes passed, and then Richard re-entered.

Paul felt intrigued. 'What's happening?'

'Watch, and you'll see. Ask Chuck to hood him and leave.'

Chuck returned to the viewing room in just seconds.

The door to the interrogation chamber opened, and a bodyguard carried in another chair and placed it five feet away from Jamal. Then he left again. Richard left the room again.

Paul turned to Chuck, 'What's happening?'

The American shook his head. 'No idea.'

Then the door to the interrogation room opened again.

The two bodyguards guided a woman. Hooded and wearing chains on her ankles, she shuffled, and the chains clanked when she moved. Paul watched Jamal. The hood moved a fraction. He sat awake and listening. The two guards placed the woman on the new chair and stood behind her.

Chuck spoke in his brash American accent, 'Who the fuck is that?'

Paul didn't speak, too busy watching, spellbound, as the room door opened yet again and Richard entered. He sat in the chair at the table and remained still and quiet, looking at Jamal. Tiny movements in the hood showed as the prisoner stretched to hear what was going on. Five minutes later, Richard stood and moved close to Jamal, then whispered in his ear.

'Your name?'

No reply.

Richard turned to the guards and nodded.

One of the men took the woman's ear through the hood and turned it sharply. She screamed. Jamal's hood jumped back when he jerked in shock and surprise.

'Your name?'

No reply.

Richard nodded at the guards once more.

The guard took the middle finger of the woman's right hand and pulled it back as far as it would go without breaking. The screams echoed through the room for what seemed like an eternity.

Richard stood next to the woman and spoke loudly, 'You are suffering because of this man. Tell him to help us, and you can go home.'

He nodded at the guard, who pulled her finger back further, almost snapping it. She screamed again, even louder than before, and then she started crying and shouting between sobs. 'Help me. Please, help me.'

Aashif Jamal shook his head and shouted obscenities.

Richard asked again, 'Your name?'

No reply.

He turned to the guards and shouted, 'Strip her naked.'

They pulled off her clothes. All the while, she screamed, 'Help me. Help me. They're going to rape me.'

Richard turned to Jamal. Had he heard something?

'What did you say?'

Through the hood, he could just make out words. 'Enough. I said, enough.'

Richard held up his hand, and the guards stopped.

'Thank you, thank you.' The woman's tears continued to flow.

Richard told the guards, 'Take her outside.' Then he sat down at the table and opened a file.

'Your name?'

Silence.

'I will bring her back and let my men have her.'

'Aashif Jamal.'

He walked over and removed Jamal's hood. 'Were you responsible for the bombing of the tube train at Kensington station?'

'Yes.'

Paul and Chuck turned to each other and shook hands, part of the team that had cracked Jamal and would take the credit for it.

***

'Jamal, I am going to ask you some questions, and if I believe for one second that you are lying to me, I will have the woman brought back in here, and you have a good idea of what will happen to her. Your three accomplices: Aabzari Maskin, Omar Jabara, and Fouad Nejam are all dead. Abbas Mahmood died under the wheels of a tube train, and Abdul Muta'al Hassain will spend the rest of his life in Belmarsh prison.' Richard paused and gave Jamal a hard stare. 'I want to know who else is involved.'

Jamal just sat there, staring at Richard. The blood all over his face had congealed, and black and blue bruising marked him. He looked dead on his feet.

Richard stared at his nails, thinking that they needed cutting, and then he looked up.

'There is no one else,' Jamal said.

Richard jumped up and shouted, 'Guards. Bring back the woman. Bring her back now.'

'Stop.'

'You have something to say, Aashif Jamal?'

Though in an obvious struggle, Jamal spoke eventually. 'There is one contact I have. I met him just once. He helped me travel to Bradford. He lives in Islington.'

'Good. His name?'

'Kaashif Bashara.'

'Does he have a codename?'

'Yes. Adhan.'

'What does that mean?'

'It is the word used for the call to prayer.'

'How old is he?'

Jamal shook his head. 'About twenty-three or four. I do not know exactly, but he is a young man.'

'Is he traditional?'

'No, he is Westernised—likes to wear nice suits, and has been here for many years.'

'How do you contact him?'

'I can't. When he dropped me off in Bradford, he told me that I would never see him again.'

Richard sat back, thinking.

'I need water,' Jamal murmured.

Richard turned to the window and pretended to drink. They got the message and sent in a bottle of water, which Jamal drank in one long gulp.

Richard got up and left the room, took a right turn, and headed to the staff quarters. He entered a small lounge. The woman sat on a hard-backed chair, sipping tea and gazing out of the window.

'You were brilliant. I hope he didn't hurt you? And thank you for all your help.' He paused. 'I know it must have been difficult for you.'

'I'm fine, thank you. How is he?'

'He's co-operating fully, and we've given him a drink. You know he will go to prison for life?'

'Yes. I still don't understand why? To kill all those innocent people. I still can't believe he was involved. We have been given incredible opportunities by this country.' Her face hardened. 'He's got what he deserved, the damn fool.'

'What next for you, Anniyah?'

'I'm not sure. I need to get away. Start again.

Something new.'

Richard smiled. 'Why don't you come and work for us?'

Anniyah returned the smile. 'Hmm. I'll have to think about that, but thank you for the offer.'

'I'm serious. We need good people.' He studied the young woman, continuing to smile. 'Well, I have to go. Keep in touch.'

'I will, thank you.' As he turned to leave, a tear rolled down her cheek. 'You promised.'

'I'll do whatever I can. I'll make sure that he suffers as little as possible.'

Anniyah nodded. 'I still love him, you know.'

'Of course, you do. He's your father.'

CHAPTER 32

Loud banging sounded at the door. Yousef, seated in the lounge and sipping at a piping-hot coffee, jumped up and grabbed his Glock from the kitchen and went to the door. Stood to the side, he shouted, 'Who is it?'

'Master, it is me, Adhan.' He sounded distressed.

Yousef opened the door and dragged him into the hall. 'Shut up, you fool.' He slapped Adhan around the face, and then took him by the scruff of his neck, pushed him into the lounge, and onto the armchair.

'Report.'

Adhan, though upset, finally managed to blurt out, 'They took Aashif Jamal. They will torture him. We are both in danger.'

Yousef looked at him, wanting to smash his face to a pulp. 'You fool. You have failed. Does Jamal know your real name?'

Adhan started crying. 'Yes. I told him, and yes, I am a fool.'

'Does he know my real name?'

'Yes.'

Yousef leapt forward and smashed his fist into Adhan's face, who covered his face, waiting for more blows.

'Listen, you fucking bastard; when I met with Aashif Jamal, you only called me Beacon. So, later on, during the journey to Bradford, you must've told him then. You madman. You've jeopardised not only the mission but also my life. MI5 will corroborate what he tells them with what they got from the Durriyah Kassab woman.' Yousef felt so angry that he shook. 'And you brought him to the road outside here. Does he know my exact address?'

'No, Master, I promise.'

Yousef strode around the room, trying to think what to do. 'Police and MI5 could come here at any minute.' He rushed to the window. 'Do you have any idea what they will be doing to Jamal?'

'Not really, Master.'

'They will torture him for information, and in the end, they will get something or even everything.'

'He is strong. He will keep quiet.'

Yousef looked at him with pity. 'You are naive and have no idea. He is untrained and will break.' Then his voice rose to a shout, 'Even I would break in the end.'

Silence hung in the air for a minute. Then Yousef said, 'What incriminating evidence is at your flat?'

'Nothing, Master, nothing at all.'

'Computer, phones, notes? Anything that could lead them to me?'

'I guarantee it, Master, nothing.'

Yousef rubbed his face. 'We have to assume the worst. Do we have anywhere safe that we can go?'

'Yes. A safe house. It is empty.'

'Where?'

'Stratford in East London.'

'We must empty this flat and move, then. Do you have a car?'

'No.'

'I want to speak and meet with control. No discussion. Organise it right now.'

'I can request that he calls.'

'Do it.'

***

Richard left the house in Dulwich and fast approached Vauxhall Bridge, on his way back to Thames House. His phone rang. He pressed the green hands-free button. 'Yes?'

He recognised Bunny's voice, 'Richard, it's a two-bedroomed flat in Richmond Avenue, Islington. He'll have gone already, but take a team and get over there now. Also, get a search team in situ and working, as quickly as possible. He will have left in a hurry, so it's unlikely but still possible that he could have left something.'

Richard felt happy; he could feel the net closing. Eager to get there, he pressed the accelerator down and flew across the bridge. He would stop at Thames House for two minutes and then leave for Islington.

With the small but incredibly strong steel crowbar, Richard broke the lock and moved slowly into the flat, followed by a search team. It soon became obvious that Kaashif Bashara had long gone. The rooms stood deathly quiet and icy cold. They moved at speed through the property to establish its vacancy. And then they relaxed and began the painstakingly slow process of searching. Richard wandered through the rooms, soaking up the atmosphere. In the kitchen, he imagined the man sitting at the breakfast bar, planning and thinking about how to kill as many British subjects as possible.

A cup of half-drunk coffee sat on the work surface. How scared had the man felt when he heard that they'd taken Aashif Jamal? Next, he wandered into the main bedroom. The bed stood unmade and untidy. Richard opened the top bedside drawer and found a packet of Paracetamol. He raised his eyebrows at three loose strawberry-flavoured condoms, a pair of glasses, and a Transport for London tube map. Lips pursed, he picked up the map. Two of the stations had rings of black biro around them: White City and Westminster. His mind raced.

Westminster had been the target, so why White City? Maybe an accomplice? His mobile beeped, and he checked the message: Car bomb in Lahore, Pakistan—sixty-five dead. Richard didn't even blink. He slipped the map into his inside coat pocket. Socks and pants filled the other two drawers. Slowly, he went back to the lounge and sat in the chair, facing the enormous flat-screen TV. A glance left and right showed no pictures, no photos, nothing to suggest that the man led anything other than a bachelor existence in London. Most probably, they would find nothing, but it would be worth knocking on the neighbours' doors to ask questions.

Two hours later, having spoken to two neighbours, he left Islington. The tenants of the flats had confirmed that the man lived alone, was young (in his twenties) and didn't seem to have a job; he also seemed to enjoy the company of women, as a conveyor belt of girls of all colours, nationalities, and ages arrived at his front door at all hours. Richard had left the search team to it and headed back to Thames House to have a chat with Bunny.

***

Yousef rushed around the flat, jamming his clothes and anything else incriminating into two large holdalls. As soon as Yousef finished in a room and shouted 'clear,' Adhan went in to check. In the bedroom, he pulled the bed out to look underneath, then checked the cupboard and drawers and, when he felt happy that the room stood empty, he shut the door. Methodically, they worked through the small flat and soon finished. Yousef took one final tour to satisfy himself that it remained devoid of any clues as to his identity.

They stood in the small hall, and Yousef spoke quietly, 'Let's go.' Then he opened the door, they left, and he locked up, then handed the key to Adhan. 'It may be useable again. You will have to wait and see.' They took a step.

Shouting reached them, as someone approached, coming up the stairs.

Mandy and one of her friends. 'Steve? What's up? You leaving?'

'Just for a couple of days. See you when I get back.' Closely followed by Adhan, he headed for the stairwell.

'Yeah, bring your friend. We can party.'

'Great idea,' Yousef called over his shoulder, as they jogged down the stairs.

When they reached the bottom, they took a left through the main door.

Adhan touched Yousef's shoulder. 'Is that the girl?'

Yousef knew what he was talking about. 'Yes.'

Adhan looked thoughtful. 'Very lovely. Such a pity that we're leaving.'

Yousef shook his head. 'Let's get out of here.' He set off at a fast pace toward White City tube station.

***

Cheri, Mandy's friend, said, 'The other boy looked handsome. Maybe we could hook up with them when they come back?'

Mandy grinned. 'Yeah, but Steve's got to get rid of that weirdo beard first. He's got a big cock and is a good fuck, but he's not coming near me with that thing on his face.'

They went into Mandy's flat, and she put Girls Aloud—The Promise on at full volume. The two danced around the lounge, singing at the top of their voices.

'Got anything to eat?' Cheri asked.

They danced into the kitchen, and Mandy opened the fridge. 'Nothing we can eat straight away.' She went to the bread bin and took out a loaf of thick-sliced white bread. 'We'll have some toast and jam.'

'Great,' Cheri said and continued to dance away, singing along with the music.

The song finished just as the two slices of bread flew out of the toaster. Mandy grabbed them and jigged to the fridge to get the margarine.

242

'I'll put two more in, Mand?' Without waiting for a reply, she slipped two more slices of bread into the toaster. 'Here, look at this.'

'What?'

The toaster stood on an old Sun newspaper, presumably to catch the crumbs.

'The picture in the paper. It looks like your Steve.'

'Don't be silly. Why on earth would his picture be in the paper?'

'Says here, the bloke is a terrorist and that he did that bombing near the Houses of Parliament.'

'Steve? A bomber?' Mandy laughed out loud, and then stopped. 'Let's have a look, then.'

Mandy pulled the paper fully out from beneath the toaster and looked at the image.

'Take off the beard, Mand, and it could be him.' This time, Cheri laughed.

Mandy didn't speak, just studied the picture closely. 'You know what, Chel, it fucking well could be him. It says his name is Yousef something or other.'

Cheri crowded her and leaned in to look over her shoulder. 'What ya gonna do?'

'I dunno. He said his name was Steve. We don't want the old bill nosing around, but if it *was* him …' Mandy thought about Steve and questioned whether that *was* his real name. He didn't work and had simply appeared one day, and now he'd done a runner.

'I suppose we ought to phone 999, but let's have our toast first; plenty of time for the call in a bit.' She opened one of the kitchen cupboards and took out a jar of raspberry jam.

An hour later, Mandy made the call; she told the operator that she thought she knew who the man in the paper was. They transferred her to the local police station and put her through to the front desk. The civil servant manning the desk took down Mandy's name and address and mobile number and a note that she thought she might know the man on the front page of The Sun. The civil servant asked what contact Mandy had had with the man, and Mandy laughed when she said, 'I fucked him, so I know him, all right. It could be him. What do you want me to do?'

'Nothing. I'll pass it onto the appropriate authorities, and they may well get in touch with you. Thank you for calling.'

The conversation between Mandy and Cheri moved onto vodka, burgers, and who they'd fucked recently.

***

The civil servant, Beth Chalmers, had a hunch. After ending the call, she telephoned the MI5 hotline for reporting sightings of the man called Yousef El-Sayed. The man at the other end of the phone had heard it all a hundred times but took down the details while Beth read them word for word. Beth even went as far as to say that she thought the girl Mandy could have something.

***

The MI5 operative thought for a minute, and then typed the details that Beth gave him onto his computer, then he marked the note as green, which meant something of interest. The information updated onto a database and sat on a screen in Thames House not even five seconds later.

***

A senior MI5 analyst, responsible for reading and grading the information, noted several interesting points. It was unusual for a sixteen-year-old girl to phone in a sighting. Also, she'd stated that she'd slept with the man — again, unusual. The man lived in a one-bedroom flat in west London and didn't appear to have a job. The analyst took a chance and forwarded the information to Richard Carpenter, adding that he felt the call had something interesting about it.

***

Richard had finished the progress meeting with Bunny and now made his way back to his flat. His mobile pinged. He switched it on, and a message appeared on the car screen in front of him. When he read it, he nearly jumped out of his seat. A girl, Mandy Smith, lived in White City. It hit him like a hammer blow: The tube map with White City circled. With trembling fingers, he pressed another button on his steering wheel.

'Yes, Richard?'

'Good news, Ma'am. A call that corroborates some other information I got from the flat in Islington. Yousef El-Sayed has been holed up in White City. I'm on my way now. Please, have a search team sent immediately. Brian Roberts has the address. The net is closing.'

'I hope so. Consider it done.' The phone went dead.

Ten minutes later, Richard flew down the Westway towards White City. His heart pounded. Kaashif Bashara and Yousef El-Sayed would be running for their lives, and that would mean that they could make mistakes. He could feel the net closing and wanted them so badly that he could taste it.

When he entered Wood Lane, he put on the blue flashing lights. The traffic moved over, and Richard screeched around the corner, into South Africa Road. Nearly there. Another right into Canada Way. Halfway down, he saw that the police had closed the road. He turned off the blue lights and slowed. After showing his MI5 pass, they let him through. He looked around. A perfect location for El-Sayed to have been — multi-cultural, working-class, everybody minding their own business. Richard pulled up behind two police cars, outside the block of flats. A police officer stood at the entrance, and Richard again showed his pass. The officer granted him access. From the foyer, he took the urine-smelling lift to the fifth floor and stepped out. Another police officer asked for ID, and he flashed his badge once more.

'Who's in charge, officer?'

'Inspector Charles Sidney.'

'Tell him I'd like a word, please.'

The officer disappeared into flat number eighteen, and a minute later, returned with Inspector Sydney.

'Hello, Charles. I'm taking charge of this location. An MI5 search team will arrive shortly. Everybody should leave, but please, keep officers on the front and back entrances. No one is allowed in until I say so, and that includes residents.'

'Okay.' The inspector nodded. 'Flat twenty is empty. The girl, Mandy Smith, is in eighteen. We haven't asked any questions yet. A female officer is with her, but all she's done is make tea.'

'The female officer can stay until my lot turn up. Thanks for all your assistance. Oh, what's the officer's name?'

'Carol Jones.'

The Inspector left, and Richard made for flat eighteen.

He stuck his head around the door. 'Carol Jones?'

The officer appeared, presumably from the lounge.

'MI5.' Richard flashed his badge. 'We've taken over this location. You're to stay until my lot come.' He smiled at her, 'Now, where's Mandy?'

'Follow me, Sir.'

Carol led him the short distance to the lounge. 'Would you wait outside, please, Carol. I'll call if I want your assistance.'

He walked into the room and shut the door behind him. Then he glanced around, noting the cheap furniture, threadbare carpets, and filthy windows. A young girl, dressed in a short brown skirt and matching top, sat on an old sofa. She looked pretty and could be a stunner with a hairdo, good makeup, and quality clothes.

'Hello, Mandy. How are you?'

'All right, but the sooner we get on, the better. I've got things to do, you know.'

'Yes, I'm sure you have.' Richard sat opposite her

in a single chair that matched the sofa in colour. 'So, tell me your story. I'll interrupt if I need clarification on anything.'

'Where do you want me to start?'

'The only place ever to start. At the beginning.'

Mandy recounted events.

Richard tried to tie down dates, but it proved difficult. 'I'm interested in the man who was with El-Sayed. Can you give me a description, please?'

Mandy laughed. 'Let's be honest, mate; they all look the fucking same, don't they.'

Richard kept a straight face. 'It's important. These people are killers. Try your hardest.'

'Young. Early twenties. Good looking. Big guy. Wore a smart blue suit. I'd say he was savvy; didn't act or look like one of those bearded weirdos.'

The suit stood out. Could it be Kaashif Bashara? Were the two of them now together? A knock at the door interrupted Richard's thoughts. Carol stuck her head around the door.

'Your mob are here, Sir.'

'Thank you. Thanks for all your help. You can go now.' He turned to Mandy, 'I'll be back in five.'

Richard went into number twenty with the search team and had a quick wander with no result. He then returned to eighteen with a female MI5 operative.

'Mandy, this is Jane. She'll be looking after you. Before I go, is there anything else you can tell me that might help us catch these two killers?'

Mandy sat there, thinking for a few seconds. 'I don't think so. I don't know the bloke that well.'

Richard had to give her some bad news. How would she take it? He took a breath in. 'Okay, so this is what's going to happen. You will have to go with Jane to what we call a safe house.' Mandy leant forward, and her mouth fell open. Richard said, 'You are a witness and can identify Yousef El-Sayed and the man who left with him. You could be in danger, and we'll look after you until we catch them and put them where they belong, which is in prison.'

Mandy looked pale with shock and could hardly speak. Eventually, she spluttered, 'What about my mum?'

'Don't worry; we'll tell your mum what's going on. So, pack a suitcase, and you can get going.'

Jane stood. 'I'll help you.' The women headed toward Mandy's bedroom.

Richard got on the phone to Bunny and brought her up to speed.

'Yes, Ma'am, definitely Yousef El-Sayed, and I'm fairly confident that the other man was Kaashif Bashara.'

'You have the witness?'

'Yes, Ma'am. The girl is being taken into witness protection.'

'Any clues as to the whereabouts of the suspects?'

'We think they may have taken the tube from White City. If you could chase up the CCTV that would be helpful.'

***

The tube journey from west to east London proved a lengthy one. El-Sayed and Bashara sat quietly on the train while it rumbled eastward.

Neither felt happy. Yousef sweated heavily, which made the palms of his hands clammy. His plans had been thrown into confusion, and now the relentless security forces had set about hunting them down. Bashara looked plain scared; in fact, terrified of getting caught and spending the rest of his life in a prison cell. Probably, the man had already begun thinking of ways to extricate himself from the situation.

As they passed Oxford Circus, Yousef noticed and, for some reason, thought of Durriyah Kassab. What a waste. Then he dismissed her out of mind. Soon, they reached Liverpool Street station, where they grabbed their bags and jumped off. Yousef's demeanour improved. Thousands of people, scurrying like ants about their business, packed the station. Just ten minutes later, they stood on the Transport for London rail service direct to Stratford.

After a short journey, they walked out of the station and into a pedestrian area. The cold fresh air hit them while they marched toward the road and bustling community. Yousef felt glad that, again, this was a working-class community that he could disappear into. Black, White, Asian, Oriental—it seemed even more multi-cultural than White City.

They turned left outside the station and walked down Great Eastern Road. Yousef, as usual, scanned the area. A Sainsbury's and a Subway outlet stood across the road. He stayed a step behind Adhan as he took in the new sights. Cars, lorries, and buses jammed the one-way system, and the vehicles caused an almost smog. Especially the red double-decker buses, some of which spewed out black smoke and fumes.

'Adhan?' He turned around, toward Yousef, but kept walking. 'Yes, Master?'

'He hasn't called yet?'

'Not yet, Master, but you will see control soon, I promise.'

'Good. There are things that need to be discussed.'

Adhan picked up the pace, and Yousef strode to match him. A little further down the road, Adhan turned into a shop service road and stopped.

'We wait here.'

Yousef didn't like it. 'We're in the open.'

'Do not worry. One minute, and we will be gone.'

Yousef, again, scanned the area. It housed a small oriental restaurant, a cinema, and a theatre. For a second, he thought about how he would like to go and see a film on the huge screen. Adhan touched his arm and broke the spell. A black Ford Fiesta pulled up alongside them, and a man shouted through the open window, 'Get in, quickly.'

They climbed into the back, and the driver pulled away.

'Allah has all the glory,' the driver said. 'Beacon, you are well?'

'I am alive, so I am well. Who are you?'

'You wanted to speak to control. Well, now is your chance.'

'First, send this one back to Syria; he needs training and some hard life.'

Control laughed. 'What do you say to that,

Kaashif?'

'I am here to serve. Whatever you wish, Master.'

'The attack at Westminster was beautiful, Beacon. I hope you can repeat it again?'

'I can, but it will require more cunning because they have my picture.'

'I have seen the pictures and, believe me, nobody would recognise you.'

The car turned left into Grove Lane and, halfway down, pulled up in front of a small terraced house. The driver jumped out, and Adhan and Yousef followed. Seconds later, they stood in the tight kitchen with the kettle on.

'You are not taking serious precautions, control?'

'You do not have to worry. These are my people. You are as safe here as if you took a stroll through the market in Deir ez-Zur.' Control let out a little chuckle.

'How is the network holding up?' Yousef asked.

'We have lost several people recently, in London and Bradford, and Jamal will be in prison for the rest of his life.'

'Yes, that's a pity. I liked him.'

'Do not be sorry for him. He will continue his work in prison. It houses many prospective new recruits, and the government kindly put them all in one place for us.' Control chuckled again.

Yousef nodded. 'That's a good way to look at it.'

'Now, we have coffee and talk some more.'

They moved to the lounge and sat down.

Control spoke first, 'Your instructions are as follows: One, you are to make one more attack on a soft target; there should be maximum casualties.

Two, you must kill the Durriyah Kassab woman; you must slit her throat and bleed her dry, do you understand?'

'Yes, and then what?'

'Then, you go home.'

Yousef smiled. 'Exactly what I wanted to hear. I miss the heat, the dust, and the comrades. The sooner, the better.'

'You have a target?'

'Yes. There will be hundreds dead and injured.'

Control closed his eyes. 'Allah be praised. Such wonderful news. You will use Adhan as your assistant.'

Silence fell for some seconds, and then Yousef said, 'He has not had the required training; he is a liability.'

Control lifted his hands and voice, 'Then, train him yourself. He will strike next year while you sun yourself on the beach surrounded by beautiful women.'

Yousef smiled. 'Let it be so.'

'Good. That is decided, then. I am happy.'

'Where did you get the scar?' Yousef looked at the line on the man's face.

Control fingered the mark running down his cheek, 'A present from a Christian with a knife. I disembowelled him in return.'

CHAPTER 33

They had, finally, transferred the mentally and physically scarred Aashif Jamal to a segregation unit at HMP Belmarsh. The taxi driver and Abd Al-Ala Ebrahimi languished in police cells at a central London high-security police station. The two of them, low grade messengers, knew little about the higher-up commanders.

Richard Carpenter worked all hours, trying desperately to locate Yousef El-Sayed and Kaashif Bashara. They had gone to ground, and the hunt had slowed to a stop. He remained living in the London flat, as Serena—enjoying life—had said that she had no interest in trying again. He missed Andrew and Harry but had messed up that relationship as well by continually cancelling visits because of work commitments. All in all, he worked long long hard hours because it felt preferable to sitting in the flat on his own, reflecting on his disastrous personal life.

Seated at a desk in one of the ops rooms on the fifth floor at Thames House, Richard thought of ways to progress the hunt for El-Sayed and Bashara. After a while, he got up and paced the room, and ended up at the window looking out across the river. Huge collections of white and yellow daffodils spread across the flower beds, throwing a little colour into an otherwise grey and miserable picture.

Atallah had returned to London, laying low, after

the capture of Jamal and the damage done to the terrorist network in Bradford. Richard kept Siddique on surveillance duty rather than have him in the Mosques; he simply didn't like him and, therefore, could or would not trust him. He hadn't seen or spoken to David Morgan for some time, and all he ever thought about was the mole without actually doing anything about it.

Still watching through the window, he swept his hair back from his forehead and checked his watch: four pm. 'Bollocks,' he muttered and grabbed his stuff from the table and made for the exit. Richard needed a drink and meant to have a good few. He almost ran to the lifts, feeling hemmed in. Fresh air and open space, that's what he needed. His whole body felt clammy, and his heart pounded. Was he having a panic attack? Worried, he took deep breaths. The lift arrived, the doors opened, and he stepped in. Thank goodness that the lift stood empty. The car stopped on the fourth floor, and two office girls got in. Sweat dripped down from his forehead. Richard wiped it away. One of the girls peered at him.

'Are you all right? You're as white as a sheet.'

'Fine, thank you, miss.' He squeezed his hands tight and hung on, waiting—praying—to escape the building as quickly as possible. The bloody lift stopped again at the second floor, and two men entered, and then they got there. The doors opened, and Richard dashed to the exit, went through the glass-panelled door, and took a deep breath. The cold air hit him and, immediately, he felt better. Eyes closed, he sucked in a deep breath of the cold air, and after taking a couple of paces, he felt much improved.

Richard crossed over the busy embankment road and sat on one of the new wooden benches, which looked out over the river. Cyclists and joggers passed in abundance, moving quickly along the gravel path. He tried to analyse what had happened, and worked it out. Overloaded, that's what it came down to. What with Serena and the boys, Durriyah Kassab, the mole, Siddique, and the workload, it had all gotten on top of him; he needed a break. A vision of sitting in a Parisian café with Durriyah, and then being on top of her, naked and thrusting, drifted into his mind. Richard shook his head and looked, again, at the river. Water calmed him. Today being Thursday, he would tell Bunny that he planned a long weekend off.

***

'Give me another whisky,' Richard said in a slurred voice, as he held up his glass to the attractive, blonde barmaid.

'Don't you think you've had enough?'

'Please, don't think I'm being rude, but why is it women in general like telling men what they can and cannot do?'

'Please, don't think I'm being rude, but most men nowadays are like grown up kids and need to be told.'

'Well, I don't.' He looked at the woman, and then smiled. 'Well, not this minute.' Then he held the up glass again.

'Of course, Sir. Single or double?'

'Let's go large, eh. What's your name?'

'Are you going to chat me up?'

'Give me the whisky. I'm thinking about it.'

'Claire.' She walked along the bar to get the whisky.

Richard watched her ample bottom sway from side to side in her tight jeans and thought of Durriyah and that his life had become such a fucking mess.

'One large whisky.' Clare placed it on the bar top. 'So, you know *my* name …'

'Richard. You can call me Rich, but I'm not.' He broke into laughter.

'What do you do, then, Rich?'

'Shhhh, can't talk about that, and if I told you, I'd have to kill you. It's all very hush-hush.'

'Sort of James Bond, then?'

Richard laughed, and then coughed when he tried to speak. Eventually, he cleared his throat. 'You could say that, or not, as the case may be. Eh? Where were we, anyway?'

'You just invited me to your place; something about wanting to check my credentials.'

Richard looked away and raised his eyebrows, not believing what he'd just heard. 'That—' He stumbled and nearly fell off the bar stool. '— sounds like an excellent idea, but I must warn you, I'm a bit pissed so might not be at my best, you know, you know what I mean.'

Claire smiled. 'Look, why don't you go home to your wife, girlfriend, whoever? I don't hook up with married men.'

'Married?' Richard shouted, 'You are not fucking

serious. That's all over. Serena's gone. Stupid cow didn't understand. The country needs me.' Then he thought of the boys and became emotional. 'Miss the boys. Have to keep busy.' He drained his glass.

'Large one, please, Claire.'

She took the glass and stood looking at him. 'Coming right up.' She gave him a single.

Richard had sat in the Bunch of Grapes on Cromwell Road since he'd arrived at five. By eight, he'd already grown drunk. Not usually a big drinker, he had downed ten whiskys, which for him, was a colossal amount.

'Got anything nice to eat, Claire?'

'Now, there's a question.'

It shot over his head. 'Steak would be nice, with fries and salad.'

Claire grabbed a menu from the back counter and handed it to Richard.

'I don't need that. Can you do a steak or not?'

'We do a Sirloin.' She read down the menu, 'And you can have that with salad and fries. There you go, perfect, and it will help sober you up.'

'No point being sober; life's a bitch, and then you—'

'Yes, I've heard that so many times.'

'Are you with someone?'

Clare ignored the question. 'Shall I order your food?'

'Yes. I'm starving. I thought you'd already done that.'

'How do you like your steak?'

Richard thought long and hard about that, and then said, 'Nice and bloody in the middle would be

258

good.'

'Richard …' Clare spoke to him like a schoolteacher speaks to children. 'I'll order your food. Now, keep quiet, please.'

He wobbled again on the stool.

'Go and sit at one of the tables. Hell, it's like having a kid.' She went off to hand in the food order.

Richard did as told and staggered over to one of the tables against the wall, by a window. He sipped at his whisky, and in double-quick time, a lovely-smelling steak and fries appeared in front of him. He wolfed down the food and felt better for it. Finished, he pushed the plate and condiments to one side and rested his head in his hands, on the table.

Soon, he fell asleep.

Someone shook his shoulder. 'Richard? Wake up. It's ten-thirty.'

The result of too much whisky, he felt groggy, but eventually sat up straight. 'Did you say half past ten?' He shook his head and took a deep breath. 'So, what are we going to do now?'

Claire looked at him for a few seconds. 'I'll be at least another two hours.'

Richard needed some company. 'I'll wait.'

Claire smiled. 'Why don't you go home, have a shower, and I'll see you when I've finished.'

Though against the rules to have non MI5 people staying at the flat, he felt desperate. 'Great idea.' Richard took a pen out of his jacket inside pocket and wrote the address on a paper napkin and handed it to her.

Not that sure if he wanted her to come, he hesitated, then said, 'You'll come over later?'

She appeared to feel the same. 'If you want me to?'

'Bloody hell,' Richard said. 'We're like a couple of kids.' He sobered even more and made a decision, grabbed Claire, and pulled her in close. Then, passionately, he kissed her on the lips. After what seemed an eternity, he eased away. 'I have to go.' Then he grabbed the napkin, screwed it up, and threw it onto the table. Without a goodbye, he left through the main door, and as the cold air hit him, thought of Durriyah Kassab. He wanted her more than anything in the world.

CHAPTER 34

'I've shown you how I like my coffee. This is shit.'

'Sorry, Master. I'll make some fresh.'

'Don't bother. It's not important.' The weak coffee had too much milk and not enough sugar, but Yousef had other things to worry about. Seated on an old grimy brown sofa in the lounge of the house in Stratford, he turned numerous things over in his mind. The smoke from his fifth cigarette of the early morning rose into the air, staining the already yellow ceiling. He still wore his white pants and tee shirt, and looked around. Immediately, he felt annoyed.

'Do you know how to fucking clean?'

Adhan looked displeased at being spoken to like a servant. 'I was going to do it this lunchtime, Master.'

'Make sure you do. This place is filthy.' He shook his head and wished himself already back in Syria.

'Master, I am going out this afternoon on a job for control.'

Yousef concentrated. 'What job is that?'

'I do not know yet, Master.'

Yousef knew he was lying but didn't pursue it. 'On your way back, get me some Arak.'

Adhan hesitated, anticipating Yousef's reaction, but then spoke, 'Control has said no more booze until the mission is complete.'

Yousef couldn't believe what he had heard. The coffee cup flew through the air and smashed against the wall, showering the room in brown liquid. He jumped up from the sofa. 'Don't fucking tell me what I can or can't have. Get the money, all the money you have, and give it to me now. Hurry.'

'Control has ordered me to look after the—'

Yousef leapt at him, punched him to the floor, and then kicked him hard in the stomach.

Yousef breathed hard and fast. 'If that money is not in my hand in the next ten seconds, I will strangle you to death.'

Adhan crawled a couple of feet, then stood and rushed to the bedroom. Then he came straight back with a large wedge of twenty-pound notes.

'That's all of it, Master. Six hundred pounds.'

Yousef peeled off five of the notes and handed back the rest. He glared at Adhan. 'For my expenses. Tell Control what the fuck you like. I'm going to shower.'

***

For ten minutes, Adhan cleaned the kitchen and lounge, and then left the flat at twelve-thirty. He looked forward to his afternoon off, away from the intense and fanatical Yousef El-Sayed. A blue sky hovered over the sunny day, although it felt a bit chilly. Adhan walked up to Stratford station and took the tube the short distance to Bethnal Green, where he turned left out of the station and took the first left into Cambridge Heath Road. Three minutes later, he walked into the towering prison-like Travelodge hotel. After he'd sauntered through reception, he got into the waiting lift and pressed the third-floor button. His heart pounded while his cock stirred. He had come here numerous times before. At room thirty-seven, he knocked, and a voice told him to go in.

He entered and closed the door behind him, and hardly had time to breathe again before she fell on him and dragged him to the pristine white-sheeted bed. The woman pushed him down and attacked his trouser belt, undoing it in a second. Then she yanked down his pants and blue suit trousers, releasing his huge, erect cock. She stopped and admired it before sitting astride him and lowering her mouth. They spent the next twenty minutes groping and fucking until both were spent. He collapsed onto the bed, taking deep breaths. Neither of them spoke for some time until, finally, he broke the silence.

'You're such an animal. I love it.'

'Yes, but do you love me? Say you love me.'

The same every time. They would fuck for three or four hours in the afternoon, and she would let him do whatever he wanted to her, as long as he told her he loved her and made it sound like he meant it.

'You know I love you.'

'Yes, I know. So, when are you going to tell your wife?'

'Carla, you know it's not that easy. I have to choose the right time, and there're the children to consider as well.'

She turned over and masturbated him. 'Are you ready yet?'

Already, his cock stirred anew. 'Of course, and then we must talk. You know how much I love to hear all the gossip from your secret service life.'

It had taken three weeks of surveillance to mark a target and follow her to a bar along the embankment. He had chatted her up, and they ended up starting a fiery sexual relationship from the first night. She was a fair bit older than him, which suited them both, and she loved his stamina while he appreciated her experience. Both rampant and aggressive lovers, when they'd finished, sweat glistened on their skin, and they panted for breath.

Kaashif rested his head on her breast and nudged her nipple with his tongue. 'So, what's happening in the murky world of spies and espionage?'

'Nothing much. The boss is obnoxious, as usual. She doesn't get any, you know.'

'Any what?'

'Cock for God's sake. Anyway, it's probably healed over by now.'

Kaashif made a surprised face. 'Ah, you're talking about Francis Matthews. What's the old love up to?'

'Usual stuff; hunting terrorists and making us all suffer every day.'

'Things aren't going well, then?'

'No, they're not. Apparently, the two most wanted have disappeared, and she's not best pleased.'

'There must be some leads?'

'Not that I've heard of. The agents are shitting themselves that there'll be another bomb.'

Kaashif nuzzled her nipple again. 'Who's the man in charge of finding the bombers?'

'Richard Carpenter; he's all right, actually, but

even he's getting crabby to talk to.'

He licked her nipple to stiffness. 'What is this crabby?'

She laughed. 'In a bad mood.' Then she grabbed for his cock, and they rolled over together, laughing.

They fucked for another two hours; he had her every way he could think of, and she loved it. Once again, they collapsed and took deep breaths to recover.

'What's happening to the woman on Epsom Downs?'

'Nothing. She's in witness protection.' His companion chuckled. 'She'll probably be there for months if not years. It could take years before it ever gets to court; that is, if ever.'

'Why do you say that?'

She chucked again. 'The targets may never be found, and if that's the case, then eventually, the woman will have to return to her old life.'

'God. She must get fed up. How can you live for months in limbo like that?'

'She's not on her own. There are a housekeeper and bodyguard.'

Adhan's ears pricked up. 'Bodyguard? What for?'

'Apparently, she's a VIP witness who can identify the two men.' She reached out and fondled his balls.

'I went to Epsom Downs once. Nice houses. Sounds like she deserves to have some luxury. Do you know the road she's in?'

'Downs something … umm, yeah, Downs Wood Road.'

Adhan jumped back. 'No. Seriously? That's where I went—number forty-eight. My God, that's a coincidence. What number is she at?'

'Three.'

Adhan smirked, and a sick smile came over his face.

Carla looked at him straight in the eye, and alarm bells went off. Her eyes grew wide with fear when comprehension dawned.

She backed away from him. 'No. No, it's not possible.' Then she backed further away and slipped off the bed. 'You are. You're one of them.'

Panic came over her, and she darted for the door.

Got her hand on the handle.

Turned it.

Didn't have time to pull.

Adhan gripped her around the throat with both hands and squeezed.

Carla tried to kick. She couldn't breathe. Adhan continued to squeeze until it was over, and then let go. Her limp body fell to the floor, and the smell of excrement filled his nostrils. He felt strange; he had killed for the first time, and it had been a woman who'd given him so much pleasure, but then he thought of other women. The world was full of women. She was just a stupid dead woman. All at once repulsed, he pulled the crumpled, semen-stained white sheet from the bed and threw it on top of Carla's lifeless body. Then he grabbed his clothes and dressed hurriedly. By the door, he stood and looked around the room. Nothing remained to help the enemy. Though his DNA lay all over the room and inside Carla, he could do nothing about that. With a deep breath, he opened the door.

***

The next morning at eleven-fifty-five, a chambermaid discovered Carla Westburgh's body. The connection to MI5 took all of six hours, and Bunny and Richard felt shocked beyond comprehension when they heard.

'Yes, Ma'am. I realise that, but we cannot even be sure it was security related.' Richard took a deep breath and exhaled.

'I'm praying it isn't, but I *am* worried. Nobody had a clue that Carla had gotten involved with someone. You would have thought that she might have told one of her friends at the office.'

'There could be a hundred explanations, Ma'am. He could have been a young black stud for hire; who knows?'

A frigid silence hung on the line, and he could imagine Bunny's face at the thought of a young black stud. Richard couldn't help a grin.

Bunny said, 'We might know more when the result of the DNA test comes through.'

It became Richard's turn to say nothing.

'What else, Richard? Give me some good news.'

'I wish I could, Ma'am. We have no further news, but we're working hard to locate the two targets.'

CHAPTER 35

Yousef stood in front of the mirror and smiled. From being a small boy, he had always liked dressing up in uniform. The thought that it would have been better if it had been an army General's made him laugh, but for this mission, it would be perfect. It had proved so easy to locate the London Cleaning Services premises in Streatham from the address on the van.

One night, he had broken in and stolen a complete uniform. Again, he laughed. There had been so many jackets, shirts, and trousers that he had even managed to get the perfect size. Though the cleaning company knew of the break in, they remained in ignorance of the stolen uniform. His information said that the police hadn't even visited the premises in response to the report, as the staff couldn't say if anything had been stolen or not.

Yousef smoothed down the front of the brown jacket, turned to look at the side view, and then saw the large LCS on the back. He disliked the brown and yellow colour scheme, but its distinctiveness would make an asset. Once he'd tidied his hair, he felt ready. This Saturday morning had dawned overcast but gave no rain as yet, which pleased him.

Adhan drove, and this made Yousef nervous; the man drove too fast and swore continuously at other drivers. Finally, Yousef had had enough.

He looked at Adhan and spoke sternly, 'I have to

teach you things, so listen carefully. Drive under the speed limit. If the limit is thirty-miles-per-hour, never go over twenty-eight. Drive with care and respect for other road users. You want to melt into the background and not be conspicuous for any reason. Do you understand?'

Adhan took a deep breath. 'Yes, but the motorists are so stupid and they …'

Yousef didn't speak, just raised his eyebrows.

'Yes, Sir. I understand.'

'Good. It is about self-control, and you must begin to learn that discipline. Now, do not speak. I need to get myself mentally right for the challenge ahead.'

Adhan said, 'Yes.'

They drove for a further twenty minutes until they got to five minutes from the target. Adhan glanced at Yousef. 'Sir, we are five minutes away.'

Yousef nodded. 'Good. I am ready.' On the street, Londoners and tourists rushed around like bees in a hive. Soon, they reached their destination, and Adhan slowed the car slowed to a halt, and Yousef jumped out. He opened the back door and grabbed a briefcase and clipboard with blank papers on it.

Then he marched the hundred yards, as though a man with a mission, which he certainly was, but not the one people would imagine. He had practised the words so often that he knew them by heart. The entrance loomed. His heart pounded. He took a deep breath and raised his hand to the old man seated in the security office. Then he called, 'Good morning.'

The old man looked at him. 'I thought your mob finished up yesterday?'

Yousef stopped and approached the window. 'Something got missed, and lucky me has had to cancel my fishing trip and come here instead. Can't get the staff nowadays.' He shook his head.

'I know what you mean. It's all these youngsters; don't know they're born.'

'I shouldn't be long, and then I'm off to the pub for a couple of pints of the black stuff.'

'Lovely. I wish I could join you. How long will you be?'

'Twenty minutes; just got to check the bars.'

'Go on through. No need to sign in.' The man waved him ahead.

Yousef marched on, sweating and heart pounding, but it had been easy and he was in. He strode along the seemingly endless corridor, and then saw a sign to the auditorium. Lighter of heart, he skipped up the steps and pushed open the door. As the magnificence of the theatre appeared before him, he stopped. Then, when loud music crashed into life from the orchestra pit, the noise jolted him back to focus. The band were practising. Quickly, he held up his clipboard and turned to head to the main entrance.

Soon, the signs to the Val Parnell Bar appeared, and he headed straight there. Thankfully, when he entered the bar, it stood empty. Yousef scanned the walls until he saw what he was after: a latticed ventilation panel near the floor. A glance around and out through the main glass door entrance showed that all remained quiet. More relaxed still, he took a screwdriver from his belt and had the cover off in seconds. Then he opened the briefcase and removed the bomb, set the timer, and placed it inside the cavity. Done, he re-attached the lattice panel, screwing it tight. The door to the bar opened just as he'd regained his feet, and a man entered. Yousef's heart jumped into his mouth.

The newcomer glanced at him. 'Good morning.' And then strolled behind the bar, uninterested.

Clammy sweat moistened his underarms and forehead. He thought about leaving by the main entrance but disregarded it; he wanted the security man to see him leave. So, he made his way back to the stairs and retraced his steps along the cavernous corridor.

Soon, he stood at the entrance. 'Cheers, then. Have a good weekend.' He waved and smiled at the old man, who—busy on the phone—raised his hand in recognition.

Out on the street once more, he took a deep breath. It had been so easy that it seemed incredible. Yousef skipped down the steps and took out his mobile.

The car stopped around the corner, and Yousef jumped into the front seat.

Adhan pulled away. 'Master, is it done?'

A slow smile appeared on Yousef's face while he sank back into the seat and closed his eyes. 'It is done. All the glory goes to Allah.'

In the lounge at the house in Stratford, Yousef relaxed in a comfortable armchair. Earlier, he had called control and said one word, 'Success.' And now, he swigged whisky straight from the bottle while Adhan sipped at a glass of beer.

'I cannot believe it was so easy.' Adhan smacked his head. 'So easy, even I could have done it. I want to do the next one as soon as possible. Maybe before you go?'

Yousef answered, slurring his words, 'You are not ready, and it is not that easy.'

'I've killed for the first time, and now I'm ready to plant a bomb.'

'You are a fool. You have no idea. To just walk into a security gate with a bomb and bluff your way through—you would pee your pants.' He burst out laughing.

Adhan went quiet, not liking Yousef laughing at him. However, feeling jubilant, Yousef dismissed his companion's dark mood.

CHAPTER 36

Bunny, behind her formidable desk, wore her usual tight, dark-blue trouser suit with a cream scarf. She felt agitated; it had been a fraught morning.

She almost spat the words, 'That terrorist bastard. I can't believe it. What was Carla thinking?' Bunny shook her head. News had come through that the virginal DNA sample matched numerous taken from the flat in Islington. The man who'd killed Carla was none other than Kaashif Bashara.

Richard rubbed his face. 'I wonder how much information she gave him?'

'That depends, somewhat, on how long the deception went on. Obviously, she'd outlived her usefulness. Otherwise, why kill her? He could have just finished the relationship. I don't understand.'

'Nor me. It could be that he didn't want anyone around who might ID him later. It's happened now, and we have to assume that they've had knowledge of our actions and intentions for a while.'

'We're fortunate that Carla didn't have purple clearance; otherwise, it would be catastrophic.'

'Was it Carla who warned them about the raid on Abbas Mahmood's shop, do you think?'

'I don't think so.' Bunny shook her head. 'She wouldn't have known about it.'

Richard gave Bunny a half smile. 'Yes, but we all know that gossip goes around the office like wildfire; she could have known we had a raid on.'

Bunny asserted her authority, 'I want us to assume it wasn't her. I don't think she was a spy. More likely, she gave information ...' She hesitated. 'While, you know ...'

Richard said, 'Sorry, what ...?'

Bunny said, 'For God's sake, Richard. While they were fucking.'

Richard just looked at her in shock; he'd never heard her swear like that.

'Yes. I *am* human, and under immense pressure. It won't happen again, I can assure you.'

To signify it meant nothing, Richard shook his head. 'They would have chosen women coming out of here, but she knew the procedures, the risks, and she had to report anybody contacting her for any reason.'

'As you so eloquently said a minute ago, he could have been some sort of rent boy or whatever, and in that case she would never tell us. Single women have needs, you know.'

Again, Richard sat speechless; he had never heard Bunny speaking like this.

'Am I shocking you?' His boss laughed. 'Don't worry. It may never happen again.' With another shake of her head, Bunny grew serious once more. 'Recap for me. Where are we at the moment, elsewhere?'

Richard scratched the stubble on his chin. 'Well, Siddique is doing the rounds of Mosques. He's not getting anywhere—'

'Why?'

Richard threw his hands in the air. 'I think,

because people just don't take to him. He has this arrogance about him, and people don't like it, so …'

'What about Atallah?'

'Laying low. We can't use him again. Whatever they think, he will be under suspicion, and it would be like feeding him to the wolves if we let him contact them again.'

In the ensuing silence, Bunny eyeballed Richard and thought. Eventually, she said, 'The needs of the organisation come first. They cannot be sure, so get him back out there working. What about Ibrahim Muhammad?'

'Nothing as yet, Ma'am. We're working on it.'

CHAPTER 37

Colin and Jane Hammond, both sixty-three, had two children—Fiona and Sophie, who had each married and, between them, had three children. They arrived at the Royal Albert Hall at seven-fourteen. Old-school, they always dressed up when visiting the theatre. Jane had chosen her favourite bright-green long dress and a matching handbag and shoes. Colin wore what he had been told to: a pair of comfortable grey trousers, blue tie, white shirt, and dark-blue blazer. They had caught the fast train from Brighton into Victoria station, London, and then taken the tube to South Kensington. There, they took the ten-minute walk at a stroll, laughing and remembering previous concerts. This night out, they'd looked forward to for weeks. All their lives, they'd been massive fans of Beverley Cosby. It would be the third time in ten years that they'd seen her performing live in London.

As they arrived at the Royal Albert Hall, they held hands and sauntered around the circular building, enjoying the coldness and looking for entrance R. They mingled with the good-natured crowd and, eventually, found 'R' and entered through the door, showing their tickets. The first port of call was to the Val Parnell Bar, where they ordered gin and tonics for the intermission. After they'd paid, they made their way into the main auditorium to find their seats. They felt incredibly excited and stood watching the seats fill up with other devoted fans. The atmosphere became electric and, soon, the auditorium filled, and then the orchestra burst into life. The couple turned to one another and smiled. They had a marriage made in heaven that had lasted for a glorious forty-three years. Again, they held hands, as the announcement came that the show would now commence.

Beverley Cosby stormed onto the stage to a tumultuous welcome of screaming and cheering, wearing a stunning, long ivory dress covered in silver sequins. Gracefully, she bowed and, immediately, the band played into her latest hit record, and then she burst into voice. Jane squeezed Colin's hand. It would be a wonderful night. The old hits got sung with a few new ones thrown in. The first half had been fantastic, and Colin and Jane felt over the moon with the atmosphere and the glorious singing. Now, at nine-fifteen and intermission time, they still had the second half to go. The couple rushed to the Val Parnell Bar for their gin and tonics.

The double wooden and glass doors stood wide open, and Jane and Colin lingered near the front with their drinks chitty in hand. Two minutes later, having gotten served, they squeezed past the huge crowd to find a space at one of the side standing tables. They chatted about the songs, about how Beverley's voice had actually improved with age, and what a wonderful first half it had been. Amid the cacophony of chatting fans, they sipped their drinks. Jane looked across at Colin and smiled. He had been, and continued to be, a wonderful husband. Of course, they'd had their ups and downs, but he'd always been there when she needed him, and she prayed that they still had many years of happiness ahead together. Colin returned the smile, took her hand, and squeezed it. Neither said anything, but knew they would make love when they returned to their detached house in Brighton. Colin lifted his glass.

'To you, Jane, for so many years of happiness and—'

CHAPTER 38

They told Hesam Atallah to go back to work. He did *not* feel happy and thought about refusing, but didn't want to jeopardise his family's future. Another option might be to disappear, but where to? It was a dangerous situation for him, but he had no choice. Wary, he popped into Brick Lane Mosque, but only stayed ten minutes. Nobody had seemed to notice or take any interest in him, and he breathed a sigh of relief. The central London Mosque would prove the big test; he visited, and once again, no one bothered or spoke to him. He left the Mosque late and headed back at a fast pace to his car at the Whitechapel car park. By eight o clock, it had grown dark, and for some reason that he couldn't put his finger on, it felt a little menacing. He quickened his pace even more and decided, then and there, to tell Richard Carpenter that he planned to leave and return to Iraq. Nervous, he rushed into the car park, which stood deathly still, with no one about. The silence seemed absolute. He fumbled for his keys and strode purposefully toward his car, put the key in the lock, turned it, and pulled open the door.

'Hesam Atallah.'

He froze. Couldn't move a muscle. Frantic, he thought about diving into the car and starting her up, and if anybody got in the way, he would run them down.

'Do not move, or it will be your last.'

His hands shaking, he turned his head and caught sight of the huge thug from the Whitechapel Muslim Centre, and behind him, the waiter from the café—his scar seemingly covering his face to make him even more terrifying.

'Shut the door and move away from the car.'

Atallah pushed the door shut and turned fully; he had to draw on all his experience and courage to remain calm. 'All the glory goes to Allah.' Eyes closed, he lowered his face and stood unmoving, waiting for what was to happen next.

'Search him.'

Massive, rough hands dug and groped in the folds of his Thobe, swept aside his penis and balls, and then moved to his arse and searched in the crack. Thank God, eventually, it was over.

The thug stood up straight. 'Clean.'

A deathly silence descended. The three men stood stock still, and Scarface stared intently at Atallah.

'So, what has happened to you, Atallah?'

'Nothing, Master. I have been ill. You know my gallstones.' He rubbed his stomach. 'Very painful.'

Scarface let out a long sigh. 'You have betrayed us. You are worse than a dog.'

Atallah bent even lower and whimpered. 'No, Sir. No, Sir. I promise. I couldn't, wouldn't, do something so awful against my own people. Believe me, Sir; it's not possible.'

'Shut up, you dog turd. I can't stand your pathetic bleating.' He turned and nodded at the huge bodyguard.

The big man moved behind Atallah, lifted his

head by the hair, and slit his throat from ear to ear with a sharp twelve-inch knife. Blood shot skyward in fountains while Atallah gurgled and fell to the concrete floor like a rag.

The two men turned and walked away as though they had killed a goat for dinner.

CHAPTER 39

The bomb detonated at exactly twenty-two minutes past nine. Colin and Jane Hammond, standing right next to the ventilation panel, were obliterated into almost nothing as the blood, flesh, and bones of almost a hundred people went flying through the air, covering all the floors of the destroyed building. Eventually, authorities would confirm them dead by identifying their wedding rings. The screaming started straight away, as men and women looked down at their shattered bodies and limbless torsos. As well as the dead, hundreds got seriously injured. The emergency services evacuated the Royal Albert Hall, as fleets of ambulances, fire engines, and police cars continued to arrive at the scene.

***

Richard Carpenter, sitting in an old but comfy, green easy chair in his flat, read a novel by Simon Scarrow. He sipped at an instant coffee and enjoyed some peace and quiet for a change. That altered at speed when his mobile pinged, and he pressed messages. He jumped up from the chair, shouting, 'Fuck.' The message told him of the bombing and carnage. He read on and saw he was to report to Thames House as soon as possible. Shocked, angry, and appalled, he threw his book onto the chair and swept out of the tiny lounge, toward the bedroom. There, he changed into a white shirt and dark-blue suit, but didn't bother with a tie. Then he grabbed his briefcase, got into his car, and two minutes later, roared out of the car park and toward his office.

***

Yousef, slouched in his chair, had started to slur his words badly. Drunk, he nonetheless kept his eyes on the BBC news channel on the TV. And then came the immortal words.

'We interrupt the current story with breaking news of a terrorist atrocity at the Royal Albert Hall in central London. Steven Granby is live from the location.'

Yousef sat bolt upright and shouted for Adhan, busy preparing food in the kitchen.

Granby came onto the screen, and behind him, Yousef could see the flashing lights of ambulances and fire engines.

'Hundreds have been killed and injured in the deadliest bombing since nine-eleven. The Prime Minister and Home Secretary are expected to arrive at any minute. The emergency services are having to cope with huge numbers of dead and injured. An emergency situation has been declared, and Doctors and medical staff are pouring into London hospitals to help with the crisis. We can now hear from the Prime Minister.'

Yousef took a long swig from the whisky bottle, and as he finished, he shouted, 'You see them bleeding, Adhan. They bleed like the hundreds they kill every day in our homes. We will kill hundreds more. Allah be praised, Allah be praised.' Then he laughed as he, again, lifted the bottle to his mouth.

'We will not rest until the perpetrators of this heinous crime are found and the full force of the law is brought upon them. Our emergency services are, once again, performing heroically in extremely difficult circumstances. We must remain strong and, once again, we send a message to the barbarians that have attacked innocent, defenceless people enjoying a night out at the theatre. We will not be beaten or cowed. However long, however much blood is given, we will prevail. You will be beaten in the end. We pray for the dead and the injured. God speed to you all.'

The Prime Minister turned and, amid vast security, made his way closer to the scene.

***

Later, Richard sat in Bunny's office.

'It's bad. Incredibly bad.'

'I'm sorry, Ma'am. We should have done better.' Richard put his hands up to his face and rubbed his eyes.

Bunny looked at him for a few seconds, took a deep breath, and then spoke, 'You are doing your best, which is all anybody can ask of you.' She paused and took another deep breath. 'I think it may be time for me to move on; the job is becoming too much for me. Hundreds killed and wounded. I can't cope with it.' She sobbed gently.

Richard sat there, stunned, and didn't know what to do or say. Eventually, he gathered his thoughts, stood, and moved to the side of Bunny's desk. 'No one could do this job better than you. You *are* MI5. We must all pull together to catch these bastards, and catch them we shall. You must, once again, pull on all your reserves of strength. We will hunt them down, and then we will arrest them or kill them.' He stared at her intently. 'Are you listening to me?'

Bunny lifted her head and wiped a tear from her eye. 'You are, of course, right. It is a momentary weakness—'

Richard said, 'It is normal. You have the weight of the world on your shoulders. I've got broad ones, so give me some extra and lessen yours.'

The red phone on the desk startled him when it rang.

'Do you want me to leave?'

Bunny shook her head, held a finger to her lips, and picked up the phone. 'Yes?'

Her grip tightened. 'I know.'

Then she nodded. 'Thank you, Sir.'

Another nod. 'Yes, thank you, Sir.'

Bunny replaced the handset in the old-fashioned cradle, and then smiled and sniffed loudly. 'Prime Minister. Said I was doing a wonderful job. Gave his full support. Will be inviting me to Downing Street for tea. Have you ever been, Richard?'

'No, Ma'am.'

'Then, you shall come with me as my most trusted lieutenant.' She looked back on form. 'How would you like that?'

'As long as it doesn't get in the way of me finding these terrorist bastards, I look forward to it.'

'Quite right.' Her face turned into steely defiance. 'Every resource, Richard. I want them found. I don't care what it takes; break every fucking rule in the book.' She stopped and turned to the side, then

spoke in a low, menacing voice, 'I want them
found. I want all the information we can get from
them, and then ...' She turned to look him square
in the eyes, 'And then you are to kill them. Do you
understand?'

'Clearly, Ma'am, and believe me, it will be a
pleasure.'

Bunny picked up the phone. 'Go to it, then.'

Richard got up from his chair just as one of the
other phones rang. Bunny picked it up and
listened. 'I see, yes, normal procedure.'

She looked up at Richard, 'Atallah, throat cut in a
car park in Whitechapel.'

Richard wasn't shocked, wasn't surprised. 'I hope
we will look after his family. I must get on, then,
Ma'am.'

'Yes, we will, and yes, you must, Richard. Keep
me informed.'

CHAPTER 40

When the call came through, Mrs Evans had felt totally shocked. 'This goes against all the protocols. I just don't understand it at all.'

Jim, the bodyguard, also felt bemused. 'I rang control. They said it's short term because of lack of staff, so that's it; we make the most of it.'

Mrs Evans tutted. 'Protocol says we should not have two clients in the house at the same time, and now you've told me they're connected to the same case ...' She flung her hands in the air as she stormed off to the stairs. 'She'll be here in ten minutes. I'll get the bed made.'

The door bell rang, and Mrs Evans opened the door to be met by a huge, black man-mountain of a bodyguard and a diminutive, rough-looking teenage girl with short, jet-black hair and dressed in blue jeans with rips in the knees and a plain white tee shirt.

Mrs Evans smiled at the girl. 'You must be Mandy. Come in, come in.'

The bodyguard turned and walked quickly back down the path, toward his MI5 silver Jaguar. Mrs Evans thought that strange, but everything about the Mandy girl turning up seemed strange. 'Would you like a cup of tea, Dear?'

Mandy didn't reply. Instead, she looked around the hall, and then at Mrs Evans. 'Got any Coke, love?'

'Oh, I take it you are referring to Coca-Cola?'

''Course I am. Jesus, what an old dump this is.'

Mrs Evans nearly had a coronary on the spot.

Mandy's attention got drawn to the stairs when the floorboards creaked.

'Hello, young lady. Although, by the way you're speaking to Mrs Evans, calling you a lady could — without question — be a serious error.'

'What you saying?' Mandy put her hands on her hips.

'I'm Durriyah. And you are?'

'Mandy. You're pretty, and I love your dress. Where did you get it?'

Durriyah smiled. She wore a simple navy-blue mini dress that showed off her long shapely legs. Already, something about the spunky girl had her liking her.

'You're quite pretty, yourself.' Durriyah strode across the hall and grabbed Mandy's hand. 'Let's go and see what drinks there are, and I can tell you all about my dress.'

Mrs Evans smiled. Thank God that Durriyah was here to take charge of the new arrival.

***

Durriyah and Mandy settled in the lounge and sipped orange juices while chatting about clothes.

Durriyah said, 'I want to hear the whole story: who you are, what you've been up to, and why you're here.'

Mandy knocked back her juice and wiped her mouth. 'Any booze in the house?'

'How old are you?'

'Old enough, believe me.'

'Hmm. I find you so interesting. I think that we can be friends. What do you think?'

'Defo. You're the only person here that I can even speak to.'

Durriyah sat forward in anticipation. 'So, let's hear your story, then.'

'Not much to say, really. Got involved with a wop who turned out to be a terrorist and ended up on the witness protection thing. I'm so fu—' She stopped herself swearing and gave Durriyah a gorgeous smile instead. 'What about you?'

Durriyah couldn't speak straight away but then rallied. Though she had to ask, she dreaded the inevitable answer, 'What was the terrorist's name?'

'Well, when I let him shag me, I thought his name was Steve, but turns out he was a lying bastard. I found out later that his real name was Yousef El-Sayed something or other.'

In shock, Durriyah moved her hands to cover her mouth.

'What is it? Do you know the lying filth?'

Durriyah sat in silence but, eventually, said, 'I slept with him as well. We had a short relationship.'

Mandy's next words showed that she wasn't into relationships, 'I didn't sleep with the bastard. He fucked me from behind in the hallway of his flat. It was all over in seconds. He did have a big cock, though.'

Durriyah had never heard anybody speak like this before and it took her aback. Intimate, personal moments weren't for broadcasting, and such language. The girl had, obviously, been brought up

in a tough environment, and Durriyah felt
determined that while they were together in the
house, she would take her under her wing and try
and make something of her.

'Mandy, I find your language disgusting, and if
we're to be friends, then it has to change. I'll help
you, whether you like it or not. So, first things first,
from now on, you will address Mrs Evans as Mrs
Evans. You may call the bodyguard Jim, and of
course, you must call me Durriyah.'

'You'll have to teach me how to say it properly,
then.' Mandy laughed.

Durriyah looked at her and smiled again. 'I'll
teach you lots of things, starting from right now.
First of all, let's go and unpack your case and settle
you into your room.'

'Haven't got much stuff, just jeans and tee shirts.'

'I've got so many clothes, I don't know what to
do with them; you can have whatever fits you.'

Mandy gave Durriyah another beautiful smile,
grabbed her hand, and all but dragged her out of
the lounge. 'Let's go, then. Come on.' Both
laughing, they grabbed the case and started up the
stairs toward Mandy's new room.

'I tell you what,' Durriyah said. 'You have a
shower, put on clean clothes, and by the time
you're ready, dinner will be served. And, believe
me, you'll enjoy the food. Mrs Evans is an excellent
cook.'

'Hope she knows how to cook burgers and fried
chicken.'

Durriyah shook her head and smiled; she didn't
want to tell Mandy that she smelt like she hadn't

had a bath in weeks. Instead, she said, 'Make sure you scrub yourself. I'll see you downstairs.'

She turned to go, but then Mandy spoke again and pulled off her tee shirt, 'Why don't you stay? We can talk.'

Momentarily, Durriyah felt excited; Mandy had full breasts, and she would have loved to have seen them without the bra and even touched them. Despite her initial response, she said, 'No. I have something to do. See you soon.' Then she left the bedroom and made her way downstairs, shaking her head. Things had changed in the house in a second, and it felt beyond exciting.

Dinner proved delicious. Homemade chicken and ham pie with broccoli and new potatoes. Durriyah thoroughly enjoyed it. Mandy pushed the food around her plate, hardly eating anything.

Durriyah couldn't stand it any longer. 'For goodness sake, stop playing with your food and eat something.'

'Can't eat this stuff.' She poked the food with her cutlery. 'What's this?' She held a piece of broccoli up in the air on her fork.

'It's called broccoli, and it's tasty and good for you,' Mrs Evans said, horrified.

'Well, you eat it, then.' Mandy threw back her chair, stormed out of the room, and ran up the stairs.

Jim didn't say a word, just continued shovelling pie into his cave-like mouth. After swallowing, he said, 'Lovely pie, Mrs Evans.'

Durriyah stood. 'I'll see to her.' Then she made for the stairs. She took a few steps and stopped.

Mandy's sobs drifted down from her room. Her heart went out to the girl, and she increased her pace. At the door, she let herself in. Mandy lay on the bed, crying. Durriyah kicked off her slippers and lay down next to her. Then she wrapped her arms around Mandy, pulled her in close, and whispered in her ear, 'Don't worry. I'm here for you. We'll be great friends. I'll look after you.' Then she kissed her on the ear and cheek. Mandy turned around and hugged Durriyah for all she was worth, and her tears wet Durriyah's cheeks. She started crying herself; two shipwrecks on the coast, seeking comfort and warmth.

An hour later, Mandy sat at the kitchen table, chomping on a quarter-pound cheese burger and chips and drinking a large Coca-Cola. Against all the rules, Durriyah had managed to persuade Jim to nip out to the local McDonalds. Now, she just sat and watched her, fascinated when ketchup spilled onto her chin. Durriyah scooped it up with her finger and stuck it in her mouth. Already, the young tearaway had changed her life drastically.

CHAPTER 41

Richard Carpenter felt more than agitated, he felt beside himself; nothing had happened, they had made no progress, and it terrified him that news of another explosion could come at any moment.

The small flat had become a prison, and he couldn't bear to stay in it except when sleeping. He spent most of his time at Thames House, going over and over the files to see if they'd missed something. Sadly, he found nothing; almost like they'd gone back to the beginning.

Bunny didn't say much; nothing to say. They sought two men in London, which had a population of about ten million—needle in a haystack sprang to mind yet again. Richard sat in the canteen, sipping another coffee and thinking, turning everything over and over in his mind. He needed to clear his head. Perhaps he could visit Durriyah again? Every day, he thought of her and felt determined to see her again soon while he hoped for a relationship in the future. A glance around the canteen showed people chatting and laughing while Richard felt miserable beyond belief. Killers on the loose, his bitch wife asking for money to pay the mortgage, and the love of his life (Durriyah) miles away in Epsom. Thoroughly fed up, he drained the cup, stood, and kept repeating to himself that there had to be something, some way forward—there always was.

***

Yousef El-Sayed and Adhan strolled up Stratford high street. On this pleasant day, people came out in force and crowded the shops. Both dressed in jeans and tee-shirts, they wore their hair short and had no beards.

Yousef said, 'It is incredible news that the two women are now together; it will make life easy for me.'

Adhan nodded, 'We have four days before the Mandy girl will have to be moved. When are you going to strike?'

Yousef looked Adhan in the eye, 'You mean *we*. You will come with me and kill one of them. It is part of your training.'

'I have killed and can do it again.'

'Yes, you are a master killer and bomber.' Yousef smiled, and then broke into laughter.

Adhan, annoyed again, hated Yousef making fun of him. They continued strolling.

Then Yousef stopped and turned to Adhan, 'The day after tomorrow, Friday, we will finish the job by bleeding out the two bitches.'

Adhan smiled falsely, and then frowned. 'I expect there will be bodyguards in the house.'

Yousef laughed. 'Of course, there will be, and they will die as well.'

Adhan didn't feel quite so sure of himself; killing women was one thing, and armed bodyguards completely different.

'Don't shit yourself. I will look after you.' Yousef laughed some more.

***

On Friday at five pm, Richard left via the main

entrance of Thames House, planning to grab a black cab and get in the Bunch of Grapes on Cromwell Road in about fifteen minutes. Would Claire be at work?

Soon, he pushed open the door and strode toward the bar, which he scanned but couldn't see the barmaid he wanted.

A tall, young redhead in a green dress appeared from the side of the bar and spoke with a lovely Irish accent, 'Yes, Sir? What can I get you?'

Richard felt unsure; if he hit the spirits too early, he would end up in a mess yet again. 'A pint of Carling sounds good.'

'Coming right up.' The girl gave him a beautiful smile.

'You're in a good mood, then?'

'No point being miserable. Life's too short.'

Richard thought about that and came to the conclusion that if all you had to worry about was pulling pints, then yes, she was right. She handed over the pint and took the three pounds fifty he gave her in change.

'What's your name, then?'

'Mandy,' she said.

Richard felt surprised. 'I've got a friend called Mandy.'

The girl smiled and laughed. 'Well, there are a few of us about.'

Richard thought about Mandy Smith, wondered where she was, and how she was coping with witness protection. His mind then wandered to thinking about Durriyah, desperate to see her again as soon as possible. Maybe a trip to Epsom would do him good. He sipped at his pint and looked around the room: a couple of old boys with half pints ... much too early even for a Friday.

***

By eleven pm, Mandy couldn't sleep. She'd been thinking about her mum and friends back in London and felt sick of the house, sick of the food, and sick of Mrs Evans and Jim. The only good news had been Durriyah, glamorous and with it, and she liked her. Never had Mandy thought she would miss her mum so much. A single tear fell down her cheek, followed by a flood.

At home, sometimes, in the night, she would sneak into her mum's room and get in bed with her for a cuddle. She wished she could get a cuddle now. With a sniffle, she wiped her eyes and made a decision. Naked, she climbed from bed and tiptoed across the room, where she picked up a white tee-shirt from the floor. Once she'd lifted it over her head, she opened the door and looked around the landing. All quiet. A little nervous, she stepped out of the door and closed it deliberately and quietly behind her. Soon, she stood outside a door further down the landing, grasped the handle, turned it, and entered the room. Inside, she shut the door and looked around the room. Durriyah lay fast asleep, her breathing gentle. Mandy smiled and took the few steps toward the bed, and then eased back the cover. Durriyah, naked, awoke with a start and eyes wide.

Mandy whispered, 'It's me, Mandy. I'm scared. I needed a cuddle.'

Durriyah smiled and slid across the bed, leaving

room for Mandy to squeeze in. Mandy took off her tee-shirt, climbed in, and snuggled into Durriyah. The bed felt warm and comforting. Arms enveloped Mandy and squeezed tight. Hands lay on her breasts.

Durriyah's breasts pressed into Mandy's back. They felt nice. Mandy moved her hand back around Durriyah, meaning to squeeze her in return, but inadvertently, she grabbed a buttock and squeezed. That felt good as well.

'I feel …' Mandy paused, then said, 'I feel lovely, and so do you.' A nervous laugh escaped her.

Durriyah touched Mandy's nipples. 'And you too, my little darling.'

Durriyah planted kiss after kiss on her shoulder and held her tight.

Mandy turned over and cuddled into the older woman, their breasts together, and entwined her legs around Durriyah's. Then she held and squeezed Durriyah's buttocks, and finally, took the plunge. She lifted her face and looked her in the eye as she moved to kiss her on the lips. Durriyah plunged her tongue into Mandy's mouth, licking and sucking her juices. Mandy, wanting more, slipped her hand down and caressed Durriyah between her long silky legs.

While breathing heavily, Mandy whispered, 'I've never been with a woman, but you're different. I like you so much.'

'And me you. Mmm, you're so sexy and gorgeous.' Durriyah nuzzled her some more.

Mandy smiled, contented, and then raised her eyebrows in surprise when Durriyah moved and

297

used her tongue to caress her most intimate place.
In heaven, Mandy groaned and closed her eyes.
***

El-Sayed and Adhan drove on the M25, headed
toward the Dartford Bridge. Rain lashed the
windscreen of the Ford Focus, and the wipers
didn't work as well as they should have. They were
on their way to kill Durriyah and Mandy.

'Shit fucking weather,' Adhan said with a scowl.

'Perfect for what we're about tonight,' Yousef
said, cheerful.

Yousef felt relaxed and in his zone. Again, he'd
reminded Adhan to stick to the speed limit and,
under no circumstances, should he do anything
that would draw attention. Adhan drove on the
inside lane at sixty-miles-per-hour, and wasn't
happy—huge juggernaut lorries sped almost onto
his bumper, and then pulled out to overtake him.

'Are you ever worried before a mission?'

Yousef thought for a few seconds. 'It is not worry
but nerves. You are nervous?'

'Yes, very.'

'Me too. The trick is to embrace the nerves. You
cannot perform at your best if you don't feel a little
nervous. Anybody who says they don't suffer
before a mission isn't telling the truth.'

Ahead, the dramatic image of the bridge came
into view. Yousef said, 'The British are great at
building everything: bridges, buildings, aeroplanes
… you name, it they can build it.'

'Yes, they're a capable nation.'

'Hmm, they've killed and raped their way
around the world for hundreds of years; arrogant

bastards, all of them. I look forward to cutting the throat of the English bitch, and Durriyah, well, it just has to be done, and then we will watch them bleed to death.'

Adhan shook his head but kept quiet. He loved women and couldn't understand Yousef getting so excited at the thought of killing them. Also, there remained the small problem of the bodyguard or guards.

Adhan drove through the cash pay-booth, throwing the coins into the basket and roaring ahead into the eerily lit night.

Yousef asked, 'You have arranged everything?'

'Yes.' Adhan nodded.

'So, what has you worried?'

Adhan took his time in replying. 'Killing, blood, the screaming; I just hope they don't scream too much.'

Yousef almost laughed. 'I'll make it quick for them, just for you.'

***

Richard Carpenter had gone back to Thames House, and now ambled trance-like through the offices. Eventually, he found an empty meeting room, entered, and sat facing the door. Then he glanced at his watch. Nine pm. So late that he'd lost track. Downcast, he felt adrift. With nowhere to go, he believed that he had lost. Despondent, he opened the file he'd brought with him and read the first two lines of the first page. Without getting any further, he sat back, took a deep breath, and exhaled slowly. Yet again, he thought of Durriyah. He would make the trip to Epsom soon to see her again.

***

'I've got so much to teach you,' Durriyah said.

'Don't I know it.' Mandy grinned. 'I never thought it could be so good with another woman.'

'Nor me. I'm very much into men, and the bigger the cock, the better.'

A bit hysterical and giddy, Mandy laughed. And then, suddenly, she went all serious. 'We should have a foursome with some big-cock hunks. Now, that would be fun.'

Durriyah smiled, but underneath, wanted to change the subject. 'We all have a dark side that sometimes takes over.' Mandy had gone quiet. 'There's nothing as good as a loving relationship between a man and a woman. You get that, Mandy? One of each.'

Mandy chuckled. 'I understand, but it's nice to be naughty sometimes.'

Durriyah turned and smiled. 'Of course. Occasionally. Now, don't you think we should get some sleep?'

Mandy laughed. 'Well, I guess so, or we could …?'

***

Yousef and Adhan had reached junction eight, the Reigate turn off on the M25. They motored up the slip road and stopped at the red traffic lights.

'How far to go?' Yousef looked at Adhan.

'Maybe twenty minutes. More, at the speed we're going.'

Yousef said, 'I must rest. Do not talk, and drive carefully.' Yousef shut his eyes—probably praying again.

Adhan, sweating, took his hands from the steering wheel and wiped them down his trousers. The lights turned orange and then green, he pressed the accelerator and pulled away. The sat nav repeated, 'Take the third exit from the roundabout.' He drove around the roundabout, taking care to get in the correct lane. An old Ford Escort banger roared past, almost clipping his wing mirrors, and he shook his hand at the other driver, and got a middle finger from the passenger sitting in the front.

'Bastards,' he shouted. If they knew who sat in the car, they would show some respect. He turned to Yousef, to all intents and purposes asleep, but Adhan knew better. The man was like a snake. You think it's asleep, but move toward it, and it rears up in defence, spitting venom and attacking with deadly intent. He took the third exit, looked closely at the speedometer, and proceeded down the dual carriageway in the inside lane.

***

Bunny wore a green trouser suit, a serious change from her usual blue. Seated at her desk, she read reports. Then the phone rang.

'That's odd. I'll look into it. Thank you for letting me know.'

For a moment, she sat stock still, and then reached for one of her phones. Then she pulled her hand back; she felt like getting out of the office. Instead of making the call, she stood, straightened her navy-blue silk scarf, and set off to find Richard Carpenter. That task proved easier said than done,

as she asked after him at various locations.
Eventually, she paged him, and he called her a
minute later.

'Where are you?'

'Meeting room six, on the third floor.'

'Okay. I'll be there in a minute.'

'What's happening?'

'I'm sure it's nothing, but I need to run something
by you.'

***

Richard felt intrigued. It was extremely unusual
for Bunny to wander around Thames House, as she
tended to summon people to her inner sanctum.

The door opened, and Bunny stepped in.

Richard stood. 'What can I do for you, Ma'am?'

'Good evening, Richard. I want to know why …'

***

Adhan pulled into the car park overlooking the
Downs at Tattenham Corner.

Yousef opened his eyes. The midnight looked
dark as coal. 'Where are we?'

'A five-minute walk from the target.'

Yousef turned and looked out of the window.
The rain came down, spitting, and the trees behind
the car park swayed from side to side in the wind.

'He knows we're here?'

'Yes.' Adhan nodded.

Yousef shut his eyes again, and then rubbed
them. Tired, he worried that the adrenalin hadn't
kicked in yet. 'I need to take some fresh air.' He
pushed open the car door and took a step out, then
sucked in the countryside air and exhaled slowly.
After a stretch, he glanced around. Two empty cars

sat across the car park, and nothing else but silence.

'Stand where you are. Do not move a muscle.' The voice came out of the darkness.

So much for nothing else but silence. Yousef had no idea where the man was. He stood stock still and let his arms hang by his side.

The voice spoke again, 'Your codename?'

Yousef calmed; he'd expected the man. 'Beacon. And Adhan is in the car.'

Silence descended again, and then the man emerged from the nearby bushes, dressed in black clothes and pointing a pistol at Yousef.

'So, you are Beacon. You have my money?'

'Yes, in the boot.'

'Tell Adhan to get it.'

'You heard the man, Adhan; get the money.'

Adhan opened his door and stepped out. Even though they'd expected the man, in the dark with a gun pointed at them, they couldn't be sure he wouldn't just shoot them.

He went to the back of the car and opened the boot, grabbed hold of one of the Glocks, and slipped it into his waistband. Then he hefted the holdall and slammed shut the boot lid.

'Walk toward me. Place the bag five feet away. Don't come any closer.'

Adhan did as instructed.

'Go and stand next to your friend.'

The man stepped forward and picked up the bag, then retreated to the bushes and put the gun into a shoulder holster. Then he opened the zipper on the bag and pulled the sides apart. Bundles of used twenty-pound notes filled it. He didn't bother to count it.

Adhan knew him to be two hundred and fifty thousand pounds better off.

In a cool voice, Yousef said, 'It's all there. I counted it myself.'

The man looked up. 'Good. Now, we will go and finish the job, but first, I must look after my retirement fund. I will be back in five minutes.' He picked up the bag and made to move.

Adhan reached for his pistol, but Yousef grabbed his hand.

'Do nothing. He will be back.'

The man disappeared into the blackness. Yousef went to the boot and took out his pistol, and after he'd caressed the handle, slipped it into his waistband.

'He's older than I thought,' Adhan mumbled, trying to calm himself.

A noise startled them, and then the man reappeared out of the darkness. He spoke in a clear, commanding voice, 'Follow me.'

***

Mrs Evans felt worried. What the hell was going on with Jim? Upstairs, on the landing, she stood at the side of the window that overlooked the front entrance. So that she could see the pavement and the path up to the front door, she'd pulled the curtain back an inch. The night had grown so late, and she felt tired, and now, just plain worried by Jim and his behaviour. Also, she remained unhappy that she had two parcels to care for, and the fact that they were both connected to the same case made it even worse.

Then she remembered that she hadn't phoned
Richard Carpenter and made a mental note to do it
first thing in the morning. Footsteps sounded on
the pavement. Jim approached the house, walking
slowly and trying to stay as quiet as he could. This
behaviour had Mrs Evans even more worried.
Then he put his hand into the inside of his jacket.
Was he checking his weapon? A chill enveloped
her from head to foot; something was very wrong.
Had that been a noise from the back of the house?
She froze. For a second, she experienced terror and
couldn't move, but then snapped out of it. She
knew what she had to do.

'Wake up. We're in danger.'
Mrs Evans had, initially, felt shocked to discover
Durriyah and Mandy snuggled up together in
Durriyah's bed.
'Wake up, quickly.'
Durriyah sat bolt upright.
Mandy stirred and looked confused. 'What's
going on?'
Mrs Evans answered quickly and quietly, 'I think
there are men breaking into the house.' To
reinforce that, they all heard a pane of glass smash
at the back of the building.
'Get up and follow me. Hurry.'
Durriyah and Mandy leapt out of bed and
grabbed tee shirts, throwing them on as quickly as
they could.
Mrs Evans led them out onto the landing and to
the bathroom. Then, with a finger to her lips, she
went to the medicine cabinet, opened it, and

pressed a button. Durriyah and Mandy watched, transfixed, when a door opened in the tiled wall. A safe room. They slid in, and the door shut behind them. Mrs Evans clicked a switch, and a low-power light came on. Though the room was small, it had space enough for the three of them. Next, Mrs Evans pressed a red button on the wall.

The room held four hard-backed wooden chairs, and the three women sat down.

Durriyah whispered, 'What's going on?'

'Jim's behaviour has been very strange, lately, and he's just come back and is at the front of the house. Someone is at the back, too. I'm not taking any chances. Don't worry; help will arrive soon.'

Dumbfounded, Durriyah said, 'Jim must know about this room?'

'No. Only the keeper of the house. And that's me.'

'What will we do?'

'Nothing. We sit tight until help arrives. Keep calm; everything will work out okay.'

Terrified, Mandy reached out her hand and grabbed Durriyah's.

***

Bunny eyed Richard. 'Good evening. I want to know why we have gone against all our normal protocols and allowed two parcels in one safe house.'

Richard gave Bunny a confused look. 'Sorry. Can you be more specific, please?'

Bunny looked as if she felt like screaming but controlled herself. 'The safe house in Epsom. Apparently, we transferred Mandy Smith there, and of course, the Durriyah Kassab woman is the incumbent parcel.'

The news shocked Richard. 'This can't be true. It goes against every protocol we have.'

'My dear, Richard. Apparently, you authorised it.'

Richard grew scared. 'I authorised no such thing. Do you think I'm mad?' Annoyed, he raised his voice.

Neither of them spoke, and it sunk in that the two witnesses in the Yousef El-Sayed case were both together and in terrible danger.

Richard leapt up, his first thought for Durriyah, and made a move toward the door.

Bunny held his arm. 'Who are the keeper and guard?'

'Mrs Evans and Jim Matthews.'

'I don't know either. Phone them.'

Richard took out his mobile and pressed contacts, typed Jim Matthews on the search bar, and the number came up.

'This number is unattainable. Please try later.'

He shut his eyes and said, 'Shit.' Then he changed the contact name to Mrs Evans and pressed the green button again. This time, he pressed speaker. It rang and rang and rang and, eventually, went to voicemail.

'I've got to get down there.' Richard opened the door.

'I'll arrange some local help.'

Richard stopped. 'No. Send agents. No police. I don't want any fuck ups.'

'Your call.' Bunny grabbed the phone and started

issuing instructions.

Richard ran down the corridor to the lifts.

***

Five minutes' walk from the house, a car parked down one of the country lanes. The windows on the black Volkswagen Golf were misted. A man sat in the front passenger seat, and a slim, attractive, red-haired woman sat astride him, moving rhythmically up and down.

'Yes, Jenney. Keep going. Oh God, that's good.'

The woman breathed hard as she pushed up and down on the man's pole. She laughed. 'And you're near retirement.' Then she sped up, and the grunting and heavy breathing got louder from them both.

Finally, the man could hold on no longer. 'Jenney, yes, yes.' He pushed up with all his strength and came to a shuddering climax, then he collapsed back into the seat.

'You didn't ...'

'Don't worry, Jim. It was good. In fact, better than good. I'm done in.'

Jim laughed. 'If Mrs Evans could see me now, she'd faint on the spot.'

'You think the old dear's never had sex? Come on; she could be a secret sex goddess.'

Jim cracked up at the thought of Mrs Evans in stockings and sexy underwear. 'I don't think so. Listen, I've got to get back.'

'Oh, so you only want me for the sex?'

'I'm completely mad about you. We'll meet again soon, I promise.'

'Good. Because I need that weapon of yours.' She

laughed.

Jim felt a little worried; he knew full well he was breaking rules, but meeting Jenney had given him a new lease of life. And the sex — it felt like being sixteen again. He made a decision to have a quiet word with Mrs Evans and put her in the know.

He opened the gate at the end of the pathway and started the long walk up to the front door. Then his training kicked in. The curtain twitched at the bedroom bay window. Mrs Evans had waited for him. With a curse, he took a few more steps, and then got shocked to the core when he heard the sound of shattering glass somewhere to the rear of the property. He stopped dead and, automatically, reached for his handgun. Terror enveloped him when he remembered leaving it behind in his room. For a second, he could have panicked, but then he took a deep breath and stepped onto the grass at the front of the house; he would have to investigate.

***

Enraged, Yousef grabbed Adhan by the throat and spat in his eye. They had made their way through woods, approached the house, and reached the edge of the back garden. Inadvertently, Adhan had stood on a broken pane of glass, which had shattered, and the noise would — undoubtedly — have been heard by someone in the house. The three men froze, waiting for lights to appear. If they came on, the mission would be over before it had even begun. The suspense felt incredible. Seconds seemed like minutes. And still, no lights came on. And no sign came that anyone in the house had stirred.

Yousef turned to the other man. 'I still don't like it. They could just be waiting for us. Perhaps, we should leave.'

The man grunted. 'No. I have plans. This needs to be concluded tonight.' Then he took a step forward, expecting Yousef and Adhan to follow him, which they did.

***

Lights flashing, Richard had already covered ten of the eighteen miles to Epsom. He'd never driven so fast in his life, careening around corners at seventy-miles-per-hour and driving through red lights with hardly a worry for other motorists. This late at night, traffic stayed extremely light, and Richard held his foot to the pedal as hard and as long as he could. Back-up wasn't far behind him, but he had no intention of waiting for them. Durriyah refused to leave his mind, and eventually, he had to block her from his thoughts so she couldn't affect his focus on the driving. The sat nav said to take the third exit from the roundabout, onto Kingston Road. Not far away, now, he screeched around the roundabout, straightened up, and then slammed his foot on the accelerator and roared away, overtaking a tiny Fiat in a cloud of smoke and dust.

***

'What's happening outside?' Durriyah asked.

'I have no idea, but we're safe in here. Only the highest authorities at MI5 have access to the whereabouts of secure rooms within safe houses. They should get here any minute.'

Mandy butted in, 'I don't mind admitting that I'm scared to death.'

Durriyah squeezed her hand, 'Don't worry; Mrs Evans has a lot of experience, and help will get here soon.'

***

Jim Matthews crept around the side of the house, hugging the building as tightly as he could. He strained to listen for any movement but could hear nothing. A twig broke when he stood on it, and he cursed to himself. After one more step, he heard something. Somebody was moving in the back garden. Why the fuck hadn't the security lights come on? Perturbed, he tip-toed a few more steps. A man came into view with, perhaps, one or two more figures behind him. Jim thought quickly, as to what could be going on. Mrs Evans must have heard the glass shattering and would have raised the alarm by now, and so MI5 people would be alert to the emergency. Perhaps the noise had scared off the intruders, and these were MI5 agents. Without his weapon, he felt paralyzed. After another moment of reflection, he decided to call their bluff. If he didn't get the right answers, he could run.

Crouched, he shouted, 'Stop where you are. I have you covered. One wrong move, and I will open fire.'

The men stopped. The one at the front turned toward him. 'Do not shoot. We are MI5 agents responding to an emergency alarm.'

Jim took a deep breath and thanked God they were friendly. Still cautious, though, he said, 'You.

The man who spoke. Walk slowly toward me. One wrong move, and it will be your last.'

The man moved confidently toward Jim. At last, he stood only a few paces away.

'My God. I can't believe my eyes,' Jim said in a loud voice. 'What on earth are you doing running around in the dark? You should be at home in bed snoring and annoying your wife.' He laughed, stood, and moved closer to the man.

'Good to see you, Jim. It's been a long time.'

'Certainly has.' Jim held out his hand, and the man shook it.

'I think we had visitors, but they must have gotten scared away. I heard breaking glass. Probably—'

Jim felt it briefly—something around his throat—and moved his hand up. Too late. The cheese wire went through his throat like a hot knife through butter. It sliced into his larynx, then cut his air supply, slicing the trachea, and then on through the oesophagus. Muscle and tissue parted when the razor-sharp wire sliced on, finally tearing his head from his torso.

***

Blood shot in fountains in every direction and covered Yousef from head to foot while the head rolled onto the grass, followed by the twitching body. Adhan turned and vomited onto the grass.

The older man stood, unperturbed; he'd seen it all before. 'Let's go. There is only one bodyguard.'

Adhan asked, 'Will they still be in the house?'

The man smiled. 'The keeper will have followed protocols and taken the parcels into the secure room. I know where it is and have the password, and so, they will come out.'

The three men picked up the pace and soon stood at the back door.

'No need to be quiet. Smash it in.'

Yousef nodded at Adhan, who went forward and kicked at the door. The older, well-built man got fed up watching Adhan wasting his time and smashed his shoulder against the door, which crashed open. Then he stepped in. The three men all entered the back of the house and waited, silent, in a hallway that led to the heart of the property. They listened and could hear nothing.

'Move.' The older man led them into the interior of the house.

***

When he reached the road, Richard Carpenter slowed, unsure whether to go in all lights on and sirens blaring or park up and go in on foot quietly. He decided on the latter, parked, and got out. Then he checked his handgun was loaded and proceeded up the road. The house stood four properties away, and he got there in seconds. The best thing would be to scout around prior to entering. Quickly, he moved to the left side of the property, stopping at regular intervals to listen. Soon, he stood at the back of the property. No lights showed, and everything seemed almost too quiet. Cautious, he edged around the back of the house, crouching as he ran across the lawn, and stumbled when he ran into something in the grass. Almost tripping, he stopped and looked down, and couldn't—at first—make it out but thought it could

be a dead animal. With his shoe, he gave it a
nudge, and then jumped back in horror. Jim
Matthews' face stared up at him, his mouth twisted
in a hideous expression.

***

Yousef and Adhan followed the man up the
stairs. At the top, the man looked around. Then he
turned to them and held his finger to his mouth,
walked a few paces, and stopped at the entrance to
what was clearly a bathroom. He pointed at both
sides of the door. Adhan and Yousef took up
station, ready. The man entered the bathroom and
looked around the tiled walls. His eyes stopped at
the cabinet, and he opened it. After staring at the
inside, he pressed a green button and waited.

A voice, a woman's, said, 'Who is there?'

The man pressed the button again. 'MI5,
responding to an emergency alarm.'

'The code word.'

The man spoke clearly and loudly, 'Abacus.'

'Thank you. We're coming out.'

The man stepped back and watched while the
tiled door opened, and a smiling Mrs Evans
stepped into the bathroom.

'We're so pleased to see you. Have you seen Jim
Matthews anywhere?'

'No sign. Let's go downstairs where we can talk.'

Mrs Evans moved to the side to allow Durriyah
and Mandy to emerge.

When Mrs Evans made to leave the bathroom, the
man held her arm and whispered, 'A word alone if
we may.'

Durriyah and Mandy stepped out of the

bathroom, and the door shut behind them. They thought nothing of it and, as they turned to go downstairs, they both stopped in shock. Neither of them could speak, as Yousef El-Sayed smiled at them.

'Hello, ladies. We meet again.'

Mrs Evans flinched when the knife cut her on the neck and ducked more quickly than the man had expected. He swung again. She backed away, and then—suddenly—sprang forward and raked his face deeply with her nails, causing him to yelp in pain.

'You fucking bitch. You'll pay for that.'

No one could save her; but, evidently, she meant to go down fighting.

He stabbed with the knife, catching her on the arm. With a scream, she flailed at him like a maniac. The man stuck the knife into her stomach and ripped upward. Shiny, grey-pink intestines spilled onto her dress and jumper. She looked down, and then raised her hand to try and scratch him once more. He slashed the knife across her throat. Blood spiralled in a fountain into the air and across the tiled floor. The woman collapsed in a heap, gurgling her death cry, and then went quiet. The fight left him panting; the woman had been strong. Then he turned, now ready to deal with the other two.

***

Richard stood at the back door, all his senses on alert, and prayed that he hadn't come too late. Handgun held out in front, he stepped into the house, scanning from side to side. Then he inched forward, straining his ears for any sound that could indicate where they were—if they even remained on the property. At the main hallway, a commotion upstairs reached him. In all the shouting, he recognised Mandy and Durriyah's voices. Thank God. Now at the bottom of the stairs, he hesitated; old, the risers would creak, yet he had no choice. Gingerly, he placed his foot on the first step. The noise sounded deafening. Both Mandy and Durriyah shouted and screamed in terror. He had to hurry. On tip-toe, spreading his legs to the sides to keep as quiet as possible, he edged up the stairs. On the landing, he moved the gun left and right. The noises came from one of the bedrooms. The bathroom door moved. Richard held the pistol straight, ready to fire.

Shock hit him in the guts. 'My God. You. The deputy director of MI5, a spy, a traitor to his country. Why, Jack?'

'You could never understand, Carpenter. I should have had the top job. Brady was always the PM's puppet, and I'm retiring soon and needed the extra cash to help with my move abroad.'

'Traitor Jack Taylor, just like Kim Philby, Donald Maclean, Guy Burgess, and Anthony Blunt. You'll spend the rest of your life in prison.'

A loud scream came from the bedroom. Richard took a step and crashed the pistol onto Jack Taylor's skull, who fell to the floor in a heap.

***

Yousef had hold of Mandy and dragged her by the throat toward the nearest bedroom. The sight of the two women had aroused him, and he wanted to enjoy them before the killing started. Behind him, Adhan pulled Durriyah by her hair. Both women yelled and screamed and tried to scratch them. Yousef ripped at Mandy's tee-shirt, revealing her naked chest, and then he threw her onto the double bed and turned to look at Durriyah. 'I'll start with the young one. You have that bitch, and then we'll swap.'

Mandy leapt from the bed, hands and nails aiming at Yousef's face. He brought back his hand and delivered a stinging backhand to her face, almost knocking her out. Then he pushed her back onto the bed and slapped her legs apart while he undid his trousers.

Adhan grew visibly excited and ripped off Durriyah's tee-shirt to reveal her in all her naked glory. He dragged her onto the bed by her hair, unfastened his trouser zip, and pushed her roughly onto her front. Left hand around her waist, he pulled her arse up into the air. Though she fought to move, he had her hair in his right hand and controlled her by pulling it so hard it made her scream.

***

Durriyah could think of only one thing: survival. 'You bastard. How did you know I like it hard and rough?' She became more compliant, which led to Adhan relaxing his grip. Then Durriyah pushed back, swaying her arse from side to side, which had Adhan mesmerised. She would survive and, if possible, help Mandy as well.

Instead of the expected penetration, a familiar voice said, 'Stand where you are, or I start shooting.'

***

Richard stood in the doorway, pistol pointed straight at Yousef. He and Adhan stood still, not believing the turn of events.

'At last, Yousef El-Sayed and Kaashif Bashara. You two terrorist scum.'

Yousef looked for options to save himself. He grabbed Mandy, held her in front of his torso, and locked her neck with his powerful arms. 'I can break her neck in a second. You'll move out of the way, now.'

When he applied pressure, Mandy's eyes bulged.

'No. Let her go, or you'll die within the next five seconds. One, two, three ...'

Yousef let her go and pushed her to the floor.

Richard nodded to Durriyah, 'Help Mandy and move out of the room. Get some clothes on and go downstairs. Help will get here at any minute.'

Yousef glared at Adhan, 'Attack the Kafir. I order it. Attack now, and you will be rewarded by Allah. Attack now.'

Adhan tensed all his muscles, ready to strike.

Richard moved the point of the gun to aim directly at him. 'One move, and you'll die with a bullet through the head. Is that how you want to go, Bashara?'

Adhan relaxed, and Richard knew he wouldn't move.

Durriyah and Mandy left the room, still sobbing and crying but recovering.

Richard wanted to kill both men. He eyed them and could see and feel the hate.

318

Yousef had noticed the concern on Richard's face. 'You like the Kassab woman?'

'Shut it, bastard.'

Yousef laughed. 'She is a wonderful fuck. I've had her every possible way even up the arse, and very delicious she is.'

'I said shut it; unless you want to die right now.'

Yousef laughed and took a step toward his Glock, which lay on the bedside table. Adhan moved a step too, but only to put more distance between himself and Yousef.

'I swear. You move again, and you will both be dead men.'

Richard grew more worried. Where the hell was the back-up? A second later, right on cue, the door opened. Bunny stood there, gun in hand.

'So, who do we have here?'

Richard smiled. 'Yousef El-Sayed and Kaashif Bashara. The scum we've been hunting, Ma'am.'

'Put the gun down, Richard.' Bunny had her pistol aimed right at him, so he had no choice but to comply.

'No, Ma'am. Not possible. Please, no. Surely. I trusted you. You're MI5. You love your country. It's not possible.' Richard felt distraught. Aside from the fact that he would now get killed, and Durriyah and Mandy would be next, he couldn't believe Bunny to be a traitor as well as Taylor.

'Love my country? A country that denied me a life? A country that stopped me loving and being loved? A service that wants me to retire because I'm past it? It's a pity it has to end like this.'

'You've been helping to catch them. You've been

on our side. You've been … no. I would have seen something. Felt something. I don't believe this.'

'It was a recent change. Things have altered. They want me to retire. Do you understand? What would I do? My whole life, I've dedicated to the service. I would die of boredom. And, having given it a great deal of thought, I'm delighted to bring down this corrupt MI5 institution and, ultimately, this sick and disgusting country. I'm sorry to include you, Richard. I actually like you but needs must. Why else would I have told you that Kassab and that slut were both here? Your death will be a hammer blow to the organisation."

Richard stood in shock, shaking his head. 'No. I can't—'

Bunny waved the gun. 'Stop the chat and get downstairs, now.'

***

Durriyah grabbed Mandy's arm, pushed open the white bedroom door, and half-dragged Mandy onto the landing. There, she stopped for a second when she came across a large, well-built man lying on the floor. Then she bent down and grabbed the knife and pistol that lay next to him. Heart thumping, she ran to the far end of the landing, and they barrelled into her bedroom. After slamming the door behind them, Durriyah grabbed a wooden chair and pushed it hard against the door, still worried and taking no chances.

Once she'd calmed a little, she stood Mandy straight and shouted at her, 'Pull yourself together. We're still in danger, and I want to help Richard.'

Mandy stood in shock and still terrified.

Durriyah slapped her round the face. 'Pull yourself together. I need your help.'

Mandy opened her eyes wide. 'Yeah, I'm with you.'

'Good, now get some clothes on. We need to make sure Richard is okay.'

Both women rummaged through drawers, grabbing anything, and ended up in jeans and shirts.

Durriyah held out the knife to Mandy. 'Take it. I'll keep the gun. I know how to use it.'

Mandy looked at the knife. 'It's—it's got blood on it. Oh God; Mrs Evans.'

Durriyah grabbed her shoulder and gave her a gentle shake. 'Keep it together. Now, let's go and see what Richard's up to.'

Mandy took the knife and followed Durriyah out onto the landing. With purpose, they walked slowly and quietly. Durriyah froze. From behind the door came talking—a woman's voice, and then Richard's. He sounded worried. They crept closer, and then the door started to open. Durriyah pulled Mandy back behind a pillar, and they watched while Richard came out. The woman behind him held a gun, followed by the two animals.

The woman spoke to the animals, 'Go and find the women and bring them downstairs. And no funny business.'

Then she leant down and shook Jack, who moaned. 'Get up and come downstairs. We need to get away from here as soon as possible.'

Richard led the way downstairs, followed by the woman. Jack struggled to stand.

The two women slipped into a different bedroom and hid behind the door.

***

Yousef and Adhan set off down the corridor. The terrorists moved down toward the far bedroom and went in. Piles of clothes met them but no women. They turned and pushed doors with their feet.

***

As they slammed doors, Durriyah could hear them getting closer. Mandy moved her feet to get comfortable, and Durriyah grabbed her arm. 'Shhh.'

***

Too late. Yousef heard the slight movement and pinpointed their hiding place. He assumed them unarmed but took no chances. Instead, he motioned to Adhan to go in first. Then he took a step back to cover the door for any eventuality. Adhan turned the handle and pushed. All seemed quiet. After a couple of steps, he cried out in pain.

***

The razor-sharp eight-inch blade bit into Adhan's shoulder, scraping onto the bone. Mandy pushed with all her might, twisting and turning the knife as best she could. Adhan screamed in agony, as the knife sliced muscle and destroyed tissue. Blood poured from the wounds, covering Mandy's hand and arm. Yousef attempted to get a clear shot at Mandy, but Adhan kept getting in the way.

Yousef yelled, 'Get out the way. I'm going to fire.'

Adhan, finally, managed to pull the knife out and fight off Mandy. He retreated a step. Durriyah stepped forward, aiming the gun at his head.

The bullet ripped through his forehead, smashing his brains into a pulp, and then exiting with flying blood and tissue from the back of his skull, hitting the wall. He fell to the floor.

***

Yousef almost panicked; it was going badly wrong. He leapt for the stairs and jumped down two at a time. At the bottom, he darted into the lounge and stopped by the door. 'The women are armed, and Adhan is dead.'

Bunny scowled. 'You bloody amateurs.' Then she rushed to the door and looked out. The bullet hit her in the chest, and she slumped to the floor, blood oozing onto her blue trouser suit.

'Jack, help me; I'm hit.'

***

Jack heard the plea. Things had gone badly. Time to make an exit. He strode to the French doors and battered them with his shoulder. The old timber gave way, and the wood around the lock splintered. Jack opened the door and dashed away, running across the lawn.

***

That left Yousef stood with his gun trained on Richard.

'Now, you will die, Kafir. You have caused so much trouble; I would like to have taken my time, but needs must. It will be a quick death.' He lifted his weapon and took aim at Richard's head. A loud explosion sounded just as his finger flexed on the trigger.

***

David Morgan entered through the French doors. 'Hello, Richard. I thought you might need some assistance.'

Richard stood there in shock; he'd thought his time had come. On the floor, Yousef El-Sayed had a massive bullet wound to his head and face; no longer the good-looking terrorist.

'You took your time. How did you know?'

'Office gossip, old boy. Always a good idea to keep one's ears open at all times.'

'What about Jack Taylor?'

'In custody. You don't think I'd risk coming to something like this without help?' He laughed.

'Thanks, David. I owe you one.'

A moan drifted up to them, and they moved toward Bunny.

David said, 'An ambulance will be here shortly, Ma'am.'

'It's too late for that. I'm done for, and thank God. I don't want to spend the rest of my life in Belmarsh. Poor Jack.'

'Jack ...' Richard paused, gathered himself, and said, 'And you, Ma'am, are traitors to your country. You both got exactly what you deserve.'

Bunny closed her eyes. After a final breath, she slipped away.

'Is it safe to come in now?' Durriyah called from the hallway.

Richard rushed to the door. 'Yes, come.'

Durriyah and Mandy appeared, and Durriyah rushed into Richard's arms, where she sobbed tears of joy that they'd survived. Mandy stood crying. David took her by the shoulder and led her to a sofa.

***

The new Director General of MI5 said, 'Take a week off. You deserve it.'

'That would be welcome, Sir. Thank you.' David left the office.

The new DG picked up the phone. 'Darling, it's Richard. I'll be home early. What's for dinner?'

He listened for a moment, and then smiled. 'Lovely. One of my favourites. Oh, by the way, I love you so very much, Durriyah.'

His smile broadened at her reply.

'I'll be home soon.' Still smiling widely, he ended the call.

Only three o'clock, and look at him, heading home.

THE END

OTHER TITLES FROM AUTHOR
CHRIS WARD

THE FOUR-PART ADULT CRIME THRILLER
BERMONDSEY SERIES

Bermondsey Trifle   http://amzn.to/1l3b3up

Bermondsey Prosseco
http://tinyurl.com/nebwtys

Bermondsey The Final Act
http://tinyurl.com/nbuahoj

Return to Bermondsey
http://tinyurl.com/jtmfec6

DI Karen Foster Series

Serial Killer http://tinyurl.com/p5ld9dx

Blue Cover Up http://tinyurl.com/mzy5f2f

Driven to Kill http://tinyurl.com/p8f9c4w

Sci-Fi and Fantasy Action Adventure

OMG Joe Warren http://tinyurl.com/jtkcusp

17783388R00187

Printed in Poland
by Amazon Fulfillment
Poland Sp. z o.o., Wrocław